DESTROYER

THE SHIFTER WAR BOOK THREE

K K NESS

BOOKS BY K K NESS

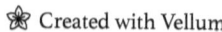

For our loved ones

~

We acknowledge the Bindal and Wulgurukaba people upon whose Country this book was written.

1

Shouts and the clash of steel rang out across the valley.

Danil hunkered amidst the towering grasses and wildflowers, moving at a cautious trot as shifters fanned out and followed. The Roldaerian border lay just beyond a gurgling stream, where a worn path meandered its way through the hills east to the village of Scara.

The fighting had to be a mile inland at least.

Danil glanced at Hafryn, noting the thin, worried line of his mouth as they sloshed through the chilly water. No Amasian shifters were supposed to be patrolling the area—not since the arrival of the Roldaerian battalion a week ago. Three hundred of King Liam's soldiers, together with as many as ten magi, were camped now at Scara. It was clear they were waiting for the Roldaerian army to leave the royal city of Aqila. Danil's only solace was that the Amasian shapeshifters were likewise gathering in Kailon to stop the Roldaerian invasion.

at didn't explain the nearby skirmish.

d the softly rolling hill, the sound of fighting

From the corner of his eye, Danil spied Blutark mutter a few soft words to awaken the glyphs lining his quiver of arrows. Soft light emanated from the large man's bow as he pushed through a dense line of purple milkweed. The flowers shivered as Elania slinked beneath them in her snow leopard Trueform, her spotted coat blending with the dappled sunlight and damp loam. Ahead, a startled flock of wrens took flight when Sonnen neared the hill. He threw the birds a disgruntled look, golden eyes flashing.

The party squatted low and waited.

Hafryn tilted his head to listen. "Fighting's over," he muttered. He pointed at a lone pine tree on a nearby hill. "That way."

They trekked along the shoulder of a hill and scarcely entered the shallow gully below before Danil spied crushed vegetation.

A horse lay slaughtered in the tall grass, arrows bristling in its side. A man lay sprawled facedown beside it. Moving cautiously forward, Danil spied more bodies, all vacant-eyed and still. The ground about them was churned up from the fight, with broken arrow shafts and abandoned swords in the dirt.

Hafryn gripped Danil's shoulder. "Ambushed," he whispered, pointing a series of spikes half-buried along the gully. Another dead horse lay skewered in the trap.

"Watch your steps," Sonnen said as he navigated past a live snare. A waxy green substance covered the spiked teeth.

Blutark fired a bolt into the grass, setting off another snare of sharpened pikes.

They moved cautiously as they examined the fight. Elania nosed out of the undergrowth to sniff out the area beyond the dead animal. The air shimmered as she transformed. "Over here," she called out, squatting beyond view.

Sonnen strode toward her, gaze moving about warily.

Danil reached them and suddenly slowed at the sight of a dead Roldaerian soldier lying prone in the clover. The soldier's red tabard was blackened, his skin blistered and charred. The surrounding grasses were scorched as if struck by lightning.

"A mage curse," Elania murmured, grimacing.

Danil's brows drew together. "An accident, perhaps?" He gazed back toward the ambushed party. "Maybe the soldier was caught by a blast meant for those poor folk?"

Hafryn crouched beside the felled man, plucking a tuft of blackened moss from the soil. "I don't think so. Likely the spell was retaliation from someone in the attacked party."

Danil gaped. "Roldaerian soldiers ambushed a *mage*?"

"Appears so," Hafryn said, frowning. He used a stick to pull loose the soldier's pouch, where a handful of Roldaerian silvers and playing dice fell out. Finding nothing of note, he added, "We should search the area more thoroughly."

Sonnen nodded. "No lingering. We might be miles from Scara, but we could find ourselves hip-deep in Roldaerian soldiers with little warning."

Taking that to heart, Danil helped to search the hill. Disquiet settled in his bones as he counted twelve bodies plus horses. Judging from the barrage of arrows, the initial attack had been thorough and brutal. Only four had survived the first wave, only to be cut down by steel.

Blutark crouched over a patch of scuffed earth and broken milkweed. "Looks like two were taken prisoner." He traced dark blood in the soil. "One's injured."

"Headed for Scara, do you think?" Sonnen asked.

Scrutinizing the surrounding hills, Blutark grunted. "Aye."

Sonnen cursed softly.

Kneeling beside a dead woman, Danil took in the careworn state of her clothes and the dirt under her nails. A glint of metal caught his eye, and he pulled a dagger from its sheath at her side. "Hafryn, take a look at this."

The wolf shifter trotted over and took the blade. "High grade Roldaerian steel," he murmured, turning the dagger about. "Well cared for, too. Typical of the Magi Guard."

Blutark looked skyward, gaining his bearings. "This close to Kailon, I'd say they planned to harvest kiandrite for themselves."

"We'd have never let them past the border," Elania growled.

It hardly surprised Danil that a mage had sought to get ahead of his cohorts. The mage caste of Roldaer needed kiandrite crystals to fuel their curses and spells. Having long since decimated the crystals in their own land, the magi had turned their insatiable hunger to Kailon and Amas.

Movement at the base of the hill caught Danil's eye. A ghostly, blonde-haired woman in battle armor stepped out of the towering grasses and stared back at him. Fine symbols and scrollwork adorned the woman's breastplate, her leg and arm bracers similarly inscribed with strange letterings. Sigils likewise painted her cheekbones and forehead. In one fist, she held a battle-axe with a kiandrite crystal embedded in the hilt.

No one else in the clearing noticed her.

The skin on Danil's arms pebbled. *A ghost...*

As if knowing she had his attention, the ghostly woman turned and disappeared back into the swaying wildflowers.

Rising, Danil gripped his dagger and followed.

"Where are you going, *fala*?" Hafryn called out, shading his eyes from the sun.

"I'm not sure."

The ghost waited as Danil shoved through a thicket of briars that tangled about his legs and cloak and pulled vengefully at his hair.

Danil stumbled to a halt.

A young woman lay sprawled deep in the grasses, so badly burned and bloodied that Danil knew she must surely be dead. A Roldaerian arrow sat lodged in her chest, its red fletching bristling in the breeze above her brown travel robes. She was blond and freckled, her face blackened and raw as if someone had mercilessly struck her with a fire curse.

The ghost stood over her, expression somber.

Cold rushed through Danil. Even with his unique abilities, he'd never seen a ghost before. He resisted the urge to make a warding sign, instead whispering, "May you find peace with the ancestors."

The ghost raised her gloved fist, light seeping from between her clenched fingers.

On the ground, the burned woman suddenly gasped, her back arching in a rictus of pain. She gave a wretched, rasping gurgle.

Danil fell back with a startled curse.

The ghost dissipated like smoke.

"*Fala?*" Hafryn pushed through the wildflowers and stuttered to a halt at the sight of the injured woman. "Merciful gods—she lives?"

Danil managed a nod. His gaze flicked over the surrounding hills, where a mournful breeze made the grasses pitch and roll in waves. The ghost was nowhere to be seen.

Hafryn ran a quick gaze over the young woman's injuries and swore. "Damned horse must have thrown her free of the fighting." He turned and called out for others to join them.

Wading through the grass, Sonnen paused at the sight of the woman, a low rumble in his chest. "Elania, if you would lend your skills," he asked.

Elania quickly knelt, grimacing as she studied the fletching wound and terrible burns. Blood appeared dark and thick as it dripped onto the soil. "The bolt has her heart." Her hands weaved a glyph above the injured woman, only for it to drift apart like gossamer.

Danil threw Elania a dismayed look. "Can't you help her?"

"There are limits to what can be healed, Danil, even with my talents." Elania's brow furrowed as she studied the burns. "Truly, it's a wonder she lives at all."

Danil thought of the woman's ghost and wondered how it had achieved such a feat.

"Is she a mage?" Sonnen asked.

They all looked to Danil.

Shifting his vision, Danil saw a waning iridescent light in the woman's belly that indicated she'd ingested the kiandrite tincture the Roldaerian magi used to power their spells. His chest tightened.

"Mage it is, then," Hafryn said, reading Danil's expression.

A glyph formed about Blutark's fingers, dark with animosity. "Is she still dangerous?"

"Not this close to death," Elania murmured, sweeping back the woman's blonde hair. The charred, weeping side of her face made her features unrecognizable. "She's barely holding on."

Danil glanced about the surrounding hills, wondering

why the ghost had gone to such effort if it was all for nothing.

"Let's get her out of the brambles," Hafryn said with a sigh. "Gently, now."

They carefully lifted the mage out of the tangling undergrowth, setting her onto a cloak in the soft grass at the base of the hill.

Blutark folded his arms, eyeing the discolored tinge to the woman's mouth. "She won't survive the journey to Kailon."

Sonnen rumbled. "Elania, if you cannot save her, may you extend her life for a time? There are questions this Roldaerian must answer."

"Not without causing more suffering," Elania said, mouth thinning. "I can only dull her senses in the hopes that her waking up won't be in agony."

Sonnen nodded, flames showing in his golden gaze. "Perhaps that is best."

Frowning in concentration, Elania drew a fresh glyph. It flared gentle blues and pinks as it dispersed over the injured woman.

With a stuttering gasp, the mage woke. Eyes wide and panicky, she attempted to flail upright but quickly dropped back, chest heaving. Her limbs trembled, her blistered lips tight in a rictus of pain.

Danil knelt and gripped her shoulder. "Rest easy. You're safe."

The dying mage fixed him with a startled look, relief flaring. "Danil," she gasped. "I found you at last."

2

"Who is she, Danil?" Blutark asked.

Danil stared down at the mage, taking her in long limbs and pale, wavy hair. Her freckled hands were unblemished and shaking as she gripped his forearm. He shook his head. "I've never seen her before."

Blood showed on the woman's lips, her breathing a wet rattle deep in her lungs. "Know what you are, Danil," she rasped. "Need you."

Unsettled, Danil leaned forward and asked, "For what? Who are you?"

Her mouth worked, trying to find words. "Lyria." A shudder went through her, blood surrounding the arrow in her chest spreading. "Mage, First Line of the Royal City of Aqila."

"Quite a mouthful," Blutark muttered under his breath.

Sonnen studied the woman, mouth set in a tight line. "Why have you come, mage? Aqila is a month's ride from here."

Lyria coughed, blood spattering.

"Easy, now." Elania laid a hand on the woman's breast,

fingers brightening with enchantments. Lyria breathed a little easier.

Danil couldn't help but wonder how much longer she had to live.

"It's the blacksward," Lyria managed. Her hand twitched at her side. "Brought it so Danil would understand. But they stole it!"

Glancing about, Danil saw only confounded looks on his companions' faces. "Blacksward?" he repeated.

Sonnen shook his head. "I know of no such thing."

A hectic light gleamed in Lyria's eyes. "Poison. It's spreading." She took a wet, rasping breath. "Danil—you must destroy it!"

"You brought this poison with you?" Hafryn asked, lip curling with a snarl.

She nodded, her grip desperate on Danil's arm.

Hafryn cursed. His pale face turned murderous.

Danil threw him a quelling look. "Who took it?" he asked Lyria. "This...blacksward?"

"Soldiers. They'll use it to ruin the deadlands."

Icy alarm threaded through Danil's veins.

Hafryn bared his teeth. "If you're here for Danil's help, why would you poison Kailon?"

"Not me," Lyria swore. She drew a shuddering breath. "There's a faction. Our mission is to stop the blacksward." She looked at Danil beseechingly. "You can save us. Save Roldaer!"

Danil leaned back, jaw clenching. Roldaer was no longer his home. It hadn't been since Magus Brianna had murdered everyone in his village and no one in the kingdom had demanded justice.

"You ask a lot of someone your kind is intent on killing, mage," Sonnen noted.

A grimace of pain tightened her blackened skin. "We know you healed the deadlands, Danil. You can do it again. You *must*."

Blutark gave a derisive snort. "This is an elaborate magi trick."

"No trick," Lyria promised, hacking up blood a globule of blood. Her limbs trembled as she collapsed back to the ground. She reached weakly again for Danil. "Promise me you will stop it!"

Hafryn gave Danil an urgent shake of his head.

"I—I can't," Danil said, mouth tight. "I'm sorry."

With a sigh, Lyria closed her eyes.

For a moment Danil wondered if she'd gone. Then movement caught his attention.

Lyria's ghost stood once more amidst the flowering foxglove halfway up the hill, her armor luminous. Her face was a mask of determination, sigils alight. She raised her hand.

Putrid wind suddenly swept over Danil. A ravenous roaring and cracking filled his ears as if an avalanche were about to tumble down the hill. From the corner of his eye, something black and viscous slithered across the ground, turning grass and soil and beetles dark and lifeless.

Danil leaped back when it hungrily reached his boots.

Hafryn suddenly gripped his elbow, steadying him as the vision loosened its hold. "I have you, *fala*." Concern shone from Hafryn's face.

Gulping for breath, Danil tasted only fresh, sun-sweetened air. No darkness gripped the hill, Danil's gaze snaring instead on a tiny rodent that scurried up a wildflower stem to munch on yellow petals.

Sonnen followed his gaze, rising to his feet cautiously. "*Videre*. What have you seen?"

Shaking his head, Danil wondered how the ghost could have possibly forced a vision upon him. As the only living *videre*, his ability to see beyond what was easily discernible had helped them to defeat and imprison Kaul. But this new vision was something else entirely.

"Oh, no," Elania suddenly gasped. At her feet, Lyria stared up at the sky, her pupils blown wide and vacant.

Sonnen rumbled low in his chest. "Our opportunity for answers is lost."

But Danil wasn't so sure. He searched the hills for the ghost but saw nothing of note amidst the bob and sway of the yellowing grasses. "I think the blacksward is real," he murmured, before sharing what he'd seen in the vision.

When he finished, Hafryn scowled. "The blacksward acts more like a living thing than a poison," he said. "If this is a magi ploy, it's far more elaborate then I'd have credited them for."

"Agreed," Blutark said. "We scarcely found the magus in time, and it's only through Elania's skill that Magus Lyria had the strength to speak."

Sonnen circled the dead woman carefully, eyeing the surrounding area before squatting with a sigh. "It is rare for the magi to sacrifice one of their own, but perhaps not if their purpose is to draw Danil out. The magi do not understand what has happened in Kailon, but they know Danil stands at the heart of matters."

"They don't even know what a custodian is," Elania agreed. "If I had to draw him out, I too might come up with something like 'blacksward'."

But Danil knew that whatever the blacksward was, Lyria had been frightened of it. If Roldaerian soldiers had indeed stolen it during the ambush, he had to do everything in his power to ensure it didn't spill into Kailon.

"The vision felt real. If there's a new threat, we must face it," he said.

Hafryn gave him an unsurprised look. "I agree, Sonnen. And there are two people who still live to tell us more about the blacksward."

"The captives," Danil said with a nod. With one injured, their best hope was that the attackers moved slowly enough to be overtaken before reaching Scara. "We must rescue them."

Elania and Blutark glanced curiously at Sonnen.

The dragon prince slid his gaze to where Danil had seen the vision, his expression contemplative. He nodded. "As you say, custodian," Sonnen said. "We follow your lead."

BY LATE AFTERNOON, they had the party of Roldaerians in sight. The soldiers moved far slower across the rolling hills than Danil expected, but the reason was easy enough to discern, with two chained prisoners hobbling behind the party.

One prisoner was an old man with cropped white hair and broad shoulders turned thin and hunched with age. He stumbled despite being aided by his younger companion. Blood matted the side of his robes and his neck underneath the chain. His companion was dark haired and showed the awkward vestiges of youth in his gangly limbs. He looked pale and frightened but nonetheless shielded his companion when a soldier raised her fist threateningly and bellowed at them to move faster.

"I sense nothing amiss," Sonnen murmured once he'd settled beside Danil and Hafryn in the lee of a boulder. The wind sighed through the pale thistleweed they used as cover.

Danil quirked a brow at the dragon prince.

"If the blacksward is curse-born, we should feel it," Sonnen explained. "I discern no poisoning or darkness hereabouts."

Nor did Danil but he felt no relief. He studied the Roldaerians as they trod along the shoulder of the opposite hill. One soldier gingerly carried a black casket. Her fellow soldiers gave her a wide berth, and even the robed magus made a furtive warding sign when she strayed too close.

Danil gave his companions a worried look.

"I see it," Sonnen murmured.

Hafryn grunted. "Blacksward, maybe?"

Danil leaned forward. "We take it, regardless." If the Roldaerians were scared of whatever was in the casket, there was little chance he'd leave it in their hands so close to Kailon.

Hafryn's eyes turned calculating. "I count less than two dozen soldiers and one magus."

"There'll be other magi among the soldiers," Sonnen replied.

Hafryn grunted in sour agreement.

The old prisoner suddenly stumbled and fell facedown, dragged by the chain attached to a soldier's mount before his young companion could attempt to lift him. Even in the distance, Danil could see the old fellow was deathly pale and slackly unconscious.

"They won't be able to get much further today," Hafryn observed, grimacing as the young prisoner valiantly tried to heave his companion upright.

A soldier dismounted and shoved the young prisoner

away. She squatted to give the unconscious man a rough slap. Turning to the robed magus, she shook her head.

The magus wheeled his horse about, face red as he waved his hands about and shouted. With a sharp nod, the lead rider lodged his pennant into the ground and bellowed orders to make camp. An array of tents was set up in quick order, while two soldiers rammed a large stake into the ground and fixed the prisoners' chains to it.

The magus stalked over to the pair and set his hands to the chains. A flash of blue light threaded along the chains, making the younger prisoner flinch. A square cage then formed over the prisoners and solidified like metal.

The magus smirked before stalking to the largest tent and disappearing from view.

The young prisoner stared after the magus balefully before turning his attention to his companion.

"Let's get out of sight," Sonnen murmured. "Hafryn, scout the area and report back."

Hafryn gave the dragon prince a lazy salute. The air shimmered before his red wolf trotted jauntily beneath the feathery inflorescence.

Retreating into the hills, Danil and Sonnen hunkered amidst the grasses to await the arrival of enchanters from Kailon. In the weeks since Danil's ill-fated journey to Corros, more Amasians had arrived to defend Kailon. Stirred by both the inadequacies of the Amasian High Council and the return of the dread lord Kaul, enchanters and common folk had sworn allegiance to both Danil and the land he was bound to protect.

Glancing back across the hills where they'd come, Danil spied a flock of sparrows drop down in the general location where Lyria and her dead companions lay. It heartened him a little, knowing Elania had sent word to camp asking

Amasians to grant the dead burial rites. It was something he expected Roldaer would never do were the situation reversed, but that hardly mattered to the Amasians who'd chosen to fight for Kailon.

Sighing, Danil turned to Sonnen. The dragon prince sat amidst the thistles, absently pulling tiny, yellow-starred flowers from his dark braid. A sheathed blade rested across his knees.

Sonnen smiled. "Rest easy, Danil. We will have the answers we need by dawn."

Danil hoped so. "I know it's madness to trust a mage's word, but—" He glanced again toward the ambush site. "Whoever did this, they meant to kill Lyria just like the others."

"I admit your ability to see her ghost has left me confounded," Sonnen murmured. "Nor do I like its propensity to show you death and ruin." The dragon prince spun a flower between his fingers, expression thoughtful. "And yet, sometimes when one's purpose is great, it is possible to push beyond the barriers of what is known and expected. As custodian and *videre,* you are a fine example."

But Danil suspected his circumstances had more to do with sheer stubbornness than any grand purpose. The wellspring within Kailon had taken a liking to him, and it never occurred to him to refute its offerings.

Sonnen's golden eyes sparkled warmly as if guessing his thoughts. "Unlike with you, however, I am not so quick to trust Lyria or her ghost. If the blacksward is truly something to be feared, she willingly brought it to us."

Danil's thoughts returned once more to the vision. "Do you also think that's what I saw?"

The dragon prince nodded. "I do not abide coincidences. Especially not with Kaul's return. The magi desire to see him reach his full power, and if the blacksward is as ravening as your vision intimated, we face a difficult test."

At least the dread lord was imprisoned within a crystalline enchantment, his location known only to Sonnen and a rare few others. It was Danil's only solace now that Roldaer's soldiers and magi increasingly took position along the border. By his judgement, they had only weeks before Kailon truly became the battlefront.

Hafryn's red wolf trotted its way through the thistleweed, tongue lolling as it approached. It pressed its large, wet snout against Danil's neck in greeting, nearly toppling him. Laughing softly, Danil pushed him away.

The air shimmered, and Hafryn was half-squatted over him with a smirking grin. "I could see the thundercloud hanging over you both from half a mile away. What grim tales have you been sharing?"

"Nothing unexpected," Sonnen observed dryly. "Have you anything to report?"

Hafryn settled beside Danil, their shoulders brushing. "A couple of soldiers are setting snares along the eastern edge of the camp. They have a bowman in one of the outer tents with his sights on the sky. A precaution, I suspect."

"No winged folk for now, then," Sonnen said. "The terrain is open enough that we shouldn't need them in any case."

With a nod, Hafryn asked, "When do we go in?"

"Darkness will be our friend."

"They may kill the prisoners before then," Hafryn warned. "There's certainly no care taken—the old man has been unconscious since they made camp."

Danil glanced anxiously at the dragon prince.

"It is a risk that we must take," Sonnen said grimly. "I

want a full contingent of enchanters at our side before we contend with whatever poison the blacksward may be."

Though he hardly wanted to wait, Danil nodded his agreement.

"Any new insight regarding the number of magi?" Sonnen asked.

Hafryn shook his head grimly.

"The leylines will warn me of any magi curses," Danil said. He sensed the leylines busily forming crystals along the edge of the settlement back in Kailon. As if knowing they had his attention, a happy greeting swept across his mind.

"We'll have to move fast on the prisoners," Hafryn warned. "The soldiers will likely kill them at the first sign of trouble." He smirked slightly. "Of course, there's a chance that the two prisoners don't want to be rescued by the likes of us."

Danil hadn't thought of that.

"We will have them talk, regardless," Sonnen rumbled. "If Lyria was indeed our ally, they will be too. In the meantime, take your ease, both of you." He rose, wiping his breeches. "The others and I will keep watch on the Roldaerians."

With a wink, Hafryn spread his cloak and motioned for Danil to settle in beside him. "You heard him, *fala*."

Danil obligingly lay back, using Hafryn's arm for a pillow. He watched Sonnen stride through the purple inflorescence, scarcely leaving a trail. "Do you think I'm right about her?"

"Who? Lyria?" Hafryn grunted, his breath warm on Danil's ear. "We don't live in a time of absolutes."

It was true. Danil needed only to look inwards. Born a

Roldaerian, his heart belonged with an Amasian wolf, while his duty was bound to the leylines of Kailon.

Hafryn propped himself onto his elbow, gazing down at Danil. The afternoon light gave his green eyes a gem-like quality. "I know what it's like to yearn for old belonging, *fala*. To lose one's homeland is a wound that rarely heals."

Danil heard the regret in his companion's voice. Their forced journey into Eyrie in the previous months had brought home to Hafryn how he could never truly return to the land of his childhood. Lifting the wolf shifter's hand, Danil traced the House glyph that was twin to his own. It took on a silvery glimmer.

Hafryn turned their hands about to kiss Danil's knuckles. "Don't mistake a mage's pleas as some pact you must fulfill, *fala*. As long as Roldaer wants kiandrite, her people will always be your enemy."

Danil nodded. Kailon was still so fragile, no matter that the leylines burbled strong and true through the land. He should be focusing all of his will on fortifying Kailon's protections and garnering more aid from Amas. But Danil recalled the desperate relief on Lyria's face when she'd first sighted him. Whatever the blacksward was, she'd died trying to warn him.

Sighing, he rested his head on Hafryn's shoulder and settled in for the remainder of the afternoon. He let his mind dip down, sinking into a newly invigorated leyline that gamboled amongst the rock below. The leyline gave a happy trill as Danil gave the streaming iridescence a little nudge toward a deep spring that fed much of the surrounding area. Flashes of purple and pale blues warmed on his chest as the first crystal sung about birds and scudding clouds.

Sunset eventually draped golden fingers through the feathery inflorescence about them before turning pink on the sharp, distant peaks of the Amasian mountains. Enchanters took advantage of the changing light to begin their arrival. Danil shifted his vision to watch the various Trueforms emerge from the grasses. Restless energy swept over the hill. Even Hafryn's wolf stalked atop the outcrop nearby, ears twitching.

Sitting up, Danil saw Elania and Blutark bent close over Blutark's quiver of arrows. Glyphs spun lazily above them before sinking onto the shafts. A pale snow leopard and oversized bear watched on with interest. Iridescent light threaded through the snow leopard, glittering like morning sunlight on water.

As moonlight limned the horizon with silver, Sonnen strode over to them, mouth determined. "It's time."

3

The tall grasses afforded them an easy way to reach the Roldaerian camp.

Hiding amidst the rustling blades, Danil could discern the symbol woven in red thread on the mage's robes. A rush of cold swept over him; Magus Brianna had once borne that same mark when she'd entered Farin and slaughtered his people.

"Kaul's underling," Hafryn whispered, teeth bared.

Four soldiers stood guard in front of the barred metal cage, where two figures huddled in the shadows.

Shifting his vision, Danil noticed a whirl of red-tinged light in the belly of one of the guards. "The soldier on the right is a magus," he muttered.

Squatted beside him, Elania nodded. "We'll deal with her first."

More Amasians spread out and encircled the camp. Danil glanced skyward, waiting for Sonnen to drop from the clouds that currently masked the moon. He suspected the Roldaerians had prepared for an attack, but facing a golden dragon was something else.

At the edge of the camp, a flash of white caught Danil's attention.

A ghostlike woman stepped out from the high grasses near where an enchanter squatted. Pale hair floated about her shoulders as she strode toward the tents, her ivory armor shining. No one spied her or the strange battle-axe she held aloft.

"Lyria," Danil breathed.

Hafryn threw him a startled look.

Then a thunderous roar reverberated across the moonlit hills, and a massive dragon hurled a ball of fire into the center of the camp. Shouts and screams rang out as the Roldaerians dove for cover. Flames shot up and consumed the canvas tents, while horses kicked the air and bucked against their tethers.

Elania raised her bow and joined in as a volley of arrows rained on the camp, each bolt leaving an iridescent trail as they arced through the air. The bolts struck the mage-guard in the chest, sending her spinning like a marionette before she collapsed into the undergrowth.

A man sprinted between the burning tents, shouting orders. The soldiers quickly rallied and scurried for their weapons.

The robed magus raised his hand, a bolt of lightning rocketing toward the dragon prince as he circled for another pass. The spell bounced harmlessly off Sonnen's golden scales before the dragon released a new fireball that sent the Roldaerians scattering once more.

"That's us," Hafryn said. He took off at a sprint.

Danil scrambled to follow, sword drawn. Growls, hisses and the pad of furred paws on the soil behind him indicated more Amasians entered the fray. They rounded the edge of the camp and launched themselves into the fighting.

Danil ducked under a soldier's wild strike before driving his blade home. From the corner of his eye, he saw Elania, Blutark and a handful of enchanters make their way towards the cage holding the prisoners.

"Watch it!" Hafryn shouted, blocking a soldier from striking Danil in the back.

Concentrating on the task at hand, Danil fought his way closer to the tents. Lyria's armor-clad ghost was there, watching. Hefting her axe, she strode into one of the tents.

"Hafryn!" he said, pointing.

Blocking a soldier's strike, Hafryn nodded.

They fought their way over with shifters at their back. Reaching the tent entrance, Hafryn said to them, "Don't let anyone in."

The shifters took up position around the tent as Danil cautiously pulled the tent flap back and stepped inside.

It was impossibly dark—far too dark considering the orange glow radiating through the canvas walls from Sonnen's fireballs. The tent was empty except for the dark lead casket Danil had seen the soldier carrier earlier in the day. No wider than his forearm, it radiated a strange kind of foulness that set Danil's teeth on edge.

Lyria stood beside the casket, her expression shuttered.

Hafryn suddenly gripped his shoulder. "Whatever you are going to do, be quick about it," he said. The sound of fighting continued outside.

"The casket can't come with us," Danil said. "It has to be destroyed."

Hafryn swore softly. "Is this something you can do, or do we need Elania and Blutark?"

"I'm not sure." Kneeling, Danil carefully raised the lid. Murky darkness roiled inside. A metallic cloud of old blood and rot drifted up. His gorge rose.

"Mage curse," Hafryn gasped, and made a rapid warding sign.

This close to Kailon, it could leach terrible evil within the fragile leylines.

Heat flooded Danil's hand, and he raised the House glyph as it burned brightly. The darkness within the casket quivered and shook. The leylines called out, a cacophony in his mind.

The glyph of Kailon brightened, flooding the area with so much light that the tent appeared to play host to the noonday sun. Squinting in the harsh luminescence, Danil set his hand over the casket. The glyph hissed and spat as it burned through the blackness. The stink of rot and putridness spewed up before it transformed into the smell of scorched earth after a lightning strike.

The light within the House glyph receded.

Blinking, Danil saw the casket reduced to nothing but a lead-lined shell. He noticed Lyria stride towards the tent entrance before dissipating like smoke

Hafryn threw his cloak over the casket and hefted it under his arm. "Let's have the enchanters take a look. See if they can figure out what the magi are up to." He motioned with his chin towards the entrance. "Time we leave this place, *fala*."

A heartbeat later, a Roldaerian soldier burst into the tent, shouting.

Hafryn whirled, dropping the casket as he blocked the first blow before striking out. His blade sliced the man's chest.

The soldier fell back with a shriek. More rushed inside.

"Come on!" Danil said, cutting a hole in the tent wall. He ushered Hafryn through.

The fighting had yet to abate outside, and to Danil's

dismay he saw the prisoners still trapped within the cage. Elania and Blutark were pinned behind a dead horse, exchanging a barrage of enchantments with the robed mage. Thick, acrid smoke plumed through the camp, the surrounding grasses on fire.

Danil fought his way to the cage. He reached for the lock and snatched his hand away when he felt a zap of pain.

Hafryn cursed and struck the padlock with the hilt of his sword.

A prisoner gripped the bars. It was the young man, his robes stained with dirt and blood. He shook his head frantically. "The lock is cursed! It won't open!"

Then a pale, ghostly hand reached between them and touched the lock. It broke apart with a sizzle.

Danil whirled to see Lyria only inches away. She stared back with intent.

Hafryn yanked open the gate.

The young man stood over his unconscious companion, fists raised. "Who are you?"

Behind them, Sonnen dropped out of the sky and raked powerful talons across a pair of soldiers.

Hafryn gave a humorless grin. "Enemy or ally—that's up to you, Roldaerian."

The young man's mouth thinned, but he nodded. "I'm not leaving Bornil." He motioned to the old man.

"That's fine, we've got enough questions for two," Hafryn said with a hard smile.

The young man gulped.

Danil bent over the old man, hand on his chest. His heart made a slow, sluggish beat. One side of his face was swollen and purple. Glancing up, Danil said, "We need Elania."

Stirring as if drawn by Danil's voice, the old prisoner

opened his eyes. Just as it had been with Lyria, his features transformed in recognition. Weak, trembling hands reached up.

Before Danil could stop him, the old man gripped the crystal hanging from his neck. It gave a tremulous trill and suddenly turned bright red in the old man's fist.

Danil gasped, yanking back, but the old man had extraordinary strength. A wild look filled the old man's as he frantically uttered something unintelligible.

A green flash drew Danil's gaze to the far end of the cage. Cold flooded him as recognition flared. "Portal!" he cried in warning.

"*Magus!*" Hafryn yelled but was suddenly tackled by the desperate young man. They crashed up against the bars, flailing and rolling.

The old mage shouted again, fist clenched tight about Danil's first crystal.

The crystal screeched. Angry red light streamed from it, sucked toward the roiling portal. With a choked cry, Danil felt the portal feed off it and drain the crystal.

A heartbeat later, the portal solidified. The air pulsed like a living thing.

The old mage gave Danil a regretful look. "Forgive me," he said and uttered new words under his breath.

Unseen hands suddenly flung Danil off his feet. The crystal snapped loose from around his neck. It shattered like glass even as green light reached out and surrounded Danil.

"*Danil!*" Hafryn roared.

Cold enveloped him, and the sound of battle abruptly became silent.

anil made a jarring landing onto gritty cobblestones. He lay still for a moment, chest heaving as dizziness made the world spin.

Instinctively, he reached out toward the leylines of Kailon. An unsettled, almost confused silence met him as the distance stretched between them. He grabbed at his throat, mourning the loss of the first crystal. The cursed old mage had forced it to feed the portal and send him... wherever this place was.

Lifting his gaze, Danil stared at grey stone buildings looming four stories over him. They were devoid of arched windows or the ornate carvings and entrances he had come to associate with Amas. Instead, the buildings were in stark disrepair, with exposed mud bricks, missing eaves and small windows boarded up with wood or mattress ticking. The door to the building opposite him hung askew off its hinges as if someone had forcibly kicked it in.

Where am I? he wondered, heart thundering as he took in the dark cobbled road cutting between the buildings. He spied movement behind one shuttered window in the nearest building.

Hands suddenly grabbed him and wrenched him up to his feet, and Danil flailed.

"Danil!" Hafryn hissed, gripping his arms.

Danil let out a cry of relief and hugged him close.

Hafryn startled, then chuckled. "You didn't think I wouldn't follow, did you?" he murmured against Danil's ear.

Holding him a moment longer, Danil pulled away to see Hafryn looking pale but otherwise unharmed.

"Come on, *fala*. We have to move."

They hurried across the cobbled road toward the shadow of an alley where rubble collected. Rodents scattered at their approach.

The stench of vomit and rotting vegetables clung about them, and Danil desperately covered his nose with his sleeve. Mildew stained the buildings where refuse sat piled high, but Hafryn hardly noticed. He hunkered behind a stack of broken wooden boards, pulling Danil down with him.

"Are you hurt?" Hafryn asked, looking him over.

Danil shook his head. "Scrapes is all. That damn mage." His eyes burned in frustration at his own stupidity. "Lyria's death, the blacksward—it was all a trap."

"Aye," Hafryn muttered grimly. "But Lyria told the truth about one thing. The blacksward is real, and you know how to destroy it."

It was Danil's only comfort.

Riders suddenly galloped past the mouth of the alley, their red tabards evident under the torches they carried.

Roldaerian soldiers, Danil realized, blood turning to ice.

The portal must have dropped them in a city somewhere within the Roldaerian kingdom. But where?

The soldiers pulled up further along the road and dismounted.

"This is the place," a woman said, her voice carrying in the quiet. "Whoever came through the portal can't have gone far. Search the area!"

Boots marched toward where Danil and Hafryn hid.

"Hurry," Hafryn hissed, trotting down a side alley.

They clung to the shadows, following a maze of alleys and small streets until the sound of clopping hooves and shouted orders were replaced by the skitter of cockroaches and rats in the alley. It was hardly late at night, but an uneasy quiet lay over the city.

"Curfew," Hafryn murmured when Danil commented on it. "Soldiers likely have run of the city. They might even be rustling up conscripts for the war."

"Conscripts?" Danil thought back to the barred windows and shattered doors of the surrounding buildings. "People are being taken by force."

"Likely so. The alternative is to willingly go up against dragons and other folk in a strange land far from home. What would you choose?"

"Thankfully, I've never had to worry about it," Danil muttered.

Hafryn gave him a tight smile. He paused in the squalor beside a crate draped with moldering blankets. Danil spied bare feet and dirty breeches, and heard a soft, steady snore emanate from within the crate.

Hafryn squatted next to the sleeping man and gave a low whistle.

The stranger sat up with a jolt, cursing blearily, and Hafryn dealt him a searing blow to the head.

"Hafryn!" Danil hissed. He watched in dismay as Hafryn

dragged the unconscious man out of the crate and divested him of his stained brown tunic.

Hafryn threw the tunic at Danil. "It stinks but you should put it on," he said before grabbing one of the rat-eaten blankets and throwing it about his own shoulders like a cape. "We look Amasian, *fala*. Hurry!"

Danil glanced down at the fine weave of his tunic and quickly shucked it off. He shuddered at the unwashed stink of sweat as he pulled the stolen tunic over his head. "Do you think those soldiers know who came through the portal?" he asked in an effort to ignore the slight damp around his middle.

"If they did, I'd expect far more soldiers," Hafryn said, searching the unconscious man's crate for anything useful. He turned back to Danil. "Here, give me your hand. We need to hide your glyph. Mine, too."

Danil turned his hand about, dismayed to see the glyph of Kailon had faded to a white scar on his palm.

"It's the distance," Hafryn said, wrapping a dirty strip of fabric over it. "Whatever the old magus did to your crystal, it sent us much further into Roldaer than what should be possible." He squeezed Danil's hand. "Don't worry, *fala*. The glyph will shine bright and true once Kailon's leylines find you again. Hopefully, we can get back home quickly."

"How do we go about that?" Danil asked tersely. "I didn't see the old mage come through the portal."

Hafryn sighed. "I don't think he planned to. I scarcely jumped through before it collapsed."

Swallowing heavily, Danil said, "I'm glad you did."

Hafryn's face warmed. "As am I." Wiping his hands, he said, "Let's get some distance between us and our smelly friend here. Then we can think about our next move."

Nodding, Danil stepped out from behind the crate. They trotted to the corner of the alley and peered out onto a darkened square. Devoid of streetlamps and heavy with shadows, it looked as rundown and decaying as the buildings surrounding it. Not even the ruined citadel of Altonas, with its broken stone and the poisoned legacy of Kaul, had felt this still and perilous.

Hafryn threw the ratty blanket over his head like a shroud and ran across the cobbles to a smaller street between two buildings. Danil made to follow but slowed when he looked along the length of the road to the distant, squat hill overlooking the city.

Surrounded by tall stone walls with black parapets, a large tower loomed over the city. In the moonlight, its domed roof looked the color of old blood.

A rush of cold shot through Danil.

All his life, he'd heard tales of the great Magi Tower. Located at the heart of Roldaer, it was where the magi trained and convened to do King Liam's bidding.

Seeing the domed roof, Danil realized the portal had dumped them in the one place he'd never thought to see.

We're in Aqila, he realized numbly.

The royal city of Roldaer.

IT TOOK another night to cautiously navigate their way west across the royal city. Daylight saw Danil and Hafryn keep hidden in small alleys or the back lots of abandoned buildings, resting wherever they dared but Danil knew it was a matter of time before they were discovered. The red dome of the Magi Tower loomed over the city. An oppressive silence lay over Aqila, almost as if the city held its breath.

"We can't stay here much longer," Danil murmured as night drew in about them. "We need horses."

They'd found sanctuary in an empty stable that looked disused for some time. Danil leaned against the end of a stall and nudged sour straw with his boot.

"It's a month's ride back to Kailon," Hafryn said, pulling ticks of straw from his braid. "And with however many magi and soldiers between us."

Danil was sharply aware. His connection to the leylines had restored during the day but still felt tenuous at best with the vast distance between them. "If I hadn't lost my crystal, we could speak with Sonnen."

Hafryn's gaze dropped to Danil's collarbone where the necklace once rested. "There's nothing for it, *fala*. We're on our own."

Danil sighed in frustration. He'd grown used to having a squad of Amasian allies at his back. He sorely missed Sonnen and his steady guidance, along with Elania's easy generosity and Blutark's stalwart presence. There were Amasians who'd followed him into the Roldaerian border camp simply because he was the custodian of Kailon.

He straightened. "Hafryn, aren't there spies still in Roldaer?"

Hafryn paused in working loose his red braid. "Patril must have some of her crows in Aqila," he allowed. "I'm not sure how we'd find them, though. They certainly aren't about to make themselves known when conscriptors are scooping up everyone they can find."

"What about in the army?"

Hafryn's eyebrows rose. "You mean the one that's readying to march on Kailon?"

Danil nodded. "It's just outside the city walls."

They'd heard the army drums throughout the day and

late into the evening. It was impossible to know how large the Roldaerian army was, but their roars and battle cries had entered Danil's broken sleep.

Tilting his head in thought, Hafryn said, "If we can find the crows, we may get home sooner. Your ability to see Trueforms will help. But infiltrating the army will be dangerous for us both."

"No worse than trying to ride across Roldaer with an army at our backs."

"Fair point," Hafryn muttered. "We stay in Aqila much longer and our luck's going to run out, too." He looked toward the stable doors, thinking. "The western gates can't be far. We'll need a diversion."

Danil straightened. "We can't have anyone catch sight of an oversized wolf. First rumor that there's an Amasian hereabouts and they'll lock down the city."

Hafryn nodded. "What about fire? We need only enough of it for the city guard to leave their posts. Nothing so big that the local peasantry becomes at risk—I know you're worried about them."

Feeling a momentary flash of discomfort, Danil explained, "The people are frightened, Hafryn. They hide as desperately as we do."

For a city so large and sprawling, few boldly walked the streets. Those who did dressed richly like noble kind, and Danil surmised they'd somehow bought a modicum of freedom.

"It's life under the boot of the magi, *fala,*" Hafryn said.

It was little different than Danil's own upbringing in Farin, where the arrival of spring had brought with it a dreaded magus whose harsh demands brought even harsher punishments. But in Aqila, the magi left their mark through curses on charred buildings and ornate statues commemorating their glory.

Hafryn threw a cloak he'd pilfered earlier in the day about his shoulders. "If we're doing this tonight, we'll need to scout first."

They soon set out into the darkening streets.

The moon was full and round above Aqila by the time they reached the outer wall and followed its curve to a sprawling market square. City guards patrolled in front of the iron gates leading to the river port. Despite the lateness of the night, traders came up from the harbor. The guards checked over the various wagons, lifting tarps and poking at bundles before letting the drivers rattle past.

Hafryn crouched under the shadowy awning of a closed stall, mouth set as he watched the gates. "Must be supplies for the army," he whispered. "They'll march soon if they're to reach Kailon by summer."

A rush of urgency swept over Danil. He pointed to some horses hitched a newel post beside the guardhouse. "What if we take those?" The polished leather saddles fairly sparkled in the torchlight. Danil scrutinized the bedrolls and saddlebags strapped to each horse with rising hope. "There might even be uniforms in those packs."

"I'd say drunken soldiers own them and are smart enough to sober up in the guardhouse before heading out to the army." Hafryn nodded. "Once we're clear of the gates, we can get rid of these rags and make ourselves look the part of Roldaerian soldiers."

It was a decent enough plan, though Danil felt a rush of nervous energy in his belly.

Hafryn's mouth firmed with resolve. "The breeze should carry the smoke over quickly enough. Wait until the guards get involved."

Danil gripped his sleeve. "Be careful," he whispered. "If they spot you, run. We'll take our chances elsewhere."

Eyes softening, Hafryn touched the side of Danil's face. "Of course." He threw the hood up over his red hair and padded silently across the edge of the market square. He disappeared into the gloom behind a row of closed stalls.

Danil pressed his back against the cold wall, heartbeat thundering as he waited. A couple more wagons trundled across the cobbles before the gates grew quiet.

Eventually, the acrid scent of smoke reached him. He turned to see an orange, flickering glow emanate from behind a nearby building. The moon turned hazy and dull from the smoke. One of the tethered horses nickered restlessly and pawed at the ground. Surprised murmurs came from the gates.

Peeking around the corner of the building, Danil saw a city guard step away from the gates and sniff the air.

The guard gaped at the sky and pointed. "Fire! Fire, damn you all!"

A handful of soldiers staggered out of the guardroom and milled about drunkenly to watch.

Then a woman bellowed, "Don't just gawp like lackwits! Get buckets before we lose half the city!"

The group broke apart and stumbled down the street leading toward the orange glow.

Cursing, the woman mounted and kicked her horse after them.

That's it, Danil thought as quiet settled over the square. Staying low, he hurried over to the saddled mounts. He placed a calming hand on one animal's twitching shoulder. Its nostrils flared as smoke stung the air. Tugging the rope loose from the newel post, Danil quickly hitched the horse's reins to the saddle horn of its quieter companion and set his boot into the stirrup.

A gauntleted fist gripped the back of his tunic and yanked him away. "Ho, now, what's this?" the guardsman chortled, wrenching Danil about. "A thief!"

Danil struggled to keep his feet as the guard heaved him past the horses and toward the gates.

"Sergeant! Another conscript!" the guardsman called out.

Cold rushed through Danil. He wrenched hard, planting his feet, but the guardsman wrapped his fist tighter around the neck of Danil's tunic and gave him a rough shake.

A scowling woman in a red tabard stepped away from the shadows beside the gates. She gave Danil a hard, assessing look.

"Caught him trying to steal your horse, sergeant," the guardsman added.

The sergeant's scowl deepened. "You won't be so enterprising with your hand cut off, thief," she snapped. She looked him up and down. "But you'll do as fodder for the Amasians."

The guardsman holding Danil grinned meanly. "Shouldn't have crawled out of whatever hovel you burrowed in," he hissed. "You're a smelly fellow, but you'll do."

A few more guards left the guardhouse to watch the encounter, their jeering catcalls ringing in Danil's ears.

Desperate rage filled Danil. Stealing horses was the easiest task considering what lay before them. He yanked hard, the tunic tearing free, only to be hauled back when the guardsman gripped a fistful of his hair.

"Steady on!" the guardsman laughed, tightening his grip until Danil's neck arched painfully.

The sergeant gave an approving nod. "Magus Tric rewards extra rations for lively conscripts. Use the manacles."

"Magus?" Danil gasped, terror flooding him. "Wait—!"

His captor struck him across the face. "Quiet, you!"

Another guard trotted over, looking bored as he pulled the metal bracers from a saddlebag and clamped them over Danil's wrists with practiced ease. A short rope attached the manacles to the saddle horn of the nearest horse.

Danil risked a darting glance but saw no sign of Hafryn in the market square. Had he been captured, also?

The sergeant and her party mounted. "Move out," she ordered.

"What about the fire?" Danil asked desperately, giving the rope a futile tug.

"That's another patrol's problem," the sergeant muttered. She smiled sharply. "Unless you had something to do with it, thief?"

Danil's closed his mouth, words caught in his throat.

The sergeant showed teeth. "Keep your secrets. Magus Tric will have you singing like a caged bird soon enough." She kicked her mount viciously.

Jolted away from the newel post, Danil barely kept his feet as he was yanked behind the sergeant's horse. The city guard formed up around him, mounts jostling in agitation. They moved out of the market square.

Danil pulled at the manacles, mouth dry as the direness of the situation closed in on him. If any magus recognized him, he was unlikely to survive it.

5

The sergeant and her patrol marched him deeper into the city.

Few people braved the dark streets, lurking about the shadows as the sergeant dragged Danil past. Those who walked or rode brazenly under the streetlamps each bore a dull bronze pin clasped to their cloaks, and Danil could only surmise the pin freed them of the threat of conscription. No one spared Danil a glance.

The Magi Tower dominated the skyline with its row of torches along the parapets. Danil expected to be taken along the winding road leading up to the stone watchtower at its the entrance, but instead he was yanked off the main street and continued east. The buildings became ornate, with curved stone accents, elegant windows and wooden boxes where small plants grew.

Danil felt the weight of each step. He knew what would happen if Magus Tric discovered his identity. The only question was whether Danil would be killed outright or brought before the Magi Council first.

Skin tightening, he resisted the urge to glance behind to see if Hafryn followed. Long experience had taught him the wolf shifter could steal through the shadows like a wraith, especially in his Trueform. His one comfort was that Hafryn didn't walk in chains beside him.

The patrol rounded a corner to find the streetlamps snuffed out.

The darkness closed in about them as the sergeant raised her fist.

They slowed to a halt.

In the gloom, Danil spied an upended wagon lying a hundred feet away, its spilled contents of pans and barrels blocking most of the street.

A guard's horse released an irritable snort, scuffing one hoof on the cobbles beside Danil.

"Sergeant?" one of the men asked, wariness in his voice.

"We go around," the sergeant said. She tugged on the rope binding Danil to the saddle horn. "Up behind me, conscript."

Danil hesitated, putting his boot on hers in the stirrup.

A flicker of movement was the only warning before a dozen riders clattered out from a side street. Each wore heavy cloths over their faces that covered all but their eyes. Yells and battle cries rang out as they barreled for the sergeant and her guards.

The sergeant shouted, drawing her sword as she wheeled her horse about.

Danil fell back and scrambled to avoid being trodden. He jerked hard on the rope, shouting in frustration as it refused to budge.

A masked rider swept past, blade flashing, and suddenly the rope was cut loose.

Not pausing to count his good luck, Danil ran for the edge of the street, only for his escape to be blocked by a guard's horse. The man snarled and swung his shield down to bludgeon Danil.

A giant wolf leaped out of the darkness and clamped powerful teeth onto the man's arm. Wrenched off his horse, the soldier struck the cobbles with a hard crack. Danil hit him in the head with the edge of his manacles for good measure.

Hafryn turned back to the fighting, fangs bared.

"No! Let's go!" Danil hissed over the clash of steel.

HAFRYN WHEELED ABOUT, loping as Danil scrambled for the side street the attackers had come from.

Danil dived when new masked riders entered the fray. Two carried a net stretched out between them, and Danil whirled as they kicked their horses toward Hafryn. "Watch out!" he shouted in warning.

Someone threw a cloak over his head. Danil flailed, struggling, but received a hard blow to his shoulder that sent a shock of numbness down his arm. He was pushed and buffeted, scarcely able to keep his feet before he was suddenly gripped about the middle and hoisted off his feet. A heartbeat later he was thrown over the neck of a horse.

Snarling and a hurt whine sounded only feet away.

"Hafryn!" Danil shouted, his cry muffled. The horse beneath him leaped forward.

The sound of fighting faded rapidly as the horse charged down a side street.

"*Hafryn!*"

Other riders surrounded him, the sound of hooves

clattering on the cobbles echoing loudly in his ears. He debated pushing himself off the horse's powerful neck but feared being crushed underfoot.

They rode hard through the streets. Danil lost all sense of direction, blood thundering in his ears. After a time, they veered sharply. The cobbles changed to sand as they pulled to a stop.

A gate clanged shut behind them.

Multiple hands grabbed him and wrenched him off the horse. Danil stumbled as they hauled him across a stone threshold. The sudden quiet was accompanied by a rush of cool felt even under the stuffy cloak. Danil spied white marble tile as he was bustled along. He dug in his boots but his captors bodily lifted him and carried him up a flight of stone steps.

Danil sensed a corridor close in about them before a door creaked open and he was suddenly hurled in. Freed of the bruising grip, he whirled about, stripping the cloak free in time to see a pair of masked strangers step back out into a plain corridor.

Danil glanced about the room in search of a weapon. It was starkly bare; a thin grate high on one wall let in a sliver of fresh air and murky torchlight. Danil turned back to his captors, teeth bared as he raised his manacled fists.

"There's no need for animosity."

A woman removed her cloth mask, revealing cold blue eyes and a scarred chin. Middle-aged and pale haired, she looked like a warrior better used to commanding a battalion than stealing conscripts in the night.

"You're among allies, Danil of Farin," she said.

Cold washed through him at hearing his name. He took a cautious step back. "Who are you?" he asked.

She smiled benignly. "A servant of Lady Osriele of Trudan."

Danil wondered if he was supposed to recognize her name. He watched her warily.

The woman motioned to her companion. They tossed a key at Danil's feet.

Danil didn't move, carefully watching them both.

"For your manacles," the woman explained.

"Thank you," he replied but made no effort to pick up the key.

She glowered but was distracted by the sound of jostling in the corridor beyond. She turned aside to make way for two strangers hauling between them a giant red wolf entangled in thick netting.

Danil's heart leaped into his throat.

Hafryn growled lowly as he was dumped a few feet from Danil.

Sliding beside him, Danil yanked the netting loose and ran urgent hands over Hafryn's matted fur. Blood showed darkly about his muzzle but Danil couldn't discern whether any of it belonged to his companion.

"Your Amasian will be fine," the woman murmured.

Danil glowered up at her. He sensed Hafryn's desire to shift but quickly pressed a knee against the wolf's shoulder in warning. "A-Amasian?" he asked with an effort.

She smiled coolly. "It must seem unlikely, but I promise we are allies to you both."

Danil's bared his teeth in hostility. "Is that why you captured us?"

"I wasn't about to pause to explain your rescue, Danil of Farin. But you are esteemed guests here at my lady's manor."

Danil cast a dubious glance about the bare room. It had all the makings of a prison cell.

"You'll understand in time," she added. "We shall speak more in the morning."

She retreated with her companion into the corridor, where she pressed on something hidden in a niche in the wall. Red-tinged light burst in the air and rapidly filled the doorway.

Terror rocked through Danil's innards. *Holy gods...a mage curse!*

The air shimmered as Hafryn transformed to stand protectively in front of Danil. He bared his teeth in readiness.

The woman smirked at the wolf shifter before motioning to her companion.

The door closed with a hard, curse-filled snick.

DANIL PACED under the moonlight streaming through the grate. Despite the red-tinged enchantment over the door, guards stood stationed in the corridor beyond. Their bored patrol had quietened as the night drew on, but he wasn't foolish enough to think them gone.

Hafryn's arms strained as he clung to the grate. "Damn these bars," he muttered under his breath. Bracing his boots against the rough wall, he heaved again, muscles coiling. He swore when there wasn't the slightest give.

Danil chewed the side of his thumb. "What if she hands us over to the Magi Council?"

Grunting, Hafryn gave up on forcing the bars. "I expect we'd already be in their dungeon if that were their plan." He carefully lowered himself to the floor. "Here, check the courtyard. There's a stable opposite us but I don't have your gift for perceiving enchantments."

Danil stepped onto Hafryn's bent leg and pulled himself up to the grate. Their prison looked down on a large, walled courtyard devoid of any greenery. A fountain in the center of the yard was dry and dusty with disuse but on the far side, flickering torchlight showed the stone-lined stables, the doors open to let in the night air. Two guards stood at the entrance, appearing surprisingly alert considering the lateness of the hour.

"What do you see?"

Danil gripped the bars of the grate, adjusting his weight as his vision shifted. The torchlight came into sharper relief, but no strange markings on the stone walls or ground caught his attention. "I'm not entirely sure I'd know it if I saw a mage curse," he admitted, regretting that they'd never tested his *videre* abilities against Roldaerian spells. Releasing a sigh, he dropped back down to the floor. "I suspect that woman let us see the one on the door."

"A show of strength," Hafryn supposed. "Though not her own strength, I suspect. Who was it she said owns this manor?"

"Lady Osriele of Trudan."

The wolf shifter leaned against the wall, boot tapping in agitation. "The magus."

"That would be my guess," Danil agreed. He peered at the door and its faint red radiance. Touching it would cause pain at the very least. But that was nothing compared to what Magus Osriele could do to them. Danil recalled Magus Ronan, who'd brandished a firewhip in Farin with skill and flare while making his victims bleed.

He shuddered.

Hafryn smiled thinly. "Being conscripted might have served us better. You'd be on your way home soon enough."

Danil thought of the bloodthirsty sergeant who'd had no qualms taking his hand. "And what was your plan? To trot after the army and hope no one noticed an oversized wolf trailing after them?"

"Easier than what we face now, don't you think?"

Settling beside Hafryn, Danil took his hand and watched the door.

At dawn came sounds of the compound waking up, with the nicker of horses accompanied by the clang of pots, hushed conversation, and a brisk sweep of a broom in the courtyard below their cell. The two guards at the entrance of the stables were joined by four more, each wearing the pale blue tabard and six-starred symbol of the Magi Guard.

Hafryn peered through the grate to study them but shook his head. "I can't make out the insignia of their mage."

Danil dreaded it was the same battle-horse insignia Magus Brianna had championed. Its connection to Kaul and his misshapen horse Trueform was clear.

Boots trod on the floorboards in the corridor, pausing at the door. Danil caught a flash of red as the curse fell away before the door opened.

Two guards stood at attention behind a manservant dressed in browns and yellows, who bowed. "Lady Osriele asks you break the morning fast with her."

The guards were stony-faced like they would brook no argument.

Wiping damp hands on his breeches, Danil rose and hurried out into the corridor with Hafryn.

The two guards filed in behind them as the mansservant escorted them up a flight of stairs to a pavilion awash with dawn light. Beads of dew clung to the edge of a large awning held aloft by four pillars carved in the shape of robed, stern-faced mages. Underneath the awning was a polished oak table and three gilded chairs with elaborate scrollwork. A warming brazier in one corner took away the sharpness of the morning air.

A woman was already seated, resplendent in a silver gown with matching satin cloak. She looked like a noblewoman freshly returned from a night of frivolity, color high on her cheeks and emerald jewels studded in her coiffed dark hair. On one gloved finger, she wore a ring with a kiandrite crystal shining a virulent red. She looked regally at ease as she motioned them toward the table.

"Please, join me, Danil and Hafryn," Lady Osriele said. The red kiandrite ring flashed in the sunlight.

Behind him, the two guards bowed to the mage and returned down the stairs, leaving just the manservant in attendance.

Hafryn was thin-lipped as he settled opposite Lady Osriele, posture watchful. "You have us at a disadvantage, my lady."

The magus smiled. "Be at ease, Hafryn. There are no magi tricks here."

A pair of servants arrived carrying a tray each; one laden with pastries, jams and compotes, the other with pots of tea. Lady Osriele motioned to the table, and the servants laid out the various plates and dishes with practiced efficiency.

Lady Osriele waited until the servants finished before giving Danil and Hafryn a benign smile. "I must apologize for your rude accommodations last night. News of your capture by the city guard reached me at a time when I was unable to lend aid. Commander Selen acted with commendable caution but I can assure you of better quarters from now on."

Danil gave Hafryn a cautious look.

Hafryn kept his gaze fixed on the mage. "Your commander said you're from Trudan. A land celebrated for its hops and bloodwine."

The mage's grey eyes brightened in delight. "You know something of Roldaer, I see." She murmured her thanks when a servant set a lemon pastry on her plate. Smoothing a napkin over her knee, she turned back to Hafryn. "Trudan is a small barony that serves me well."

"You're a long way from home," Hafryn said.

"Aren't we all?"

The servants retired down the stairs, soon replaced by a new server who arrived with a small tray bearing an elegant ceramic bowl filled with steaming water. A glass stirrer and square of silk cloth also sat on the tray, along with a stoppered bottle made of pale wood. Osriele took each item with gentle hands, laying them out before her with grace. She wiped the rim of the cup before folding the silk cloth once more. Each move was delicately restrained and meditative, and Danil watched with growing fascination.

Lady Osriele unstoppered the bottle and with the tip of the stirrer dipped into the contents.

Danil saw a familiar iridescent shimmer on the tip of the glass rod. He gasped. "Kiandrite."

Beside him, Hafryn gave a low growl.

Osriele dipped the kiandrite-dusted stirrer into the cup, moving it through the water in three slow concentric circles. She tapped once on the rim of the cup, allowing the last drops of water to fall back into the cup, before carefully wiping the stirrer and setting it aside. She took the small bowl in both hands, head bowed for a few long heartbeats, before taking a measured sip.

Danil's vision shifted as he traced the path of the kiandrite flecks into her belly.

The mage gave him a bemused look over the rim of her cup. "I understand you don't require mage-crystal infusions, Danil. I would like to know how this came about."

Folding his arms, Danil asked, "Is this why you've taken us prisoner?"

"Curiosity only," she said mildly. "Now, please, do eat."

Danil leaned back as a plate was set before him. With a flourish, the servant set down stuffed bread brimming with raisins and another pastry layered with silken custard. Danil's belly rumbled. The last day had been grim foraging through the city's detritus.

"You're a generous host," Hafryn allowed, though he scarcely looked at the food presented on his own plate.

Osriele inclined her head. "My servants will have baths ready for you both, also." She looked over their stained tunics, assessing. "I have no idea how you came to be in the royal city or how long you've managed to stay hidden, but I'm glad of it."

Danil raised a dubious eyebrow. ""Attacking the city guard is reckless even for a magus—your guards risked a painful death if caught."

She nodded and used the napkin to dab her lips. "The Magi Council can never know who called for your rescue. But, Danil, your exploits in the deadlands have given me hope. I need you to fulfill a similar task for your homeland of Roldaer."

A ball of unease formed in Danil's belly. "I'm no longer Roldaerian, my lady."

Osriele nodded, unsurprised. "Among my brethren, you're called Danil the Traitor. You defied the will of the magi, and in doing so betrayed our King. You consorted with our enemy, and bedded them, too," she added with a brief glance at Hafryn.

Danil felt his cheeks burn. Beside him, Hafryn seethed.

Osriele stroked the rim of her cup slowly with long fingers. "I know the truth is far more complicated. You've been likewise betrayed, Danil, when you only acted in good faith for your kingdom." She leaned back. "I know what happened in Farin."

Danil felt old grief form as a lump in his throat. He swallowed heavily. "Then you know why I care little for what happens in Roldaer now."

Her grey eyes appeared knowing. "And yet here you are."

"What are we really doing here, magus?" Hafryn asked, his arms folded.

"Call me Osriele, please. I hope to be friends."

Danil glanced at the teacup dubiously. He was confident that he'd never call a mage anything other than an enemy.

"I see I must be frank. Very well." Osriele sat back in her chair, expression troubled. "There is a poison spreading across Roldaer." She looked between them. "A dark and merciless poison where nothing survives and nothing grows once it moves on."

"Sounds like a magi curse," Hafryn muttered. His flat expression gave no evidence he knew of the blacksward Lyria had died to warn them of.

"A curse is something I can contend with," Osriele said with a shake of her head. "This is something that resists all spells. The devastation it has wrought is very similar to the deadlands. Or at least what the deadlands once were."

Danil kept his face free of expression.

Osriele regarded him carefully. "I've heard tellings of what the deadlands have become. Life runs rampant where only barrenness once ruled. That is your doing, Danil."

He shook his head. "You overestimate my hand in Kailon's return."

"I don't think I do." Osriele regarded him a moment longer before she sighed. "The poison is spreading rapidly across Roldaer. If it cannot be stopped, it will destroy the kingdom entirely."

"Still not seeing how this is our problem," Hafryn said.

She smiled slightly. "War has gripped our two lands, Hafryn Wolfkind. Do you not see a connection?"

"Aye. It has to do with the magi and their plot to see Kaul rule over us all."

Osriele tilted her head. "I understand that Kaul Mage-Kin was fortunately defeated in the deadlands."

Glancing at Hafryn, Danil firmed his jaw. They weren't about to tell the magus that Kaul lay imprisoned rather than dead.

Osriele took a sip of her tea before continuing. "Not every mage sees the poison as something to be defeated. According to the Magi Council, Roldaer has grown increasingly useless. But not Amas—it has the power that we crave."

"Kiandrite," Danil surmised.

Osriele inclined her head. "But the Magi Council cannot gain control of Amas alone. We need the services of the army and the common people of Roldaer." She raised her eyebrow. "What better way to ensure the peasantry's wholehearted commitment to war than with the knowledge that they cannot turn back? That their kingdom no longer exists, consumed instead by an unstoppable evil?"

"You're saying the Magi Council wants to see Roldaer destroyed," Hafryn said with a scowl.

"A necessary loss when the goal is Amas and its mage-crystals."

Danil stared at her in astonishment.

Osriele raised her chin. "But I will not sit idle like the Council and pretend to wring my hands as the devastation spreads. Roldaer is my home and my responsibility." She turned her gaze to Danil. "You may be a traitor to your kingdom, Danil, but to save your Amasian friends, we share a common purpose—the saving of Roldaer."

6

Osriele took them downstairs to the second level of the manor. They strode along a corridor looking down on the central courtyard, where more horses marked the arrival of new soldiers. The corridor itself was artfully decorated with painted floor tiles and accented wood paneling framing tapestries of banquets and dance halls. Incense burners sat outside a closed door, and Danil caught the scent of mixed herbs before the mage ushered them inside.

Gilded chandeliers and wall sconces kept the windowless room well lit. The floor was partially carpeted, with a few couches arranged near the fire for comfort. A strange, staff-like pedestal sat in the center of the room. It had clawed prongs designed to hold something but currently sat empty.

Danil's gaze was locked on the walls. A shimmering map of Roldaer sprawled across the four walls, spanning from the south and eastern oceans to the border of Kailon. Small rivers and hills were evident across the map, along with hamlets and towns and the roads that interconnected them.

Stepping closer, Danil thought he saw waves moving in the southern Hermsa Sea.

Taking off her rubied kiandrite ring, Osriele strode to the pedestal and set the ring within the clawed housing. She muttered a few words, and angry light spat out to all corners of the room. Danil instinctively ducked.

Hafryn cursed in surprise, turning slowly about.

Blinking, Danil saw that the map now included ugly black splotches covering the interior of Roldaer. It had a strangely viscous, shiny appearance. Danil caught a vague waft of rotting flesh and foul water. He backed up a step. "It's blacksward, isn't it?"

A flash of relief crossed Osriele's face. "So, my people reached you after all!"

Mouth thin, Hafryn quirked a brow at her.

"I sent a party of three magi and their private guards," Osriele explained. "Their task was to see that you understood the direness of our situation."

"By bringing blacksward to Kailon?" Danil asked, voice sharp.

Osriele looked undeterred. "Would you have believed them otherwise?" she asked. "I figured you could achieve what we have failed to do and destroy the blacksward. I know I was right, Danil."

Danil glanced again at the map. The border of Kailon was clear of the festering black splotches that marred large swathes of Roldaer.

"One of my allies, Magus Bornil, discovered a way to seal portions of blacksward within lead boxes. He journeyed with a sample to the deadlands to find you. I was able to track the blacksward until it suddenly disappeared a few days ago." Osriele gave him a searching look. "But you already know this."

Danil wasn't about to explain how he asked the leylines of Kailon to burn away the contents of the casket.

Osriele sighed. "As you can see, the blacksward has taken hold over much of our prized farmland. Entire towns are gone." She strode to one wall where Aqila sat beside a large river. She tapped an area of the map far to the south of the royal city. "The first sighting of the blacksward was within useless territory along the coast but it has steadily spread from there. I daresay it is only by luck that it's yet to touch Aqila."

"Luck?" Danil asked.

"Indeed. The Magi Council isn't responsible for the blacksward—they simply don't wish to stop it. Their goal would be more difficult if the Magi Tower itself was under threat."

"What's the origin, then?" Hafryn asked. "If the blacksward resists magic, it's because magic has played a part in its creation."

Osriele gave him a thoughtful look. "That I can't say. It emerged last spring. Some magi volunteered to find a solution, and even visited the deadlands to see if the devastation there was of a similar nature."

Frowning, Danil said, "Any magi who came to the deadlands in recent months ended up in Farin—they'd have taken part in the attempt to resurrect Kaul."

She nodded. "I believe you know Magus Brianna and Magus Ronan. They were part of our initial search to understand how the blacksward came to be."

But Danil knew that Brianna's quest in Farin had nothing to do with blacksward. He wondered if Brianna had used the poison as an excuse to search for Kaul's relics and the wellspring.

Hafryn rubbed his chin. "Someone knew of the travel

party you sent to find Danil, Osriele. They were attacked before they reached Kailon—not by Amasians, either."

"If others are working against me, I assure you I would not be standing here now. The Council is swift in its handling of traitors." She peered at the map. "There may be others who can track blacksward just as I have done."

Then they would also know what had happened near Kailon. Danil didn't like showing his hand to the magi, especially when he had done something that no magus seemed capable or willing of doing.

"Your Magi Council will move rapidly now that they know the blacksward can be stopped," Hafryn said. "What do you think, *fala*?"

Danil made a slow turn of the room, following the spread of darkness across the map. "Will stopping the blacksward truly end the war?"

Osriele raised her chin. "Yes. If Roldaer heals as you have done with the deadlands, our people will have no reason to fight."

Danil glanced questioningly at Hafryn.

The wolf shifter shrugged. "You owe Roldaer nothing. Kailon is your duty."

But if protecting Kailon meant saving Roldaer, Danil was ready to risk it.

Movement interrupted his thoughts, and Danil smothered a gasp. Lyria's ghost stood beside a section of the map where the black looked thickest. Her armor reflected flames from the candlelight. The kiandrite crystal in her axe cast iridescent light across the map, flaring brightest across a tract of poisoned land. Danil felt compelled to move towards it. Underneath the black was a tangle of streams, estuaries, and marshlands that filtered out toward the treacherous Hermsa Sea.

"It's the Fens," Osriele said, watching him with open curiosity. "A place of no importance, just brackish water and poor farms with few good folk to work them."

Danil drew closer to Lyria. The crystal in her axe grew brighter, coalescing on a tiny dot of rock on the coast. "What about here?" He tapped the map.

Osriele moved closer, thumbing her lip in thought. "An abandoned spire, I believe. It's surely been empty since living memory. I can't even recall its name."

Lyria gazed somberly at the coastal spire before drawing Danil's gaze to a stretch of black elsewhere in the Fens. The tip of her axe pressed upon it.

The crackling growl of an avalanche rolled over Danil. He stilled, breathing catching in his lungs as the cloying reek of rot and fouled water suffocated the air. His heart ratcheted in his chest. The blackness upon the map called out to him, harsh whispers booming in his ears.

Too late, Hafryn leaped for him. "Danil, don't—!"

The darkness shot up and consumed Danil whole.

7

Rain hissed as it struck broken stone pillars and crumbling stone. A platform stained black with mold sat surrounded by thorny scrub and deadened trees.

Danil took careful steps past Amasian guards standing at attention under flickering torchlight. Patril, the crow commander of Altonas, stood among them, hand resting on her sword. She and her companions remained unaware of Danil, their attention fixated on the platform.

Powerful glyphs warded the steps, spreading in concentric circles across the stone toward a palely glowing prison of kiandrite. A cold wind sent damp leaves skittering up against Danil's legs.

Within the kiandrite prison, Kaul slept.

Even stripped of his monstrous helm and armor, the dread lord radiated darkness. Painted silver glyphs covered his broad hands and scowling face.

A whisper of movement made Danil turn.

Three cloaked figures stood on the edge of the platform. Darkness cleaved to them, making it impossible to read their features under their shadowed hoods. The closest figure appeared impossibly large and bore an ornately-pommeled broadsword, while his companion held forth a wooden staff with a milky-white orb that cast sickly light over them all. The other figure was indistinguishable under their cloak, though they hunched like an old woman bowed with age.

Reeking foulness swirled about them, though Patril and her fellow guards were unmoved by the strangers' arrival.

One figure pulled back their hood, revealing a white-haired woman with darkly glittering eyes.

Danil stepped back as recognition flared. "Videre," he breathed.

During the Great War, she had used her powers to help Kaul bury the glyphs meant to stop him. With her help, the dread lord had defied time and death to return to Kailon. It was only with the aid of the leylines that Danil had been able to defeat him.

The videre smirked.

But why are we here? Danil wondered, returning his gaze to the imprisoned dread lord. Something had called him to this strange place.

Glancing down, he noticed the glyph on his hand pulsed black to match the lichen staining the platform. The thick scent of rot churned about him. His gorge rose.

The figure holding the milky-white orb raised their staff high. Sickly light flooded the platform.

A powerful force suddenly gripped Danil's wrist. Sweat gathering, he was forced to raise a trembling hand and press the glyph of Kailon hard against the smooth crystal imprisoning Kaul. The stench of death plumed around him.

With a resounding clap, the crystal prison cracked.

Kaul's eyes snapped open.

8

Danil fell back with a jolt. He struck the carpeted floor, breath shuddering. Gazing up, he suddenly saw Lyria crouched over him, her expression furious.

He scrambled back.

Suddenly Hafryn was there, shaking him. "Danil, what happened?" he asked urgently. "You faded out just like—" He stopped suddenly, throwing a sharp look at Osriele, who sat frozen with a startled expression on her face.

—*Like when Kaul had first reached through the void*, Danil thought, shaking.

Lyria stepped back, facade implacable. Her armor flashed sharply in the candlelight before she was suddenly gone.

Bile burned in Danil's throat.

"Steady, now," Hafryn said, helping him sit upright.

Taking a gulp of air, Danil said, "Forgive me. I-I'm not sure what happened."

Hafryn shook his head, lips white. He turned to Osriele. "The last few days have been rather trying. He needs rest."

Osriele hesitated, then nodded. "Being portalled such

distances affects everyone differently, especially those with a magical bent. Let me send for a healer. We can continue this later." She opened the door and motioned to the manservant waiting outside. "Show them to their rooms."

The manservant bowed deeply.

Hafryn threw one of Danil's arms about his shoulders and eased him upright.

The world whitened for a moment as blood hammered in Danil's ears.

"Find your feet," Hafryn murmured in his ear, steadying him.

The dizziness passed, and Danil sucked in shaky breaths. "I can make it," he said, swallowing. He needed to tell Hafryn everything he'd seen.

Looking dubious, Hafryn helped him down the corridor, trailing after the manservant. They took a new balconied walkway that looked down on a smaller, private courtyard with a tinkling fountain.

They entered a room filled with streaming sunlight. Danil vaguely noted the soft tapestries and ornate furnishings before Hafryn eased him down onto a raised bed thick with feathery down. He sank into it with a sigh.

Hafryn turned to the manservant. "I need a water basin and cooling cloths."

The manservant bowed and closed the door after him without sliding the lock into place.

Hafryn raised an eyebrow at that before turning back to Danil. "A vision hasn't taken you like that since the dread lord was defeated."

"I saw Kaul in his kiandrite prison. His *videre* was there."

Hafryn sank onto the bed beside him. "The woman from the Great War? How's that possible?"

Danil quickly recalled the other hooded figures he'd

seen, again tasting the foulness that had emanated from them. He swallowed. "I don't understand it. Patril was there, too."

Frowning, Hafryn pushed sweaty hair from Danil's forehead. "She and her finest crows guard over Kaul's prison." He suddenly sighed. "If your vision indeed sent you there, it's possible you saw some sort of true-telling."

"Then Kaul's awake," Danil said in alarm. "The prison won't hold him for much longer."

Hafryn scrubbed his hands over his face in weary frustration. "The vision took you only after you touched the map. I can't help but suspect a link between the blacksward and Kaul."

Danil nodded, wondering at that as well. He spoke of Lyria's ghost and how she'd pointed to the abandoned spire on the coastal edge of the Fens.

"A magi ghost—just what we need. She's not here now, is she?" Hafryn asked, shooting a wary look about the room.

Danil shook his head.

Hafryn relaxed slightly. "There was a time when our greatest problem was your innate ability to find kiandrite in the deadlands, *fala*."

Danil missed the simplicity of those days, too. But then he wouldn't have Hafryn at his side. "We need to discover who Lyria was."

"Osriele should know," Hafryn said, though he wrinkled his nose with unease.

Their conversation was interrupted by the arrival of Osriele's healer. Dressed in green robes and carrying a satchel, the venerable mage had kindly lines about his mouth as he set a basin of fragrant water on the side table. Wet cloths pressed to Danil's forehead brought blessed relief.

"No spells," Hafryn growled.

The healer-mage ignored Hafryn as he took Danil's face in his hands and examined his eyes with disconcerting intensity. He then turned Danil's wrist and pressed a finger to the pulse. The mage's gaze lingered for a moment on the glyph on Danil's palm.

Danil glanced at it, also, dismayed by the pale, scar-like mark. By habit he wriggled his fingers, wishing to see flashes of blues, yellows and pinks whirl across the surface.

Hafryn gripped Danil hand, intertwining their fingers together and blocking the glyph from the healer's view.

Danil threw him a startled glance. The wolf shifter stared warningly at the healer, teeth partly bared.

Clearing his throat, the healer left off his examination and said, "It appears you have a mild bout of mage-fever, young man."

Danil blinked. "Mage-fever?"

"Too much spellwork has left you drained beyond healthy reserves," the magus observed. "You'd do well to learn how to better pace yourself."

Danil shook his head in confusion. "But I haven't—"

"What can be done for it?" Hafryn interrupted, giving Danil's hand a warning squeeze.

"A tincture of mage-crystals will make things right," the healer-mage said. He rifled through his satchel.

The thought of drinking kiandrite like a magus made Danil shudder. "I won't drink it," he said.

The healer paused, his bushy eyebrows rising. "Your only other choice is to stay abed for a few days."

"Better," Hafryn said.

Danil gave a short nod of agreement.

"I shall recommend a bath be brought in at haste, then,"

the healer continued. "With all due delicacy, one can smell you both from the stables."

Hafryn released an amused snort. "We'd be grateful, healer."

Satisfied, the man made for the door.

When he was gone, Hafryn turned back to Danil with a frown. "Spellwork?"

"Obviously not," Danil muttered, settling into the soft downy bed once more. It eased the tension in his shoulders like a warm embrace.

Hafryn made a slow study of him. "He seemed to think you were a magus. Or an apprentice, at least."

Danil gave him a baleful look.

Raising his hands, Hafryn said, "Such assumptions could be useful. Don't be quick to discount it."

Danil sighed. "The healer might believe I'm magically drained but I think it's because I'm so far from Kailon." He couldn't help but reach west toward the leylines. A faint whisper reached back, though it was so remote that it slipped like gossamer between his fingers.

Hafryn stroked his jaw. "No custodian has ever traveled so far from their House," he admitted. "Some custodians are known to roam, but all leylines in Amas are connected. No one's ever truly separated from their House."

"There aren't any leylines in Roldaer," Danil said. It felt like dead, silent land when his mind swept across it.

"Only empty channels," Hafryn agreed. "The magi have much to answer for."

Danil turned his head on the pillow to study Hafryn. "Do you really think Osriele wants to stop the blacksward?"

Hafryn hesitated. "If she's part of the quest to spread it, we'd be in the Magi Tower dungeons right now. That doesn't mean we can trust her." He settled beside Danil and tucked his arm under his head. "The Magi Council's plan is impressive, though—to force Roldaer to invade because the kingdom is a poisoned ruin."

"We have to stop the blacksward," Danil said.

With a grunt, Hafryn said, "I'm guessing we're headed for the abandoned spire."

Danil threw him a startled look.

Hafryn's mouth quirked. "That's where your ghost wants us to go, yes?"

"Lyria's not my ghost," Danil replied uncomfortably. But he couldn't forget her fierce expression when the kiandrite from her battle-axe glittered across the map.

"She's decided you're the one destined to fulfill her quest. Were I a ghost, I'd likely choose you, too," Hafryn said.

Danil snorted.

The door opened again as a line of servants entered; two carried a large wooden tub that they set opposite the bed, while more servants brought in steaming buckets of water. They filled the tub in rapid order, the fragrant steam of peppermint filling the room.

A new servant came in with towels and clean, pale robes, which she draped over the back of a chair. She set a tray of sandsoap on a stool and bowed before ushering everyone out and closing the door once more.

Waiting until the tread of boots faded, Danil gingerly swung his legs off the bed. He held his breath for a few heartbeats, satisfied when the room hardly spun. The heated water called to him like a longed-for lover. He padded to the door and set the lock.

Hafryn watched with interest from the blankets when

Danil pulled his tunic over his head, shuddering at the grease and stains when he dropped the rags to the tiles.

Lowering his breeches, Danil said, "There's more dirt on me than an alley cat." He turned slightly, rubbing his flank. "See?"

"I surely do," Hafryn said, eyes growing heated. "Roldaer's got her grubby hands all over you."

Danil chuckled as he clambered over the rim of the tub. "This will certainly set things right." Fragrant water swelled around him. He stretched out languidly. "There might even be room for both of us."

"Oh?"

"Plenty of soap, too." Danil raised an eyebrow archly.

Hafryn grinned and launched off the bed.

To Danil's surprise, he drowsed for much of the day. Servants came with the midday and evening meals, and at Hafryn's urging, they both ate well. The wolf shifter took to lounging in the stuffed chair beside the bed, his bare feet on the blankets and fingers tapping restlessly on the armrest.

The next time Danil woke, Hafryn was dressed in longs sleeves and breeches, hopping on one foot as he pulled on polished boots. A candelabra on the nightstand cut through the darkness, while a deep silence indicated it was likely late in the night.

The low murmur of voices passed outside their door.

Hafryn threw a tunic at Danil's head. "Get dressed, *fala*," he whispered.

Throwing off the blankets, Danil followed after him, grimacing at the cold tiles underfoot.

Hafryn cracked open the door, allowing in a sliver of

light. The voices grew louder now, but Danil saw no one on the balcony overlooking the courtyard. Gazing down, he spied saddled horses outside the stables, along with three Magi Guard dressed in red tabards. They stood at attention, with one holding the reins of a fourth horse.

Danil cautiously edged back into the shadows.

"Come on," Hafryn whispered.

Taking careful steps and hugging close to the wall, they followed the corridor to a reception room, where firelight streamed from the open doorway. Danil recognized Osriele's voice coming from within, her low murmur respectful and restrained. The other voice was a man, one that Danil didn't recognize. He risked a peek inside and saw Osriele seated on a divan in an elegant formal room with stiff-backed chairs and a small table with a pot of steaming tea.

If Osriele noticed them, she gave no indication. Her companion sat with his back to the doorway, his balding pate gleaming in the firelight. He wore a red woolen robe, and Danil felt a rush of cold at the realization that it was another mage.

"You were missed at the Magi Council meeting this day, my lady," the man murmured. "I was tasked with seeing to your wellbeing."

"I can assure you there's nothing for you to report back to the Council, Lord Heron," Osriele took a demure sip of her tea. "As you can see, I am quite well."

The mage inclined his head. "You can understand our caution, my lady. The city is abuzz with rumors. The filthy Amasians have sent assassins among us. As the king's cousin and treasured heir, you must be protected."

Danil stilled at the revelation, while Hafryn cursed softly beside him.

"I assure you, my lord, my guards are most capable." She

tapped a long finger against the arm of the divan. "They have served me long before I became heir."

"Of course. However, the city will be stripped of its safeguards once the army has begun its march for our glory," Lord Heron said.

Osriele gave a low hum. "I understand that will be in the next few days."

"Preparations are moving apace," Lord Heron agreed. "I will have more guards brought to you."

She smiled coolly. "I won't see my private manor overrun, my lord. So many guards would serve only to leave it feeling like a prison."

"That is not our intent, your highness."

She smiled slightly. "But you make a fair point. Perhaps staying in Aqila is no longer a wise choice." Osriele gave him a mild look. "What news of the hunt for the Amasian wolf in our fair city?"

"Ten feet tall and with fangs the stuff of nightmares," Lord Heron said with a shudder. "He attacked during a melee with the rebels." His bald pate reddened in the firelight. "The city guard grows lax in their task of conscription."

"That's something under your command, is it not?" Osriele asked, eyebrow raised.

The man folded his hands into his lap and straightened. "The city patrols are being suitably punished," he said. He tilted his ear toward the plastered ceiling as if listening to something. "Do you have guests, my lady? I sense another magus."

Osriele shook her head, grey eyes amused. "An apprentice is here following the loss of his master in the deadlands last month. He's convalescing until a new master can be found."

Danil wondered if they spoke of him. Hafryn squeezed his elbow in alarm.

"That's most generous of her highness. We suffered a heavy blow with the deaths of so many of our kindred magi. The Traitor of Farin is proving a bigger problem than expected." Lord Heron took a hearty gulp of tea. "Still, what is a deadland scavenger to the might of Roldaer?"

Hafryn gave a low hiss, mouth pinched.

"Indeed, Lord Heron. And rumors of Kaul Mage-Kin still persist."

"You're well informed, as always. The high priestess assures me that her plans are moving to fruition."

Osriele gave a soft, disbelieving chuckle. "Come, now, my lord! Kaul was defeated and is now missing—likely dead, if the shifters have any sense of self-preservation."

"He's not so easy to kill, your highness," Lord Heron said smugly. "We need only concentrate on our own task."

"You mean seeing Roldaer fall." Her fists balled in her lap.

The other mage lost his smugness. He set down his tea. "I understand the loss of Trudan to the blacksward was difficult for you. We have all suffered. Our glory will be in restored when the Amasian blight is vanquished."

Osriele inclined her head but her gaze remained sharp.

"But the evening grows late." Rising, the magi lord gave Osriele a deep bow. "I will press upon your hospitality no longer, your highness. Thank you for the tea."

"You're most welcome, Lord Heron." Osriele smiled benignly. "My man will show you out."

Lord Heron bowed once more, and Danil saw him smile thinly.

Hafryn shook his arm and motioned for him to hurry. They trotted back along the balcony on silent feet, closing the door to their room just as footsteps sounded on the stairs.

Pressing his ear to the door, Danil listened to the mage command his men to mount up. The sound of hooves and the creak of the outer gate opening echoed across the courtyard before the mage and his three men left the manor.

Footsteps sounded outside the room before Osriele stalked inside. She closed the door hard behind her and scowled at them. "Are you both curse-addled?" she hissed. "Lord Heron is a member of the Magi Council! Had the inclination struck, he'd have found you in a heartbeat."

Hafryn folded his arms. "It wouldn't have mattered unless you told his lordship who we are, highness."

Her shook her head in disbelief at him. "There is a likeness of your lover hanging from the walls of the Magi Tower. Do you know what fate will befall Danil should he be found?"

A terrible chill gripped Danil's innards.

"If you speak true, princess, you're taking quite the risk in harboring us," Hafryn said, though he looked pale and sickened.

She muttered an oath under her breath. "Roldaer is my home. My birthright. I will not abandon it. If that means I must go against my fellow magi to ensure it remains hale and strong, then that is my fate."

"Highness or no, you'll end up in the dungeons of the Tower with that kind of talking," Hafryn observed.

She raised her chin. "No slight to your kingdom, Hafryn, but I have no wish to live there."

"Happy to pillage it though," Hafryn observed.

Osriele said nothing to that, her mouth thin.

Danil folded his arms, unsettled. If they were truly to form an alliance with Osriele, he knew it could only be temporary. No matter if they cleansed Roldaer the blacksward, the magi's need for kiandrite would still endure. Kailon would remain at risk.

"How is it that you're the heir to the throne?" Hafryn asked, eyes narrow. "You're of an age to King Liam."

"We share a grandmother," Osriele said tersely. "His Majesty has yet to sire children, and his previous heir met an unfortunate end while training for battle. Now I'm expected to remain in Roldaer while the war takes its course."

"Dangerous, wouldn't you say, considering your Council's plan for your beloved kingdom?" Hafryn observed.

Her mouth tightened. "Tragedy has a way of bringing folk together."

"You must be well-regarded, then. I can't imagine anyone mourning a dead magus."

Osriele's smirked warningly. "I wouldn't be so smug, wolf, considering your wellbeing very much hinges on my own."

Hafryn curled his lip. "And I wouldn't—"

Stepping between them, Danil said, "Enough. This isn't how alliances are made. No matter our differences, we share a common goal. The blacksward must be overcome—for the benefit of Amas and Roldaer." He glanced sharply at Hafryn.

The wolf shifter looked unhappy but offered him an accepting shrug. "We either deal with it here or at the border."

It felt wiser to deal the blacksward at its root, rather than striking Kailon with the Roldaerian army at its heels.

Osriele looked between them, her features lifting in

hope. "Then we're agreed? You'll heal Roldaer as you have done the deadlands, Danil?"

He wasn't sure if that was possible. The damage done by the spreading blacksward could well be permanent. But the alternative was too devastating to leave unchallenged.

"We'll do all we can."

9

Preparations were painfully slow when undertaken in the shadows of the Magi Council. Supplies intended for the Roldaerian army made their way into the manor under cover of night, while the number of guards taking residence in the stable gradually swelled to over thirty as the days progressed. Danil chafed at the slowness of it all, his gaze often turning west where the murmur of leylines was a fleeting whisper.

When more riders arrived late in the afternoon, Danil and Hafryn were escorted to a new room where a plain map of Roldaer was laid out on a polished oak table. The new map showed the kingdom's terrain in miniature scale, from the lakes of Plenir to the jagged mountains bordering Kailon.

Standing beside Osriele at the table, a middle-aged woman appeared ready for battle, wearing a dark leather cuirass with a silver gorget and bracers over her forearms and leather breeches. Russet brown fur lined the hood of her cloak, her blond hair pulled back in a tail. A shield and spear leaned against a nearby chair.

She gave Danil and Hafryn a hard, unwelcoming stare, her blue eyes like hard gems, and Danil suddenly recognized her as the woman who'd rescued them from the city guard.

"This is Commander Selen," Osriele said mildly. "She's been with me since I first attained my magi robes many years ago."

Commander Selen bowed stiffly. "Grace to you both."

Danil bowed awkwardly in return, while Hafryn watched her with a wolf's quiet intensity.

"The commander will be joining us on our quest, along with a select handful of her most trusted guards," Osriele explained.

"I'd prefer a full guard complement, my lady," Commander Selen said, wary gaze assessing Hafryn.

Osriele merely shook her head. "Three guards, commander, as we discussed. Any more will draw too much interest. Hafryn and Danil here will make up the appropriate numbers for a travel party befitting a mage of my standing."

The commander inclined her head, though she looked dissatisfied. "If that's your wish, my lady."

Osriele returned to the table. "Now, shall we discuss how best to cleanse Roldaer of its poison?"

Drawing close, Danil set his gaze over the map. He felt instinctively drawn south to the same rocky outcrop Lyria had pointed to, where the Hermsa Sea bordered a sprawling basin of streams and estuaries. He tapped the parchment roughly where Lyria's kiandrite had focused all of its iridescent light. "This place."

"Again, you insist upon an abandoned spire," Osriele murmured, her head slanted in curiosity. "It's called Isfil—

there are few records about its former purpose, though I believe it was once a place of magi learning."

"We'd have to journey through the Fens to reach it," the commander said, studying the map. "In such a worthless scrap of mud, we're likely to come upon brigands and outcasts."

Hafryn folded his arms. "If I recall correctly, the blacksward has a heavy presence there."

"Much of the surrounding Fens is in ruins," Osriele agreed. She glanced at Danil. "I'm uncertain of your insistence that we journey to Isfil. There are other places in Roldaer where the suffering is greater."

Resisting the urge to look at Hafryn, Danil said, "I can't explain it, my lady. But if you wish for our help, there needs to be a measure of trust."

Commander Selen folded her arms and muttered something under her breath.

Hafryn gave her a hard look. "We're here at your mistress's behest, commander. If you take our advice only when it's convenient, we've got little chance of success."

"It's not my duty to take you at your word, wolf," the commander replied coolly. "Lady Osriele is my one responsibility."

Raising her hands, Osriele said, "Our task is too great to hold onto old enmities. Commander Selen, I expect you to select only guards who can work with our new allies."

The commander pressed a fist to her breast, blue eyes stubborn. "Yes, my lady."

Satisfied, Osriele turned back to Danil. "The Fens are more than a month's ride from Aqila. The army could well be at the deadland border by then, and the blacksward will surely follow in its wake. I admit your insistence that we go to Isfil is...puzzling."

Hafryn rubbed his chin, a look of discomfort crossing his face. "Danil can see into things that we can't, Osriele. Kailon's thrived because of it. If his instincts point him to an abandoned spire, then we must make all haste there."

Curiosity crossed Osriele's features. "Perhaps you're seer-touched, Danil. That will be most useful on our journey."

Danil forced himself to shrug, not inclined to explain his abilities as a *videre* to a magus, even one who professed to be an ally. "I'm peasant born, my lady. My abilities surprise no one more than me."

Her curiosity only sharpened.

Hafryn cleared his throat. "As Osriele says, we don't have the time to ride across the countryside for a month." He glanced across the table at the magus. "Have you anyone who can portal us to the Fens?"

Danil stilled, part dreading the answer.

The commander laughed in astonishment. "You are brazen, wolf!"

"It's a fair question, Selen." Osriele looked at them both, thinking. "I haven't the skill to portal us there. It is a unique ability that very few magi have."

Thank the gods, Danil thought. The landscape of the coming war would be very different if every magus had the skill to transport soldiers deep into Kailon.

"But the ancient system of pillars still work," Osriele continued. "I believe one such pillar would see us arrive near the Fens." She returned to the map, searching. "Here. An old waypoint sits on the edge of the marshlands near the crossroad leading to Jaffen. From there, it's a week's ride to the coast."

Feeling a rush of anxiety, Danil glanced questioningly at Hafryn.

"If that's the best option," Hafryn said with another unhappy sigh.

Osriele paused gravely. "I must warn you that for us to use the system of pillars, the nearest one we can access is in Aqila. Within the Magi Tower, to be precise."

Danil's stomach dropped. Even hidden from sight, the tower was a heavy presence in the back of his mind.

Hafryn scowled derisively. "You expect us to enter the Magi Tower willingly? When every magus within knows what Danil looks like? Surely you jest!"

The commander grunted. "I can ensure Danil remains unnoticed."

Hafryn gave a disbelieving snort.

Chin raised, Osriele said, "As you said, Hafryn, there must be a measure of trust between us."

It was asking more of Danil than he felt willing to give. But no alternative was likely to present itself, and he couldn't renege on his duties as both custodian of Kailon and friend to Amas. They had to risk the Magi Tower.

Hafryn raised a questioning eyebrow at Danil, mouth tight.

Shaking himself, Danil said, "We use the pillars to get as close as we can to Isfil."

Hafryn sighed but looked unsurprised.

"Very well," Osriele said, rolling up the map. "Your bravery is commendable, Danil. Both of you."

The commander folded her arms. "Our arrival at the Magi Tower will raise questions. We can say you're retiring to the summer palace for your safety, my lady. With Aqila emptied and the army on the march, the royal heir will indeed be at risk. No one need know our true destination."

Osriele inclined her head in agreement. "Organize a

suitable retinue, then. And inform the Magi Tower of our impending arrival."

"I'll need until the morning to make final preparations, my lady," Commander Selen.

"See it done."

The commander saluted crisply before taking up her shield and spear and marching out of the room.

Hafryn canted his head, green eyes narrow. "Can we expect spells that alert your brethren of an Amasian in the Tower, Osriele?"

She released a soft, startled laugh. "I promise you, Hafryn, no mage believes your people would dare."

Hafryn smiled, showing teeth. "Clearly, they're mistaken."

anil pulled on the buckles of Hafryn's leather cuirass, glancing up when his friend grunted. "Not too tight?"

Hafryn tested the armor, twisting and bending as a cockerel crowed at the dawning sky on the street outside the manor. "Osriele must have spent a pretty coin to outfit her personal guard like this." He suddenly winked. "We'll see by day's end if I've got chafe or smell like a tannery."

Danil studied the entirety of Hafryn's outfit, inspecting the leather arms guards, tooled belt and matching Roldaerian wayfarer boots. A yellow ribbon meant for Osriele's guard tied back Hafryn's red hair.

"You look ridiculous," Danil said.

Looking mildly affronted, Hafryn said, "At least I have a sword." He raised it, testing the balance. "It'll do, should there be a need."

"Let's hope not," Danil muttered, tossing him a fawn cloak. He fastened his own matching cloak and tucked his dagger out of sight in his boot, yearning for a more familiar blade.

Hafryn picked up a pair of ceremonial helms left on the

table. Plumed feathers dyed yellow bristled from the top. "The commander has no love for us, but she's certainly thinking ahead," he observed. "I don't want us entering the Magi Tower with people able to see our faces. Yours in particular."

It still alarmed Danil that so many magi knew his face. It was only by chance that he hadn't been recognized before Commander Selen and her guards had rescued them. He thumbed the hinge of his helm's visor. "Will you really be the first Amasian to enter the Magi Tower?"

"Willingly, perhaps."

Danil drew his attention away from the visor and peered closely at Hafryn.

"Don't you remember Talis? The vole shifter who was taken on our journey to Altonas?" Hafryn prompted when Danil gave him a blank look. "He was probably brought through the Magi Tower before being sent to places unknown."

A ball of guilt formed in Danil's belly. He hadn't thought of the young man since Kailon had awakened. "What do you think happened to him? I don't understand why magi would take Amasians at all."

"We haven't discovered the reason either—not even our spies," Hafryn said. Putting the helm on his head, he lifted the visor. "Amasians have been taken for years." His green eyes were darker than normal. "Keep your wits about you. With your ability to see Trueforms, you may be able to find them when all other efforts have failed."

Danil nodded, feeling a rush of responsibility.

A quiet knock on the door stalled any further conversation. A servant bowed and offered to escort them to the stables.

Danil put on his helm before stepping out into the

corridor. They followed the servant down the stairs and across the courtyard to the stables. Inside, Commander Selen busily addressed two dozen guards in the same attire as Danil and Hafryn.

The commander paused at their arrival and gave them both a hard look. "You're late. The sun is already up."

Hafryn bowed as the sky grew pink overhead. "Apologies, commander."

Commander Selen's nostrils flared. "For the time being, if I address you, you will place your fist on your chest and say 'yes, commander!'" she ordered. "Isn't that so, guardsmen?"

Behind her, the row of guards pressed their fists against their armored chests and shouted as one, "Yes, commander!"

Danil could feel Hafryn roll his eyes beneath his helm. The wolf shifter nonetheless made a crisp imitation of the guards' movements, and Danil hurried to do the same.

Still looking displeased, Commander Selen turned back to the guards who had their horses saddled and ready. "You are Lady Osriele's personal protection. I have briefed you on the task at hand. If you fail me, there will be an accounting."

"Yes, commander!"

"You will speak to no one about our new arrivals. They are our allies and will be treated as such."

"Yes, commander!"

It was impossible to know whether they meant it.

Apparently satisfied, the commander turned and nodded at a stableboy holding the bridles of two bay mares. The boy offloaded the reins to Danil and Hafryn.

"The Housemaster assures me there are sufficient provisions for you both in the saddlebags," the commander said. "The caring and upkeep of your horses are your own responsibility."

Hafryn checked over the saddlebags and stirrups before nodding to Danil to mount.

Swinging up, Danil gave his horse a gentle pat on the neck and glanced about.

The guards ignored them, busy with final preparations.

Osriele arrived dressed in brown travel robes with gold trim. She looked over her personal guard and gave a two-fingered signal. They quickly mounted as the stableboy emerged with a black gelding.

Once mounted, Osriele steered her horse to where Danil and Hafryn waited. "These are my most trusted guards. You can be certain of their discretion and loyalty. Although, Hafryn, I must ask you not to speak once we leave the manor—at least until we are free of the city. Your Amasian accent will likely betray us all."

Hafryn inclined his head. "Of course, my lady."

Osriele nodded in satisfaction. "Let this be the day we turn the tide against the blacksward and all who would see it prevail," she declared.

Commander and the guards pressed their fists to their chests.

Osriele motioned for the party to ride out. The personal guard quickly formed position around her. Danil found himself behind and to the left of the mage, with Hafryn at his side.

The gates opened out onto a cobbled street lined by more compounds and gated manors. Danil was unsurprised to discover they had been brought into the wealthier quarter of the city. The pale, swept cobbles blazed like gold in the gathering light. The surrounding buildings, though squat and plainly shaped, nonetheless had individual touches like painted doorways, tiled walls and even frescoes depicting events like feasts, a boar hunt and noble folk lounging about a courtyard filled with fountains.

The city guards hereabouts were equally better kempt, their uniforms crisp and blades showing ornamental hilts with various gems and animal-shaped pommels. They paused in their duties to bow as Osriele and her party rode past. Noble folk and servants likewise appeared to recognize her, sweeping aside or dropping to their knees with soft murmurs of 'your highness' and 'Lady Osriele'.

Osriele stared regally ahead, ignoring the spectacle she caused as they rode along the main road headed for the towering stronghold that loomed over the city.

Danil had to resist the urge to fidget in the saddle when they reached the flagstone archway at the base of the gravel road leading up to the Magi Tower. The dark walls loomed over them, blocking out the morning sun. Danil glimpsed the red dome marking the tower itself. Soldiers were evident upon the parapet, while white birds circled in the thermals above.

Climbing the gravel path, the city gradually dropped below them. Flat roofs and neatly rowed streets spread out toward the river harbor, where ships and barges navigated the brown water.

But Danil's gaze snapped west, past the city walls to the adjoining fields. A mass of tents, pennants and training corrals sprawled far into the horizon. Soldiers trained on horseback but were scarcely more than dots and flapping pennants in the distance. Closer to the city, trained soldiers harangued scrappy lines of pikemen and fighters into battalions.

Danil felt a sick sort of astonishment at the size of the

army. There had to be tens of thousands of soldiers and conscripts readying to march.

Hafryn pulled up beside him, posture tight.

"We're to fight that?" Danil choked out, voice hardly a whisper as the magnitude of what they were up against swept over him. It scarcely mattered that more and more Amasians had volunteered to protect Kailon.

This army would crush them all.

GUARDS WEARING red tabards watched from the rampart above as the party rode under the Magi Tower's massive iron portcullis and into a bailey. Inside was surprisingly austere, with no banners or intricate statues and carvings; just a spare expanse of cobbled stones, grey walls and battlements. And guards—so many that Danil felt sweat bead under his braid. Hafryn appeared relaxed beside him, the feathery plume of his helm swaying jauntily as they followed Osriele's lead.

They passed under the heavy shadow of the tower itself. Danil tilted back his head to see that not even a single window or arrow-slit was evident along its ominous height. Four heavily-armored men watched the party with distrust as they passed under the arched gates. Shifting his vision, Danil saw flecks of kiandrite in their guts. Knowing they were magi, he quickly glanced away.

Osriele led them through a second gate and into a smaller courtyard.

Tormented whispers swirled around them. Danil glanced about sharply. The courtyard was unremarkable save for two stone pillars driven deep into the ground. Shards of red crystal dotted the pillars. As if sensing Danil's gaze, the tormented whispers grew louder, turning into murmurings of suffering and longing for deep groves and running streams. Danil caught vision of a blue lake and the spires of Corros. The crystals were likely stolen from Amas long ago.

His horse skipped sideways in agitation, chewing at the bit. "Steady, now," Danil murmured shakily. He gave the mare's neck a rub.

Heavy footsteps behind them marked the arrival of a balding, robed man and his retinue of guardsmen. Danil recognized him as the mage who had visited Osriele days before.

Lord Heron hurried toward the pillars, sweating. "Your Highness! Where do you go at such short notice?" he asked, panting as he reached them.

"I'm taking your advice, Lord Heron," Osriele said mildly. "It will soon be unsafe in the royal city. I wish to retire to the summer palace at Sorben until the time our king calls upon me."

Commander Selen pressed a fist to her chest. "A briefing package was delivered to the Magi Council before dawn, my lord. For the safety of Her Highness, I will not welcome any visitors to Sorben while she is in residence."

"Of course, of course," Lord Heron said. Though sweating, he looked relieved. "The royal city will be poorer for your absence, Lady Osriele."

Osriele inclined her head. "As it will when you leave with the army, my lord."

Lord Heron motioned to the pillars. "Please, allow my companion to awaken the portal. A parting gift, if you will."

Danil suddenly noticed the cloaked woman standing to the side of guardsmen. The furred depths of her hood made it impossible to see more than the delicate line of her chin, though something about her was vaguely familiar.

Osriele wavered, then inclined her head.

The cloaked woman raised both hands high above her, muttering deep guttural words. The pillars ignited, turning angry blood-red as a shrill scream filled Danil's mind. He clenched both fists in his mount's mane in an effort not to reel. The cloaked woman cried out triumphantly, and bile flooded Danil's mouth when the red portal burst into being between the two pillars. The tortured kiandrite screeched, gouging at the back of his mind.

Hafryn's pressed his horse up close to Danil, his hand reaching out to steady as Danil slid sideways in his saddle.

"I'm fine," Danil whispered shakily and righted himself. *Going through the portal may be another thing, though*, he thought.

Lord Heron bowed deeply. "Safe journey to you, my lady," he said a flourish.

"And to you and our glorious army, Lord Heron."

Osriele didn't look back as she sedately nudged her horse between the pillars. The rubied portal rippled and pulsed as she entered, flanked by Commander Selen and another guard. The rest of the party moved to follow.

Biting heat prickled Danil's skin as he neared the dense red void. He glanced back at the cloaked magus, his breath hot under his helm. She stood with her hands folded beneath the sleeves of her robes. Danil felt the sharpness of her gaze.

Turning back, he nudged his horse and rode through the threshold with Hafryn at his side. Brittle ruby light blinded Danil's vision as a thousand stinging nettles scraped across his skin. Gasping, Danil pushed through, buffeted by a sour wind that whirled about and solidified into a single, frantic voice.

Custodian! it called.

Danil and Hafryn emerged on the edge of a field. A dirt road cut a meandering path toward a line of trees and a small town on the horizon.

Danil slumped over in the saddle, lungs raw and heaving.

"What was *that?*" Hafryn asked. He wrenched off his helm, his red hair sticking damply to his temples.

"Kiandrite," Danil rasped. "Enslaved by the magi."

Hafryn's features grew perplexed. "The portal that got us to Aqila felt nothing like that."

Danil couldn't explain it, either. Perhaps it had to do with the magus who created the portal, or that the kiandrite at the Magi Tower had experienced centuries of suffering. He shakily wiped his mouth.

The portal rippled as a handful more riders emerged. Heartbeats later, it closed in a shower of red sparks.

"Ride for Sorben," Commander Selen ordered a fine-boned guardswoman, who was busily loosening the straps of her breastplate. Another rider handed the guardswoman a brown and gold travel robe that was twin to Osriele's own garb.

"Stop for no one," the commander continued, twisting in the saddle to acknowledge each guard in turn. "Secure the palace and ensure no one enters or leaves. The life of Her Royal Highness depends on it."

"Yes, commander!" the party hollered.

Osriele smiled. "You all honor me. Safe travels."

"And to you, my lady," one of the guards called out.

Commander Selen inspected the newly attired

guardswoman and nodded in satisfaction. "Corporal Gala has the lead. Move out!"

The brown-robed guardswoman wheeled her horse to the front of the party. The majority formed up behind her and left at a gallop, leaving behind only three guards, Osriele and Commander Selen.

Hafryn folded his arms and watched the party gallop toward the distant town.

Osriele turned back to the two pillars. "Now for our true destination." She removed her glove to reveal her red kiandrite ring. She pressed it to the stone of the left pillar and muttered a handful of unfamiliar words. The rubied kiandrite resentfully woke once more as a new portal took form.

"Will your Magi Council be able to track us through the pillars?" Hafryn asked.

Osriele shook her head. "No. It's one of the advantages of using the pillars, though I have little doubt someone will come through to confirm that I reside in the summer palace."

"Corporal Gala will play the part," Commander Selen said. "Lady Osriele has always been private, so her seclusion won't raise many questions, so long as we don't tarry."

Taking that as an order, the first of the remaining guards kicked their horse forward and into the swirling ruby light of the portal.

The portal growled and sizzled in Danil's mind. The remaining Roldaerians seemed incapable of sensing the kiandrite's suffering, instead following after the lead guard.

Watching them disappear, Hafryn leaned back in the saddle, reins loose. His mouth quirked. "Here's our chance, *fala*. Kailon lies that way." He pointed to the horizon of fields and flat land.

"Tempting," Danil said without much intent.

Snorting, Hafryn nudged his horse. "Come along, custodian," he sighed before disappearing through the portal.

Danil took a bracing breath before kicking his horse into a trot after him. The same biting, buffeting wind pulled at his braid, his skin smarting. Harsh, mournful whispers tugged at his cloak.

Then the portal released him.

Blinking rapidly, Danil took in a sudden expanse of reedbeds interspersed with dark waterways. Insects buzzed and waders skimmed across the murky surface. The air was heavy with the scent of mud and rotting vegetation. Danil unsnarled his cloak and grimaced at the scudding clouds.

Osriele and her guards milled on a scrap of earth between the reeds. Skirting the edge of the water was a road scarcely wide enough for two horses to ride abreast. It appeared rough-hewn and supported with river-smooth rocks brought in from elsewhere.

Danil turned back to the pillars as the portal closed. Red filaments cobwebbed throughout the stone like a poisoned wound. The breeze carried mournful whispers of ill-treatment and anguish.

Heart aching, Danil pulled off his gloves and traced the healing glyph he'd seen Elania create for Lyria. He let it discretely drop past his horse's shoulder and onto the muddy ground.

May you find peace, he thought, and felt the House glyph on his palm burn hot.

The abused kiandrite turned momentarily iridescent. The whispers stuttered in surprise.

"Danil," Hafryn hissed. The wolf shifter moved his horse

between Danil and the party, blocking him from view. "You need to stop whatever you're doing."

In the short distance, Osriele and Commander Selen studied Danil intently, expressions flat. The three guards muttered lowly, voices lost in the breeze.

Hafryn gripped the pommel of his sword as he watched the Roldaerians. One pale-eyed, broad-shouldered guard with a wayfarer bow looked ready to shoot them from their horses.

"We're wasting daylight, commander," Osriele suddenly said, turning her horse about and up onto the muddy road.

Giving Danil a narrow look, Commander Selen nudged her horse up beside the mage. "Private Ruslin, stay here until sunset and report if anyone comes through the portal. The rest of you, form up. We don't want our lady on the road at nightfall."

A guard dismounted beside the pillars to wait. He threw Danil and Hafryn a wary look, stepping wide of their horses.

Danil waited until the young man was out of earshot. "I'm sorry," he murmured to Hafryn. "I couldn't leave the kiandrite to suffer."

Hafryn kept his gaze fixed ahead on Osriele riding beside the commander. "Just be wary. Allies can become enemies at the merest twist of an enchantment."

Danil nodded, swallowing.

"Let's not fall behind," Hafryn said, nudging after the party.

Following, Danil glanced down as heat still radiated from the House glyph. The markings were still pale like an old scar, but for a moment, he saw iridescent light dance across the surface.

11

By late afternoon the road took them into the village of Camrin. Shuttered huts and a thatchless, decaying trade hall showed that the village's finest days were long ended. A scrawny sow and two piglets lay in the mud at the center of the road. The few peasants who called the village home watched the party distrustfully when they pulled up in front of the wooden inn.

"Charming place," Hafryn muttered as he gazed up at the inn's rotten, dripping eaves. "Are we certain we want to spend the night?"

Osriele pulled off her riding gloves and dismounted. "It's our last opportunity for a proper meal and bed before we enter the Fens, Hafryn."

The inn bore a faded sign of a hare and axe over the entrance. A single lantern hung unlit by the rusted door handle. Dust covered the shuttered windows, and only dim light came from within.

"We might prefer the Fens, my lady," Commander Selen observed gruffly.

Danil had to agree. Even the inn at Farin had been in better repair.

Dismounting, Osriele said, "Perhaps so but here we are."

"I see a stable 'round back, my lady," one of the guards said, leaning in his saddle.

"Excellent, Corporal Gethin. You and Private Ruslin see to the horses."

The two men waited for everyone to dismount before leading the animals around the side of the inn. Commander Selen put her shoulder into the door to nudge it open.

Inside, arched beams and a large stone fireplace harkened to old opulence, but the floorboards were worn and deeply scratched, and the rickety tables and chairs promised little comfort. A small, sputtering fire shed uneven light across the aleroom, offering little warmth for the pair of farmers slouched over their tankards.

A stout, rosy-cheeked woman beamed as she strode from behind the bar. "Worthy guests at last! Come in, come in! Take your ease."

Bemused, Danil loosened his cloak and settled at a table near the fire. Hafryn sat opposite him, considering the ale barrels with intent.

"We're in need of rooms for the night," Osriele said, setting her gloves on the table.

The woman put her hands on her hips. "Plenty to choose from, I'm afraid. Times are grim. Fair folk such as yourselves don't travel these parts anymore."

Osriele nodded. "We've seen little sign of travelers on the road. I daresay things grow worse further south?"

"They do indeed. Not even the army's recruiters bother us for fear of what happens at night." She waved her hand. "Let me rustle up my finest ale and I can tell you all about it.

Stew's not much but it's just about ready to come off the hob if you're in need of an honest meal."

With a smile, Osriele said, "You have our gratitude."

Bowing, the barkeeper retreated to the bar and busied herself with setting up a row of tankards.

Hafryn leaned forward, hands clasped on the table. "What do you make of that? Sounds like the blacksward isn't the only problem hereabouts."

Osriele settled in her chair and daintily clasped her hands in her lap. "She likely speaks of displaced bandits and rabble. I understand the blacksward swept through parts of this region some months ago."

"We shouldn't have sent so many guards to Sorben," Commander Selen muttered under her breath.

"Our presence draws enough attention," Osriele dismissed softly. "A contingent of guards would see people running for fear of being conscripted to face Amas."

"Cowards," the commander said, throwing a dark look at the two farmers. "I've yet to see a shifter worth fearing."

Danil expected Hafryn to bare his teeth at the insult, but his companion appeared remarkably content in his seat. Hafryn knew how to bide his time.

With a few curt mutters, the farmers scraped back their chairs and made for the door, their ales unfinished.

The commander watched them leave suspiciously. "Ania, go help Gethin and Rus bring in the saddlebags," she ordered the female guard leaning conspicuously beside a front window.

The guardswoman all but saluted before taking the corridor leading out to the rear stables.

"Your soldiers are hardly discrete, commander," Hafryn noted.

"They won't need to try to be for much longer," Osriele

said with a quelling look at Selen. "There are very few towns between us and our destination."

"Fat lot of good that'll be if those men go scampering off to the local brigands with tales of easy pickings," the commander said. "At least Ania and Ruslin grew up in these parts. They should have an inkling of where the boltholes are that brigands tend to use."

A foaming tankard was placed in front of Danil.

"Brigands?" the barkeeper chortled, ale sloshing across her tray. "If only we had so easy a foe!" She set the remaining tankards down and sopped up the mess with a rag.

"You mentioned dangers at night," Commander Selen said. "But I saw no indication that the village has been recently under attack."

The barkeeper set her hands on her hips and smiled, but there was an uneasy tension about her shoulders. "Indeed so, but folk are fearful all the same."

Motioning to an empty seat, Osriele said, "Please, join us, friend. The meal can wait."

The barkeeper hesitated. "Well, supposing since you're my only customers now," she said amiably, setting her tray against the leg of her chair as she got comfortable. "Name's Emiline."

"Osriele," the magus replied, shaking the proffered hand.

Emiline looked her over. "You have a soft look about you, Osriele, so I'll not frighten you with the details even if you do travel with harder sorts—not that I'm prying, mind!"

Danil smothered a snort into his tankard. The barkeeper wouldn't be so free with her assessment if she knew who Osriele really was.

Osriele's mouth quirked. "You clearly have a care for

your patrons, Emiline." She put a pair of silver coins on the table and pushed them toward the barkeeper. "All the same, I'd prefer to know if I'm courting trouble on the road."

Sweeping up the coins with practiced efficiency, the barkeeper said, "It started not long after the blight took the Dunmere farm out by the marshes. Evil thing, that. And spread quickly!" She shook her head. "Folk were packing up and making for the northern baronies. Can't blame them, mind. It's a hard life near the Fens."

Osriele nodded sympathetically.

Resting her elbows on the table, Emiline continued, "Turns out folk aren't leaving. They're *disappearing*. The Dunmeres came by on their way out wailing about some creature taking their girl. A creature with glowing eyes and teeth as long as your forearm." She made a warding sign across her chest. "Wouldn't have believed them if I haven't had occasion to hear it myself. Cursed thing hunts at night."

Commander Selen leaned forward. "What does the thing sound like?"

"Like no worldly creature I've ever come upon." Swallowing, the barkeeper threw a wary look at the closed door. "Just days ago, Thomber the Cowherd went missing. Some of his herd were seen up by the crossroad. He'd never abandon them."

"You're talking about the crossroad leading into the Fens, yes?" Commander Selen asked.

Emiline straightened, her eyes somber. "Don't go in there if you care for your lives, friends. The blight's strongest in the Fens. It's where the creature roves." She rose abruptly. "Now, let me fetch your meals and send my boy up to prepare your rooms."

"Three rooms shall suffice," Osriele murmured.

The barkeeper sketched a bow. "Wonderful. Do stay as long as you please."

Hafryn watched her slip out of the aleroom, fingers drumming on the table pensively. "She's frightened." He glanced at Osriele. "Are there rumors of strange creatures in other places the blacksward has taken?"

Osriele shook her head. "It's the first I've heard of it."

"Probably a stray dog looking for scraps," Selen muttered. She took a sip of ale and grimaced.

Danil shook his head. The remoteness of Camrin reminded him of his former village. "This isn't the noble quarter of Aqila. Peasants are made of sterner stuff. If Emiline says the Fens are dangerous, we'd do well to heed her warning."

Tilting her head, Osriele asked, "What would you have us do, Danil? It was you who insisted we ride for Isfil."

But it had been Lyria who'd insisted they journey to the spire. Danil would rather be in Kailon shoring up his defenses and seeking out enchanters to help quash all trace of the blacksward. It surprised him that Osriele was questioning their quest when she and Lyria had surely discussed it long ago.

Sighing, Danil said, "We'll have to hope that your guards and Hafryn are enough."

"And we two are not without our talents, Danil," Osriele added with a slight smile.

Danil nodded, thoughts once again straying to the errant ghost. "Were you and Lyria close?"

If Osriele was surprised by the question, she hid it well. "Our paths crossed because we shared a similar desire to save Roldaer. I knew little of Lyria personally, other than she had a deep hatred for the blacksward—likely because she also lost her lands to it."

"She was nobility, too?" Danil asked.

Osriele shook her head. "When a magus receives their robes, they're gifted a parcel of land. Should their offspring prove lacking in magical ability, the lands return to the crown. It encourages proper breeding among magi to safeguard the power of our spellwork."

Danil wrinkled his nose. It sounded rather dull and heartless, and no doubt robbed others of their rightful lands.

"Of course, there are aberrations such as yourself, Danil," Osriele continued, her gaze contemplative. "Had you been born anywhere but on the border, I expect you'd have been discovered early and raised appropriately."

Glancing at Hafryn, Danil said, "I'm glad to have remained unnoticed."

Hafryn's green eyes turned warm. His knee brushed against Danil's under the wobbly table. "As am I, *fala*."

"Well, you're hardly unremarkable now," Osriele observed. "Lyria convinced me that you're the answer to what ails Roldaer. She died believing that. I do hope she wasn't mistaken."

Danil held her gaze. "So do I, Osriele," he said as the barkeeper bustled in from the kitchen with a steaming tray of meals. "For all our sakes."

THEY RETURNED to the road the next morning, following its meandering path between water-logged trees and hummocks of sedge and reeds. Birdlife ran rampant in the marshes, with lily dancers and long-legged storks hunting for insects and small fish. The crossroads was an innocuous junction with a trail cutting away from the

main road and heading between the shifting waters of
the Fens.

Hafryn rode at the head of the party with the
commander, keeping watch for the creature that had left the
barkeeper in Camrin so spooked.

Danil found himself riding beside Private Ruslin.
Though they were of a similar age, the guardsman was
taciturn and surly, pale eyes cold. There was something
familiar about him that Danil couldn't quite place, but
Ruslin rebuffed his stilted attempts at conversation, his gaze
set fixedly ahead. Eventually, the road widened enough that
Ruslin could nudge his horse past the two other guards and
settle in the middle of the party.

Danil stared after him, nonplussed.

Corporal Gethin slowed his horse until they rode side by
side. Unlike Ruslin, the man seemed amiable enough, his
twin braids swinging back and forth with the sway of his
mount's gait. At least he appeared not to take offense at
Danil's very presence.

It only made Danil scowl and wonder what he'd done to
so insult Ruslin.

"You could be mistaken for brothers," Gethin said
mildly, his voice a slow, rolling brogue. "Or cousins, at least."

Danil threw him a startled look. "Beg pardon?"

Gethin pointed with his chin. "Ruslin."

Glancing ahead, Danil noted the other guardsman's dark
braid and pale skin. Paired with Ruslin's grey eyes, Danil
supposed there were similarities. Still, he sighed in
irritation. "Half of Roldaer has our coloring," he pointed
out.

Gethin studied Danil's nose, the line of his chin and
mouth. He shrugged. "Rus sees it, too. Probably scared your
wolf will take a fancy to him."

Danil felt his scowl turn thunderous.

"I'm teasing," Gethin said, mouth twitching. "The wolf clearly sees no one but you."

"I can assure you, Hafryn misses nothing," Danil muttered.

"Glad to hear it." Gethin looked out over the reeds, a crease forming between his brows. "I don't understand why Lady Osriele sees fit to be out here, but I expect you to protect her as surely as I'll protect Hafryn Wolfkind."

Danil observed him, not sure if he should feel threatened or reassured. "Of course."

"Then we'll get along well," Gethin said with a weighted smile.

Instinct told Danil he rode beside a dangerous and loyal man. He wondered what Osriele had done to earn such devotion.

Late afternoon brought biting insects intent on any exposed skin. The horses flicked their tails in swift agitation, and Danil hunched under his cloak as hungry insects buzzed around his head. Not looking forward to a grim night, Danil complained about there not being an enchantment he knew of that could offer them relief.

Hafryn huffed a laugh as they set up camp on a scrap of muddy earth to the side of the road. "It's called the ability to shift, *fala*. Amasians aren't so tasty then."

Osriele approached to hand Danil a small jar of unguent. "Repellent from our kind host last night. She assured me that a campfire will also draw away the worst of the midges."

"Perhaps not wise considering what else may be in the Fens," Hafryn pointed out.

"My thoughts exactly, Hafryn."

Danil opened the jar and rubbed a portion of the oily

salve over his exposed skin. It smelled faintly medicinal, heavily laced with garlic. He handed the jar to Hafryn, who murmured his thanks.

Osriele continued to watch Hafryn, her gaze thoughtful. "I've never had the opportunity to ask one of your people, Hafryn, and our tomes are somewhat biased. But I understand your senses are enhanced when you take on your animal form."

"Some," Hafryn allowed, rubbing salve on the back of his neck.

"Like a wolf's nose and an eagle's eyesight," Danil said.

"And a dragon's rage," Hafryn added with a humorless smirk.

A few feet away, the guardswoman Ania cast a suspicious look at the sky.

Danil idly wished to see a flash of gold and broad, mighty wings. A sudden, hard yearning for Kailon took him, and he pushed his mind toward the leylines. Fleeting whispers reached back, and Danil felt warmth flood his House glyph.

"I'm aware you both call Prince Sonnen of Corros a friend," Osriele said, amusement in her tone. "I hope to meet him one day when the situation isn't so fraught."

"Let's both pray for the day, my lady," Hafryn said with a slight bow. "Although you must understand that he won't tolerate the way you use kiandrite."

"You mean mage-crystals? I understand your enchanters don't need to ingest them to create their magicks."

Hafryn nodded. "The crystals are a part of us, the result of generations of living and loving and dying upon the soil in which kiandrite thrives. Those who become enchanters do so at the kiandrite's wishes, not because we bend it to our will."

Osriele shook her head mockingly as she set up her bedroll. "You make it sound like mage-crystals are living things with minds of their own."

"How else would you explain Danil?" Hafryn questioned. "Until a few months ago, he was a Roldaerian peasant, but tales of his exploits have reached Aqila. And yet, he refuses so much as a mouthful of that tea you so crave."

Osriele gave Danil a sharp look.

Shifting uncomfortably, Danil said, "I never asked for the abilities I now have, but kiandrite can be...insistent."

Osriele's frown deepened.

"It's like the ring you bear," Danil tried to explain, pointing to Osriele's gloved hand. "The kiandrite's red now from having its power used against its will. But it wasn't always that color."

Hafryn grunted in agreement. "The ring looks like the sort that's passed on through the generations. I'll bet a handful of gold coin that when it first came into your family, it shone like sunlight on water."

Osriele blinked. "There are certainly tales in the Trudan archives." Her brow furrowed. "But how could you know, Hafryn?"

"The ring is of Eyrie design, for a start. Probably taken during the Great War. As for the kiandrite itself, certain colors have meaning—blue for contentment; pink for the heart. Red shows that the kiandrite has experienced trauma, that it's been forced against its will."

"Now you're suggesting that mage-crystals have emotions," Osriele said with an astonished laugh.

"Not as we experience them, but they're no less valued," Hafryn replied. "Your ring will eventually shatter and die, Osriele. Kiandrite can only be forced for so long."

"Your ways are very strange, Amasian," the mage said.

Danil thought of his first crystal and how it had shattered after being forced to portal him and Hafryn into Aqila. He swallowed an ache in his throat and pushed his mind toward the ring, wishing it comfort.

The rubied kiandrite all but snarled. Raging hatred slammed against Danil, the crystal so twisted with pain and anguish that even the slightest mental touch brought it new, raw agony. It shoved Danil away, rejecting him with a slap.

Danil jolted back in surprised dismay. '*I can help you,*' he thought.

'*Begone, mage!*' it shrieked.

Startled, Danil withdrew to see Hafryn give him a curious look.

Commander Selen returned then from scouting the nearby rushes. Her mouth was a grim line as she pulled her mount to a halt. "Get the saddle back on Lady Osriele's horse, Ania," she ordered. "We may not be staying here tonight."

"What is it, commander?"

"There's signs of blacksward near the road up ahead. It's perhaps a week or two old. I think it best we be cautious before setting up camp."

Danil threw Hafryn a worried glance. "Why does it matter how old the blacksward is?" They'd only seen the small sample trapped within the casket, but Danil couldn't forget its ravening hunger.

"It means it should have finished consuming everything in its path, but there may yet be some active sites," Osriele explained. "If we are fortunate, only the destruction it has wrought will remain."

"We're wasting daylight, my lady" Commander Selen said, turning her horse about.

Osriele raised a hand. "They should see for themselves, commander."

Selen faltered before bowing in grim agreement. They quickly broke camp and returned to their mounts.

Gethin waited for them further up the road. He pointed to a large clump of dead reeds in the distance. The water surrounding it was unnaturally still.

By habit, Danil shifted his vision but saw nothing of note. He shrugged at Hafryn.

The commander gave Gethin an obscure signal. "Let them see for themselves."

Gethin quirked an eyebrow but pressed a fist to his chest. "Yes, commander." He drew his sword and jumped onto a nearby hummock of sedges. "Step where I step. Careful, now, the reeds may yet hold remnants of the blacksward."

Ania and Ruslin took up sentry on the road, sitting tall in the saddle with bows ready while the rest of the party took a wandering path to avoid the water. Ignoring the itch between his shoulders, Danil trailed after Gethin in the squishing mud.

The clump of dried reeds hid a broader swathe of death stretching back a few hundred feet. Gossamer-thin, black cobwebs clung to decayed tree-stumps that looked to have died centuries ago. The remnants of a small, furred animal lay in the shadow of its former burrow, too slow to escape the poison. A wet, fusty stench clung to the air. Not a single insect or bug traversed the dead, ashy foliage.

"Look at this, *fala*," Hafryn murmured, crouching beside a fragile, star-shaped sedge. The tiny, wilted leaves were grey and powdery.

"Is it wise to be so close?" Danil asked as the hairs on his arms rose.

"All of its potency is gone," Osriele murmured. "The blacksward essentially dies when there's no more life to feed upon."

Hafryn touched a dead frond and cursed softly when it disintegrated. Pale dust floated onto the water.

Osriele took on a haunted look. "I fear that such ruin can never be undone."

Danil carefully traced a healing enchantment and sent it over the dead fronds. It was like sweeping his hand over empty air; there was nothing for the glyph to cling to.

Sighing, he looked out over the swampy water and wished he knew of powerful enchantments. Only now, seeing the devastation, did he fully grasp what was at stake. It was much worse than the deadlands had ever been.

But why had Lyria urged him across the Fens in search of an abandoned spire? He needed to be where his abilities made a difference. There were places in Roldaer of great importance, ones that if saved from the blacksward could offer hope to common folk and stop the desperate invasion.

But he'd trusted Lyria's ghost as implicitly as he did the leylines of Kailon. Having survived on blind luck and instinct for so long, it never occurred to him that he'd eventually make a mistake. Out here, there were no leylines to rise up and salvage the day. He had to face the grim prospect that he'd likely sent them on a fool's errand.

One that would cost them all dearly.

12

The ruinous touch of the blacksward left its mark throughout the Fens. It swept across sections of the road, forcing the party to navigate across sucking mud and copses of leafless, wizened trees. The slowness of the journey set Danil's teeth on edge. They had days of travel yet before they reached Isfil, and he still had no inkling of what to expect once they got there.

Midday heat brought with it the rising stench of baking mud and detritus as they rode up onto a small trail. It led them to three huts perched on stilts above the water. Decaying wood railings and rat-sized holes in the thatch walls indicated the villagers had abandoned the place some time ago. The door to one hut hung askew, groaning softly as it swung back and forth. Inside, the contents of the hut were strewn across the floorboards, with dented pots beneath an overturned table and crates emptied.

Commander Selen raised her fist. She watched the quiet huts distrustfully.

Hafryn stood in the stirrups for a better view. "The place

looks ransacked—and I don't think by rodents seeking to make a new burrow."

The commander quirked an eyebrow at Osriele.

Osriele sighed. "We should rest the horses, regardless."

Danil took the creaking, uneven steps up to the shuddery walkway framing the furthest hut. Old fish scales and broken netting on the railing indicated that the former inhabitants had likely been fisherfolk. With Hafryn behind him, Danil eased open the door. Inside was a mess, with shelves toppled and old baskets spilled across the coarse floorboards. To Danil's untrained eye, it looked like a knife had been used to slash open an abandoned sleeping pallet. He threw Hafryn a questioning look.

His companion took a slow turn about the room. "Wouldn't have thought brigands would take an interest in a hovel like this," he observed, easing past a fish trap hanging by a hook from the rafters. "Someone expected to find valuables."

Danil lifted the edge of a basket to inspect the shredded the remains of clothing underneath. At least there were no bloody indications that someone had died over paltry trinkets.

Hafryn rested his hands on the rear windowsill. A pensive line showed on his brow. Behind the huts was a thin, snaking trail that led towards a shadowy copse of trees. "The path looks recently disturbed," he murmured.

Danil came up beside him but saw nothing amiss. "How can you tell?"

Hafryn leaned his hip against the windowsill, mouth quirking. "If you recall, I used to have no trouble finding you in the deadlands. Admittedly, you left a trail easy enough for a blind wolf to follow, but there was a time or two when I steered you from danger as well."

"Is that so?" Danil raised a skeptical eyebrow. "You once chased me into a meltwater stream." He pointed. "You stood on the bank while I almost froze to death."

Hafryn sniffed. "Must have been a different wolf."

"You weren't in your Trueform," Danil countered. "Or wearing clothes, for that matter."

"Ah, so you were overwhelmed by the grandiosity of all this," Hafryn said, gesturing at himself.

"Hence the screaming," Danil replied dryly.

Hafryn huffed a laugh.

Finding nothing else of note, they eventually made their way outside once more, where the song of insects buzzed louder. Clattering down the steps, they headed behind the hut and past a small vegetable patch of wilting greens.

Hafryn paused beside a tuft of grass, where boot prints tracked deep in the mud. "See here?" He traced the damp edge. "It's fresh—today, even."

Danil looked towards the trees uneasily before glancing back at where Ania stood guard near the horses. She ignored them, watching Osriele as the magus moved under the stilts of one hut. Danil turned back to see Hafryn already striding along the path, hand on the pommel of his blade.

Within the copse, whiskery moss draped over low-hanging, gnarled branches. A spring-fed pool sat was framed by dark rocks and brown lichen. The smell of damp loam tingled Danil's nose.

Hafryn walked the edge of the pool, touching crushed lichen and disturbed rocks. He paused when signs of the boot prints abruptly stopped in front of a dark hole that disappeared under the rocks. He blinked up at the twisted branches overhead, expression contemplative.

Drawing closer, Danil saw a few nicks carved in the slab

of pale stone above the burrow entrance. The marks curved and straightened in odd places, much like a glyph.

Seeming not to notice, Hafryn returned to studying the boot prints. He squatted, prodding the ground.

The glyph-like marks stirred. Angry red light burst out of the stone and zigzagged across the earth to Hafryn's boots.

"Hafryn, watch out!" Danil cried, leaping.

The ground shuddered and collapsed under Hafryn. He dropped into the darkness, hitting hard earth with a pained grunt.

Danil skidded to the edge of the hole. "Hafryn!" A moment of silence passed as he tried to stare into the darkness. Directly opposite him, the glyph-like marks ceased their virulent red glow. "*Hafryn!*"

"I'm alright, *fala*," Hafryn called up.

Danil's vision adjusted to see the wolf shifter clamber to his feet amidst a tangled mass of twisted tree roots and rocks.

Shaking dirt out of his braid, Hafryn stretched gingerly but looked to have garnered little more than a few scrapes. "Don't look so fretful. It's just some animal burrow." He looked about, nose wrinkling. "Smells like its last occupant died in here, too. The old entrance looks caved in. Here, help me up."

Relieved, Danil settled on his belly and stretched his arms down.

Clambering onto a broad tree root, Hafryn made to grasp Danil's forearms but paused. "Here, now, what's this?" He hopped down and scratched at the dirt along the wall of the burrow.

Danil caught a flash of gold as Hafryn fished out a long chain with a circular amulet covered in mud.

"Now, this is no fisherman's trinket!" Hafryn said, using the hem of his tunic to wipe away some of the grime.

Cleaned, the medallion glistened with small blue gems inset at even intervals along the edge. A large crack marred the bottom half of the amulet, almost as if an axe had struck it in some long, forgotten battle.

"How did it end up down there?" Danil asked, leaning further over the edge as damp soaked through his tunic.

"The burrow's former occupants must have carried it in for their nest. There's animal hair and the like hereabouts, too." He scoured away more dirt until the amulet flashed in the murky light. Hafryn pulled the necklace over his head and reached up for Danil's arms once more. "Here, let me up."

Grasping his forearms, Danil heaved him up and caught another glimpse of the amulet. Tiny markings dotted the edges between the blue gems. Save for the jagged crack, the center was smooth and unpolished as if newly made.

"Damn thing's heavy." Hafryn idly pulled at the necklace to take it off. He froze, his brow furrowing deeply before he gripped the amulet tight and yanked. "Strange—it won't come off." He ran his fingers along the chain in search of a clasp.

"What? Let me try." Danil gripped the amulet.

Sudden, scalding agony clenched him in a vice-like grip. A dark presence clawed toward him through a veil of poisonous ash. Danil snatched his hand back with a gasp, barely keeping to his feet.

Hafryn stared at him, white-faced. "*Fala...*"

Danil cursed softly. "It's magicked."

Sweat gathered on Hafryn's temples. "To do what?"

Danil shook his head mutely, the taste of poisoned ash filling his mouth. "I don't know. But it's powerful." Far too powerful to be left abandoned and forgotten in a burrow deep in the Fens.

Branches suddenly broke above them with a clattering thump, and Danil whirled in time to see a blue-tipped owl drop out of the trees.

Hafryn shoved him back, blade drawn and teeth bared.

The air shimmered, throwing sparks across the muddy ground, before a cloaked woman rose to her feet. A flash of red hair and venomous green eyes made Danil step back in alarm.

"You idiots," Merlias hissed. "You have no idea what you've done!"

13

"What are you doing here, Merlias?" Hafryn hissed.

The Eyrie enchanter's green eyes turned murderous when Hafryn pointed the tip of his blade at her throat. Danil hadn't seen her since their victory against Kaul, though he knew she'd acted to save Kailon only at Councilor Viren's bidding. Now, her owl Trueform sat upon her shoulder, wings slightly flared and feathers puffed.

Merlias' fingers twitched as if she yearned to weave a cruel enchantment. "I was going to ask you the same thing, exile. Last I heard, you and the custodian were lost in Aqila."

Danil straightened. "Sonnen knows where we are?"

"Oh, I'd hardly say that," Merlias said, lips curling. "If you intend to return to Kailon, custodian, you've made quite the detour."

Heart sinking, Danil forced himself to look her over. Mud tracked high up her boots and breeches, her wayfarer cloak torn in places from a hard journey. He folded his arms. "It was you, wasn't it? You ruined the huts while searching for something."

She sneered and turned her back on them.

"I suspect we already found what drew her out here, *fala*," Hafryn muttered. The amulet sparked blue and gold against his chest.

Merlias gave a derisive snort and whirled back at them. "The burial mound and its shiny bauble were lost to all since the Great War. Typical that you would be the ones to stumble upon them."

Danil glanced at the stone slab with its strange markings. It had grown quiet, with nary a shimmer of red light since Hafryn had emerged with the amulet around his neck. "What do you mean by 'burial mound'?"

The Eyrie enchanter's face darkened with fury. "You really are idiots."

"Or blessed with luck—it appears we have what you want, Merlias," Hafryn quipped, although there was a growing uneasiness to his features.

"Don't be so quick to gloat, exile," Merlias snapped. The enchanter's gaze flitted momentarily to the amulet. "You won't like the path you're now on."

Danil folded his arms. "Viren obviously sent you. What does he want with the amulet?"

"That's hardly your concern," the enchanter replied. "Kailon's leylines need their custodian now more than ever. You must return and take up your duties before the Roldaerian army reaches the border."

It wasn't anything he didn't already know. He looked at the Eyrie enchanter hopefully. "Can you get word to Sonnen, then? We're headed for a spire—Isfil."

Merlias gave a careless shrug. "Never heard of it."

Danil couldn't tell if she was lying. "Please, Sonnen has to know what's happened to us. If he could meet us there—"

"No." Merlias' gaze fell upon the amulet on Hafryn's

chest once more. "If you won't heed my warning, custodian, you're on your own."

The air shimmered as she leaped and transformed into her owl form.

Danil instinctively jumped after her, hands scrambling, but the blue-tipped owl easily wheeled into the branches with a derisive hoot. He yelled up at her in frustration.

"You won't catch her, *fala*. Owl enchanters are too quick for that."

"She could help us!" Danil said in frustration.

Hafryn shoved his sword back in his sheath, mouth thin. "It pains me to say it, but even if Merlias wanted to, she couldn't get news to Sonnen at the speed you'd like. There are few enchanters in Amas with the skills Elania has to send messages across distances, and Merlias isn't one of them."

Scrubbing a hand over his face, Danil growled, "She could have at least explained why Viren wants the amulet." The more they knew of it, the better their chance to see Hafryn free of it.

Hafryn grunted. "Old enmities die hard, even when we share a greater foe."

Sighing, Danil returned his attention to the amulet. He shifted his vision and saw tiny red sigils writhe across the polished surface.

The air behind Hafryn suddenly coalesced like mist as Lyria drifted out of the tranquil pool. Having avoided the party since Aqila, Danil was surprised to see her draw near and brush ghostly fingers over the necklace. The kiandrite crystal on her battle-axe flashed as if struck by sunlight.

Hafryn grimaced and rubbed his throat.

Danil watched Lyria hopefully, but with her face turning somber, Lyria merely stepped back and faded amidst the trees. He released a frustrated growl and lifted his hand, letting the House glyph glow upon Hafryn's throat. The amulet darkened with menace.

"*Fala,* don't," Hafryn gasped. Sweat beaded across his brow, his body taut as if coiled with pain.

Danil quickly lowered his hand, paling with dismay.

Hafryn let out a ragged breath. "Damned thing must be cursed." He swallowed heavily. "Let's not try it again."

Shoulders sagging, Danil said, "If it's cursed, there may be another who can remove the amulet."

A grimace of discomfort crossed Hafryn's face. "Never thought I'd willingly seek out a mage's expertise."

"Osriele's our ally now," Danil argued. "And I don't like how the amulet is affecting you."

"Nor I," Hafryn muttered. He shook his head at the slab of stone blocking the entrance into the burrow. "Merlias said it's a burial mound. But for who? And why were they buried with this thing?"

Danil could only hope that whoever had last worn the amulet hadn't been driven to their death because of it. He suppressed a shudder. "Perhaps there's something hereabouts that we all missed."

They searched the small boulders surrounding the burial mound. It was remarkably ordinary, with even the strange markings on the stone all but faded.

"There's nothing here."

Rising from in front of the slab, Danil sighed in frustration. "Let's get back to the others, then. This place makes my blood cold."

Returning to the huts, the rest of the party was already mounted and waiting.

Commander Selen wheeled her horse about as they reached their mounts, her scowl deepening when her gaze fell to the amulet. "That's quite the trinket, wolf. Where have you two been to find such a thing?"

Sharing a glance, Danil and Hafryn told the party how they came upon the amulet, but by silent agreement made no mention of Merlias.

"Most strange," Osriele said, turning her horse about to face them fully. "Certainly not something our absent fisherfolk would be harboring."

Danil looked at her hopefully. "Do you know what it is?"

She leaned back in the saddle. "It's Roldaerian in design, but I don't recognize the markings. Nor do I know of an amulet that fights against removal." She studied him a moment before dismounting. "May I see, Hafryn?"

Mouth thin, Hafryn gave a tight nod.

Osriele gripped the necklace in her fist, muttering a few sharp, grating words. Danil saw the amulet awaken before red spears of light thrust into Osriele's fingers.

Hafryn flinched, face whitening.

"Fascinating," Osriele murmured. "If I didn't know that it's quite impossible, I'd say that the amulet has a hatred for my spellwork." She released her grip and massaged her hand against her side as if it pained her. "Perhaps if we were in in the royal city, we'd discover a way to remove it."

Danil could only stare at her in dismay. "Is there nothing you can do?"

"Not without causing Hafryn significant pain, and I have no wish to inflict that on either of you." She shook her head. "It could well be that even death may not release you from its power, Hafryn. For now, I fear the amulet is yours to bear."

A SEA BREEZE swept across the marshes as the party drew closer to the coast. The shifting water transformed into estuaries and deep streams lined by scraggly pockets of forest and rushes. The winding road forced them to cross the brackish, waist-high water numerous times throughout the day.

Danil had to force aside his frustration at the slowness of their journey. Hafryn rode hunched in the saddle beside him, hair damp about his face. A red line showed across the back of his neck where the amulet pressed down on him. Shifting his vision, Danil could see the amulet's flaming red light.

"I'm fine, *fala*," Hafryn murmured when the party was forced to stop on the banks of a fast-flowing stream. The water was too deep to cross without losing the horses.

Cursing, the commander ordered Ania upstream to look for a shallow, sandy ford.

Danil glanced suspiciously up at the sliver of sky visible through the knotted foliage. Merlias might have demanded they face the trials of the amulet alone, but she wasn't the type of Amasian to abandon her quest—especially when Councilor Viren was the one commanding her. She would be back for the amulet in time.

"I've seen nothing of her, either," Hafryn murmured, too low for others to hear.

Nudging his horse closer, Danil said, "She'll come back for the amulet."

Hafryn grunted, looking remarkably unperturbed.

Danil studied him more closely as they waited for the guardswoman's return. There was a sweaty paleness under the wolf shifter's freckles that set his teeth on edge.

Osriele nudged her horse beside them on the sandy bank, her gaze sharp. "Are you taking ill, Hafryn?"

"Nothing that can't be overcome," Hafryn replied with a weary smile.

"I'd offer you a healing remedy, but I fear what the amulet would do to us both," Osriele said mildly.

Hafryn's smile turned genuine. "It's a kind offer all the same, Osriele."

She looked him over. "Perhaps we'll find what we need in Isfil, since we're only days away. It's possible that whoever lost the amulet was a magus seeking to understand its purpose. Isfil was once celebrated as a place of both knowledge and respite. A shame that it's fallen into disrepair."

"I imagine the journey to Isfil was arduous even in at its height," Danil said.

Osriele wavered before shaking her head. "There was a time when the magi's one purpose was to serve the land and our people. All of Roldaer enjoyed clean wells, reliable roads and bountiful crops. Our journey to Isfil would have been rather enjoyable." Her gaze turned distant with regret. "Relics still remain throughout Roldaer, if one knows where to look. But the old ways are far behind us."

Hafryn studied her contemplatively.

Thudding hooves drew their attention upstream as Ania approached at speed.

Commander Selen nudged her horse forward, her hand on her blade. "Report, private."

Sweat showed on Ania's forehead, her dark braid askew as she motioned with her chin toward the forest lining the stream. "There's something you need to see, commander," she said grimly.

The party followed the guardswoman under the canopy of rough, knurled branches. The soil was hard-packed with dry mud, the tree roots twisted and snaking across the surface. Ania led them deeper into a grove where the burbling estuaries grew muted.

Old blood painted the soil black. Flies buzzed in the air over a body that lay in shredded pieces between the trees. Massive slashes showed in the remains of the dead man's tunic and breeches, and Danil thought he saw bone. He covered his mouth and nose with his sleeve, trying not to gag.

Hafryn's horse danced sideways, its nostrils flared. "Our missing cowherd, perhaps?" He studied the body with interest.

Ania motioned to a bare patch of dirt a few feet away. A large paw print, wider than Danil's hand, gouged deep into the mud. Six points above the pad indicated powerful, oversized claws. "Looks like the barkeeper wasn't exaggerating about a night creature, my lady," she said to Osriele. "It herded this fellow off the road and trapped him between the quickmarshes. Took its time eating him, too."

Leaning over the saddle, Danil tracked the prints across the soil. "It's headed for the coast."

"Just like us." The commander stroked the pommel of her sword, watching as Gethin dismounted to examine the area closely. "Could we be facing another Amasian?"

Danil threw her a startled glance, fearing that she somehow knew of Merlias after all.

"It hunts like a soldier," Ania said, giving the surrounding trees a wary glance. "But it lopes like a cat. Ain't like anything I came across growing up in these parts."

Hafryn snorted. "No Amasian can take on whatever form this creature has."

"So says the Amasian," Ruslin said lowly.

"Trueforms are only real animals like dragons, wolves and barn owls," Danil explained, feeling a flash of irritation on Hafryn's behalf. "This print doesn't match any creature I can think of."

"I assume you're no better versed in animal spoor than I am, Danil," Commander Selen said dryly. "But you make your point. Whatever this thing was, it made short work of this poor soul."

Gethin rose from his examination of the body, muttering, "We shouldn't linger."

The commander smirked. "Frightened of a kitty, corporal?"

Gethin pointed at the exposed, shattered bones strewn about the grass. "The creature crunched through bone to reach the marrow, commander."

Commander Selen raised an eyebrow. "I don't see the importance."

"It's not merely a predator," Gethin replied tersely. "It has a taste for people."

14

To Danil's surprise and alarm, Lyria took to haunting their steps as the day continued. She lingered at the edge of Danil's vision, slipping between the trees or appearing far in the distance behind them. He could only guess at what her intent was, but feared her increasing interest was connected somehow to the amulet. His only solace was that Merlias seemed to have truly left them to their fate, although instinct warned him not to be complacent.

Hafryn rode beside him, doing his best to hide his discomfort. The neck of his surcoat protected much of his throat, but Danil caught sight of a patch of reddened skin chafed raw under the weight of the amulet. He worried what effect the amulet could have over Hafryn in just a few more days, much less however long it took to see it removed.

They paused to water their horses at a stream that ran clear of algae or brackish water. Lyria stood knee-deep in the water, head cocked as if listening. Not even the horses sensed her presence, bending their soft noses to the current beside her.

Danil checked his mount's muddy hooves and shook his head. The Fens were as dreary as Commander Selen promised back in Aqila. Sparsely populated and uniquely smelly, it hardly seemed worth the effort. "Why here?" he murmured to himself.

Hafryn quirked an eyebrow.

Danil released a frustrated breath. "If I wanted to force all of Roldaer to march into Amas, this is hardly the place I'd start. Why not in the northlands where the farming is rich? Why not the royal city itself?"

Rubbing his chin, Hafryn said, "It is rather odd." He dropped his voice. "Perhaps Merlias isn't the only one seeking the amulet, and the blacksward is being used to find it."

"Well, unless they know of a gentle way to remove the amulet, they'll have to fight through me to reach you," Danil said but couldn't shake the notion that he'd overlooked something important.

Hafryn's mouth twitched. "My gallant defender."

"Pity I can't defend you from yourself," Danil said dryly, returning to inspecting his horse. "Even Merlias thinks we're fools."

Hafryn snorted. "That's practically a compliment from an Eyrie." Running his gaze down Danil, he added, "A few ribald ballads might be more suited to you than compliments, however. Travel suits you."

Danil stopped his work and chuckled. "Ballads, Hafryn? No need to scare the Roldaerians with your warbling."

With a sniff, Hafryn said, "It'd probably be educational, *fala*. There's even one song about a lusty wanderer and a winsome wolf—"

Hurriedly clapping a hand over Hafryn's mouth, Danil said, "Sing it to me later."

Hafryn's green eyes twinkled over his hand.

A soft chuckle came from behind them.

Danil turned in surprise to see Ania at the edge of the stream with her horse.

"Forgive me for overhearing," the guardswoman said, her cheeks turning pink. "It's just that you sound very much like my fathers."

Startled by the admission, Danil said, "Amasians aren't so different to Roldaerians. They love and fight just as fiercely."

Ania looked between them, expression thoughtful. "The old tales are still spoken at night hereabouts. Easy enough to imagine an Amasian lurking in the rushes to snare the unwary."

"Some of us lurk much better in alerooms and royal courts," Hafryn quipped.

"I imagine so," Ania replied with amusement in her voice.

Their conversation was interrupted by a strange tinkling sound upstream. Traveling at speed across the water's surface was a small glass orb. It held a slightly red tinge.

Danil straightened, instinctively raising his House glyph. Power flooded through him.

"All is well, Danil," Osriele said mildly from further along the bank. "It's just a glory sphere."

The orb swept past Danil so close that he felt its breeze against his cheek. It landed on Osriele's outstretched hand. Taking slow, cautious steps up the bank, Danil looked at the glass orb with interest. "What does it do?"

Osriele smiled slightly. "Call it a message ball, if you will. They're sent to all magi whenever there's glorious or momentous news. I believe your Amasian enchanters have something similar." She withdrew a small pin from her hair and pricked the glass. It shattered into tiny fragments and revealed a rolled parchment within.

Danil thought of how Elania often whispered into balls of light, sending them to allies located miles or days away. He deeply regretted not mastering the skill.

Unfolding the parchment, Osriele ran her gaze over the contents. She sighed. "So it has begun. Commander, we must hasten our pace to Isfil." She balled up the parchment and threw it into the water. It caught on a rock before spinning downstream.

Commander Selen nodded and ordered Ania to check the road ahead. The guardswoman pressed a fist to her breast and mounted.

Watching Ania leave at a trot, Danil asked, "Has something happened?"

"Roldaerian glory, apparently," Osriele muttered, her features softly mocking. "The army marches for Amas."

Cold rushed through him. Hafryn moved behind him and offered silent support. "How long before the army reaches the border?"

"A month would be my guess, considering its sizeable presence. Perhaps less, if the Magi Council ushers it along."

"They'll portal everyone to the border," Danil whispered.

Osriele shook her head. "The ability to portal is rare and taxing. All magi with the talent will be held in reserve until the first battle truly begins."

But that was little comfort to them all. Danil had seen firsthand how magi could flood a campsite with soldiers without warning.

"We're running out of time."

15

Danil woke to a light, brushing touch across the back of his hand. He flailed a moment before his vision became accustomed to the darkness.

Lyria crouched beside him in the shadow of the dying embers. She looked more solid than usual, the paint on her cheeks and forehead sharply evident.

Sitting upright, Danil glanced about the camp. It was relatively quiet, the hummocks of reeds shivering gently as a briny breeze danced across the water's surface. Hafryn was on his side a few inches from Danil, his face tight even in sleep. Pressure marks from the necklace lined his throat. On the opposite side of the embers, Commander Selen lay asleep in a roll of blankets only a few feet from Osriele, the hilt of her sword within easy reach. The shadowy outline of a sentry guard was visible on a mound of grass on the edge of camp, and by the cant of their hips Danil judged it to be Ania. The other two guards were buried deep under their blankets to fend off the buzzing insects. All was well.

Impatience flashed across Lyria's face before she reached out and pressed a finger to Danil's temple.

A shattering roar filled his mind like the side of a mountain collapsing into the sea. The cloying odor of rotting flesh latched onto him, threatening to consume him. He flinched back, gorge rising.

Lyria watched him intently, hand outstretched.

Clambering to his feet, Danil expected to see blacksward rolling towards them from the marshes. But in the silvery moonlight, the hummocks were devoid of anything beyond dipping inflorescence, stunted trees and a few chirping crickets. He swallowed heavily and turned to give Lyria a questioning look.

The ghostly presence was gone.

Danil released a shuddering breath and bent to gently shake Hafryn's shoulder.

The wolf shifter flinched awake, scrabbling for his dagger.

Danil gripped his wrist. "Easy," he murmured, unnerved by the wildness in Hafryn's eyes. "We need to rouse the camp."

Hafryn sank back and wiped his face with a shaking hand. He cursed softly under his breath.

"What is it?" Commander Selen called out softly.

Danil glanced across the camp to see the commander already on her feet. "We have to leave," he said. "Now."

Osriele stirred, pushing away her blankets when the commander apprised her of the situation. "I sense nothing amiss," she murmured.

The commander let out a low whistle and quickly received a whistling reply out amidst the rushes. "Ruslin reports that all is well," Commander Selen said.

Osriele tilted her head, her face curious in the moonlight. "Is it an enchanter compulsion, Danil? Your hand glows."

"No, I—" He frowned, glancing down at the light streaming onto the ground. The House glyph was a warm, steady presence. Through it, his connection with Kailon grew stronger. "I can't explain it, Osriele."

"Trust Danil's word," Hafryn said gruffly to the Roldaerians as he tied up his bedroll. He handed Danil a pair of riding gloves. "We can't stay here."

Danil threw him a grateful look.

Osriele studied them both before motioning to her guards.

Cursing, the commander turned and bellowed for Ruslin to come in from sentry duty as they broke camp and saddled the horses. Dawn was still hours away when they took to the road, and the horses were fractious and surly from having had little rest.

"Are we to continue for Isfil, Danil?" Osriele asked mildly.

Danil glanced about. A sense of urgency clawed at his throat, but he had little notion of where to turn. "Our quest hasn't changed," he allowed.

Commander Selen muttered something under her breath and kicked her mount to the head of the party. "Gethin, you have the rear."

They moved at a steady trot as the moon dipped behind the trees. Frogs and crickets sang in counterpoint among the moonlit stalks.

Scarcely a mile later, Danil caught a flash of white in the distance. Lyria stood on a game trail cutting towards a copse of trees. He slowed his mount. "We need to enter the forest."

Glancing at the looming dark, Commander Selen released a long, drawn out sigh. "This is most unwise, my lady."

"Nonetheless, we are here," Osriele replied calmly. She

removed her riding glove to expose her rubied kiandrite ring in preparation. "Please, Danil, lead on."

Danil watched Lyria stride into the trees and nudged his mount after her. He had little idea where she was taking them.

As they ducked under the low-lying branches, Commander Selen pressed ahead until she rode at Danil's side. "No tricks, traitor," she murmured.

Danil gazed at her sharply.

The commander's gaze remained fixed on the trail ahead, her expression smooth as if she'd never spoken. "If any harm befalls Princess Osriele, I will tear both you and the wolf asunder," she promised.

Mouth curled, Danil said, "If you distrust us so much—"

"I do," Commander Selen said quietly, guiding her mount around a large, knobby oak. "You'd be wise to remember it."

Danil glowered but closed his mouth. He had no urge to explain himself. He didn't regret becoming the custodian of Kailon. No one driven by hatred of the Amasians could cow him.

They rode in tense silence. The forest held nothing of interest beyond knotted roots and dark mud. Though Danil searched for her, Lyria had long faded between the trees.

Wondering if he'd roused everyone for nothing, Danil startled when the commander raised her fist. "Wait here."

The party drew up behind them and came to a halt.

In the sudden quiet, Danil heard chanting. It sounded guttural and raw, shouted in a language he didn't recognize. It came from just beyond a copse of trees east of the trail.

"That's no magi spell," Osriele observed tightly.

Commander Selen swung out of the saddle and quietly drew her blade. She pointed to the three guards and made a closed fist gesture. They slid off their horses and disappeared into the brush.

Nodding at Hafryn, Danil did the same.

They moved toward the noise, Danil scanning the trees for people. The air felt close and still, with scarcely a rustle of leaves to break the unnatural stillness about the place.

The guttural chanting grew louder and more fervent. Flickering torchlight showed through the trees before they were close enough to hunker down on the edge of a clearing.

A red-robed magus stood near the center, chanting rapidly. Surrounding him was a circle of Magi Guard dressed in ceremonial armor.

The hairs on Danil's arms stood up. "What are they doing in the Fens?" he whispered.

Osriele settled in the undergrowth beside him, eyes wide. She shook her head mutely.

A guardswoman stepped forward and ceremoniously held up a small cage. The mage opened the latch and snatched out a tiny brown bird. Still chanting, the mage used a long and sharp pin to pierce the bird's chest. It fluttered once and then collapsed, its blood beading onto the needle.

The mage's voice rose to a crescendo as he slammed the needle into the ground.

Black, tar-like liquid welled up from around the needle. It quickly spread like a tide, dragging along with it the smell of rotting corpses and poisoned water. The ground tremored and erupted around the magus, but he remained untouched by the black liquid, a satisfied smile on his lips.

"No," Osriele gasped, horrified realization evident on her face.

The mage began a new incantation as he stretched his

arms wide. The black liquid swept to the circle of guards, who scrambled and fell with tortured screams underneath the swelling darkness.

"Blacksward!" Commander Selen hissed, wrenching Osriele up and away. "Flee, damn you all!"

Hafryn was pale and shaking as he scrambled to his feet. "The bloody magi are creating it themselves!"

Danil froze in dismay as the blacksward continued to swallow more of the clearing. It swarmed toward him and his companions.

"Hurry, Danil!" Osriele cried, tugging desperately against the commander's grip. "Do as you have done on the borderlands!"

Heart thundering, Danil planted his hands into the damp soil and reached for the leylines far away in Kailon. The House glyph brightened as he turned his thoughts to burning the blacksward clean. Heat traveled through his arm and into the earth. Kailon reached for him in a tumult of whispers but suddenly fetched up against the vast emptiness that was Roldaer.

The first trees crunched and groaned before collapsing under the poisonous blacksward.

"It approaches, *fala*," Hafryn hissed. "We can't stay here."

Danil clenched his eyes shut and shook his head. "Kailon's too far. I need more time." The smell of death burned the back of his throat. He reached again for the leylines, mental fingers scrabbling. A fragment of iridescent light reached out.

Hands suddenly gripped Danil by the shoulders and wrested him from under the brush. "No—!"

"Run, you idiot!" Hafryn snarled, shoving him hard.

The blacksward swept over where they'd crouched only

heartbeats before. The magus trailed after it, voice rising to a fevered pitch.

Danil staggered through the brush. Terrified horses cried shrilly from somewhere ahead, the chanting magus only a short distance behind. Desperate, Danil weaved a blocking enchantment and threw it behind them. The blacksward swept over it, undeterred, and Danil felt the hot spark of the glyph die out. He yelled in despair.

Gethin emerged from the trees with the horses in tow. His eyes turned wild as he took in the spreading tide of darkness. Cursing, he bent and hauled a weeping Osriele up behind him.

"Get her out of here!" the commander ordered.

Danil numbly let himself be shoved up into his saddle before Hafryn mounted his own horse. Ruslin skittered past them, white-faced with vomit on his tunic.

"Where's Ania?" Commander Selen yelled, turning back toward the clearing. "Ania!"

The blacksward thundered toward them, tearing down trees and consuming every leaf, bark and stem.

"She's lost!" Ruslin yanked hard on his horse's reins. "We must flee, commander!"

Selen wavered, mouth thin.

Between the trees, the red-robed magus trod sedately after the blacksward. The land behind him steamed and wailed.

"To the road," the commander ordered, cursing bitterly as she wheeled her horse about.

They galloped back to the game trail, the stench of death bearing down on them. The blacksward moved with gnashing fervor as they veered sharply onto the road.

The blacksward slowed only when it struck water,

writhing and curling as it sought a new path through the reedbeds.

Commander Selen threw a sharp look over her shoulder and gave a yell of triumph as they finally drew ahead. But Danil knew the blacksward was not finished destroying the surrounding landscape.

And he was helpless to stop it.

16

Outriding the blacksward forced them to forge their own path as they hastened on toward the coastal spire of Isfil. The noxious stench of rot assaulted Danil's nose as he gripped the reins and guided his horse over the rough terrain. The miles stretched on, a dark silence hanging over the group. Hafryn was a hard line of tension riding ahead of Danil, his fury a palpable force around him. Danil left him to his anger, concentrating instead on navigating the long reeds that whipped at his legs as he passed. Ahead, the estuaries coalesced into a sprawling basin that spilled out into the sea, the brown sediment of the Fens striking up against clearer waters.

Commander Selen ordered a stop to rest the mounts when the midmorning sun burned away the last touch of dew. Sweat and mud lathered the horses' flanks, their nostrils flared and legs trembling with exhaustion. Danil quietly set a protective glyph over them, ensuring their lower limbs would not become further shredded by the unforgiving rushes.

In a damp clearing, Gethin gently eased Osriele down

from the saddle. The woman was blank-faced and pale, her gaze distant. She seemed to have little care about her surroundings, letting herself be swaddled in blankets while Gethin and Ruslin set up camp and took to heating a kettle of kiandrite tea.

Danil dismounted gingerly, exhaustion sapping his bones. The blacksward felt like a hungering shadow in the back of his mind, and he couldn't help but look over his shoulder warily.

Hafryn stroked his horse's pale nose, murmuring to it softly before uncinching the girth and pulling the saddle loose. The wolf shifter worked in short, sharp movements, teeth clenched.

The surrounding marshes looked peaceful enough, but Danil wondered how long it would be before the blacksward and its mage found their way here. Desperate for a distraction, he worried loose a bur in his mare's mane before grabbing a clump of dry grass and using it to rub down the worst of the mud. He watched Hafryn as the wolf shifter worked on his own animal.

"You're angry," Danil said eventually.

Dark green eyes met his over the back of the horse. "You nearly let yourself be killed."

Danil felt his mouth pull downwards. "Fighting the blacksward was nothing like before," he admitted. It had been so much more virulent and ravenous.

"That was obvious the moment you tried," Hafryn muttered, briskly wiping dried mud from the horse's rump. "It nearly had you. I never thought you'd be so reckless."

Danil gaped. "Why else are we here if not to stop the blacksward?"

Hafryn snorted bitterly. "We should leave the magi to ruin themselves."

Danil threw a quick glance at Osriele looking wan and heartsore. "How can you say that?" he hissed. "They're destroying Roldaer!"

Hafryn shrugged, mouth thin. "The magi have done as they wished for centuries. The kingdom's grown powerful because of it, but now the blacksward's a reckoning for them all."

"But it's never the magi who suffer!" Danil protested, voice rising.

Gethin looked up from where he worked on the fire, a frown on his face. Noticing Danil's look, he raised a pot of water in question.

Danil shook his head. He had no stomach for herbed tea.

Dropping his voice, Danil continued with a hiss, "It's always peasants and farmers who suffer when they get in the magi's way. It's whole villages like Farin."

Hafryn gave him a sobering look. "Farin's gone, *fala*. You chose Kailon as your home. I thought you loved it there."

"I do, but—" He stopped, forcing down the lump in his throat. Every beat of his heart told him that failure to protect Roldaer would surely doom them all. "I fear what will happen if it's not stopped. Surely even you can see they won't stop with the ruin of Roldaer. That magus—his face. He was *enjoying* it."

Hafryn's mouth remained pinched but his furious currying slowed. "There must be something more to the blacksward than just the desecration of Roldaer and the impetus for war. A power of some kind, maybe." He turned tired eyes to Danil. "We're missing something."

Danil nodded. "I feel it, too."

"Something was different when you cleansed the blacksward near Scara," Hafryn noted broodily. "Perhaps it's the proximity to Kailon. We can't know until we get back there and you take up your duties as custodian once more."

"You're suggesting that we abandon our quest," Danil said, focusing his attention on a spiked burr trapped in his horse's mane.

"Osriele swore to us that the blacksward had nothing to do with the magi. That it wasn't a magi curse. Perhaps she lied to drag us even further away from Kailon," Hafryn said. "We need to return home. *Fala,* you have to let Roldaer go."

"Like you did with the Eyrie?" It was out before Danil could stop it.

Hafryn's face shuttered. "You strike low, Danil. The Eyrie always act in the interest of Amas."

Danil glanced at the amulet, thinking of how Merlias had so disdainfully left Hafryn to suffer. But he couldn't poke at that particular wound. Guilt lanced through his belly. "I'm sorry. I can't let the magi destroy Roldaer. I *can't.*"

Hafryn shook his head. "Roldaer doesn't deserve your life."

Glancing away, Danil watched Ruslin wade through knee-high depths to reach a hummock of sedges sitting high in the water. Even in the distance, he could read the haunted expression on the guard's face as he took up sentry duty. The man's grief over Ania only firmed his resolve.

"Who are we, Hafryn, if we stand aside and do nothing?"

Hafryn sighed in defeat.

A short distance away, Commander Selen knelt to give Osriele a steaming cup of tea. They spoke quietly for a time before the commander strode over to Danil and Hafryn, her face grave. "Forgive my interruption. Lady Osriele would speak with you, Danil."

Hafryn sighed and returned to scrubbing his mount free of dirt, his movements brisk and curt.

Heartsore, Danil trailed after the commander.

Osriele sat on a cloak swaddled in furs and looking pale with sorrow. A bowl of stew sat untouched beside her. She reached out and took both of Danil's hands in hers, smiling wanly.

"Are you well, Osriele?" Danil asked, kneeling opposite her.

"You're kind to ask, Danil, when we both know who is the cause of this land's suffering," she replied, deep shadows under her eyes as she shook her head. "I had no idea the Council's betrayal ran so deep."

Danil swallowed. "It should have surprised me less than it did, too."

She nodded, her tears moistening her cheeks. "My brethren have wronged you many times, Danil. I swear I'm not one of them." Her grip on his hands tightened, pleading. "Our task remains unchanged."

Danil glanced again at where Hafryn worked. The ache grew fresh and sharp in his belly. "I know."

At least now they knew the cause of the blacksward, though Danil had never heard of a magi spell capable of such destruction. "Do you recognize the curse the mage used?" he asked, recalling the guttural cries as the blacksward formed.

Osriele shook her head. "His words weren't of the Old Tongue." Seeing Danil's confused look, she added, "There are very few spells that don't use our oldest homeland language. Our words combined with mage-crystals are the foundation of our magic."

Danil frowned. "But I didn't see any kiandrite."

"Nor I. The spell needed the bird to create it." She let out a sigh, and Danil sensed how hopeless she felt. "I know little about death magicks. I foolishly believed they were anathema to even my most overzealous of compatriots."

Danil gazed down at their clasped hands. A glimmer of light leaked through from his palm. "I thought I knew how to destroy the blacksward," he murmured. He'd felt the power of the House glyph charge through the soil as the blacksward slithered towards him, but it hadn't been enough. "I couldn't stop it, though. It would have killed us all if we'd stayed."

"And yet you sensed what the mage planned to do long before the blacksward was created," Osriele pointed out. She studied him with a mixture of confusion and purpose. "You're still the key to changing our fate, Danil. I can feel it. A deadland scavenger shouldn't be at the center of all things, but here you are."

Danil didn't know how to explain Lyria's part in it all. He glanced away. "I'm sorry for Ania."

"There will be a reckoning, Danil," Osriele said, dark resolve firming her voice. "For all magi."

"THE CREATURE HAS GOTTEN AHEAD of us, my lady," Gethin said after a generous amount of swearing. "And it appears to have gathered friends."

The dark-haired corporal leaned over the saddlebow to point out the spoor of large, cat-like animals crisscrossing the road.

The marshes had given way to patches of redwood forest and large estuaries where plump fish meandered in the currents. A salty breeze carried with it the brine of the ocean, indicating they couldn't be far now from the coast.

Sliding from the saddle, Gethin followed the spoor until

the marks disappeared into the surrounding brush. "It's impossible to tell how many."

"Ania would know," Ruslin muttered just loud enough for Danil to hear.

Out of everyone in the party, the guardsman acted most haunted by Ania's death, and Danil wondered if they'd perhaps grown up in the same Fens village together. Already close-lipped and surly, Ruslin was now a dark shadow riding on the fringes of the party.

"The spoor looks fresh," Hafryn noted. He dismounted and tracked another set of prints further along the trail. "Could be trouble if the creatures are hungry or brazen enough to attack large groups."

Taking that as a warning, Gethin wordlessly unstrapped his wayfarer bow, slipping the pieces together with practiced efficiency.

The commander motioned to Danil. "Check Ania's saddlebags. She always carried a crossbow."

Eyebrow raised, Danil went to the spare horse tethered to Ruslin's saddlebow. The guardsman ignored him as he opened Ania's saddlebags and pushed aside linens and packets of trailbread.

"Do you have any experience with a crossbow, Danil?" Gethin asked as he moved his horse closer.

"Some. Not with one as fancy as this, though. Even the deadlands had its predators." Danil wasn't going to say that those predators were primarily Amasian, despite Hafryn's tell-tale smirk.

At the commander's orders, Gethin showed Danil how to set the crossbow and load a bolt. The corporal nodded in satisfaction after Danil made several successful shots. "Good. Don't load it until you mean to shoot it," he warned. Noting his tight features, Gethin gave Danil a shoulder bump and whispered conspiratorially, "And for the sake of my unborn children, don't aim it me."

Danil nodded, giving the Roldaerian a tight smile as he mounted his horse once more. The crossbow creaked softly as he rested it across his thighs.

Commander Selen made a quick perusal of her map. "We should be out of this forest in another mile or so. Then it's clear to the coast."

"Lead on, commander," Osriele ordered. "This forest makes me nervous. I'd rather we have some warning should those creatures decide to attack."

The road itself was patchy and overgrown, forcing them to navigate their horses around sharp-bladed grasses and dark-leaved sedges. A bitter wind cut through the trees, creating a soft moan that set Danil's teeth on edge. Osriele wasn't the only one to think this forest was unsettling.

Strange gouges in the soil caught Hafryn's attention. He bent in his saddle to examine them before releasing a sharp hiss. "Ride! The creatures are—"

An unearthly screech filled the air.

Danil spun in the saddle as a massive, cat-like creature launched from the redwoods to land beside Hafryn. Easily the size of a horse, its possessed scaly, armored skin and fangs as long as Danil's forearm. A bronze helm covered much of its snout and forehead, with only its pointy ears and glowing eyes visible.

Taloned claws slashed at the air where Hafryn's head had been only moments before, the wolf shifter having launched himself backward off his horse to the ground with a harsh curse.

"Run!" Hafryn bellowed as he drew his sword.

A second creature launched itself from behind the trees with a feral snarl, this one taller than the first. It landed on Ruslin, causing the man and his horse to collapse under the weight with a sickening crunch. The man shrieked, instinctively raising his arm as the creature sought his face with its gaping maw. It chomped down on his forearm, the sound both wet and harsh as Ruslin howled. Using his free hand, the guardsman pulled a short sword from his waist and stabbed frantically at its unnaturally glowing eye. It gave a jarring screech before shaking its massive head, sending Ruslin hurtling into a redwood with a thud. It followed, seeking to finish the stunned man.

Danil shook himself free of his horror, fixing a bolt and firing the crossbow at the creature's hide. It reared in shock and turned slitted orange eyes in Danil's direction.

Danil's horse reared, kicking the air in terror as the beast loomed over them. He fought the reins, the crossbow slipping from his hands as he struggled to stay on.

Hafryn blocked a swipe from the first creature before propelling himself toward Danil, falling to his knees to slide under the threatening creature. With a snarl, he drove his sword deep into the giant cat's belly, twisting harshly to cause more damage.

Black blood oozed from the wound, emitting a hot stench that instantly had Danil gagging. The creature released a bellowing howl, turning to face the new threat with a snap of its jaws.

Arrows pelted the wounded creature as Gethin took position behind a fallen tree. "Selen!" the dark-haired man roared at the commander as she swiped at the first beast's flank with her sword from atop her horse. "Your spear!"

One handed, she freed the spear from where she'd secured it under her leg and threw it to Gethin, never pausing in her strikes at the first creature.

Gethin leaped forward, snatching the spear from the air and thrusting it into the second creature's exposed throat.

Danil leaped off his rearing horse to join him, scooping the crossbow up from the forest floor he ran. Setting it again, the bolt released with a hard 'snick' only to ricochet off the larger creature's helm. It stood over them and roared, swiping the air with claws sheathed in blackened steel.

"Shoot for the belly and throat!" Gethin shouted, releasing another brutal thrust into the creature's side.

Arms raised high, Osriele shouted something guttural from behind where Selen kept the first beast busy. Her kiandrite ring burned bright red. An unseen force buffeted both creatures and sent them reeling from the group. The injured one staggered and shook its head as if to clear it while the first growled deep.

Hafryn and Gethin took the opportunity to attack the stunned larger beast, working in tandem as Gethin thrust his spear at its throat while Hafryn went once more for its belly. It screeched, unable to handle the double assault as Hafryn thrust up and back, aiming for the creature's heart. It collapsed with a wet groan, the wolf shifter only barely leaping out of the way in time.

Danil reloaded the crossbow and aimed for the smaller creature as it stalked after them from behind.

Hafryn spun to meet it, his blade scouring a deep wound across its foreleg. He unleashed a flurry of blows, far faster than Danil imagined possible. The thwarted creature caterwauled angrily, metal claws slashing before it finally skittered back. A growl reverberated through the trees with such ferocity that Danil felt it vibrate in his chest.

The air about Hafryn flickered. A heartbeat later, a dark cloud gathered and transformed into a vaguely man-sized shape.

Danil blinked.

The specter followed Hafryn like a shadow, mimicking each parry and blow as he set upon the remaining creature, until Danil could no longer discern who acted first.

Grinning wildly, Hafryn tracked the injured animal. It bared its fangs, muscles tightening as it prepared to launch once again. Hafryn met it in the air, steel ringing out as his blade struck and passed through the animal's helm. It crashed and hissed threateningly as Hafryn raised his sword once more, the amulet on his chest shining bright and bloody, and plunged the sword through the creature's skull. His shadow drove its blade down at the same moment, triumphant.

Black tar and putrid blood streamed across the ground as the creature finally stilled.

Breath heaving, Hafryn looked towards the trees, green eyes fierce as if expecting another attack. His blade dripped with gore.

Danil made his way over to him, wary of the shadow figure. It tracked his approach with an eerie amount of awareness.

Hafryn appeared unaware of the strange entity.

"Hafryn," Danil said quietly. He touched Hafryn's sleeve, avoiding the blackened blood spattering his friend's tunic.

Hafryn's grip on his blade turned white-knuckled as the shadowy figure stepped close.

"*Fala*," Danil said, carefully setting his hand over the top of Hafryn's. Eyes on the shadowy figure, he instinctively raised his House glyph. White-hot heat flooded his palm.

'*Begone*,' he commanded, unleashing a blast of light.

The shadow threw back its head and gave a soundless yell, whirling away into the trees.

A heartbeat later, Hafryn returned to himself. Blinking

rapidly, he dropped the blade. "What happened? Gods, what's that stink?"

Danil frowned, drawing close. "You killed them," he said. "That—their blood is putrid."

Almost like the blacksward, he thought.

Hafryn gazed about at the carnage, green eyes troubled.

Osriele emerged from behind Commander Selen's protective stance. "You were able to kill when my spells had little effect, Hafryn."

"It was nothing," Hafryn said. His gaze fell on the dropped blade with a strange hunger.

Danil studied him uneasily, his gaze finally dropping to the blade as well.

Blood from the dead creatures began to pool together, slinking across the forest floor to meet in inky blackness. The fetid smell of old rot thickened, and Danil barely held back the urge to gag as he took a worried step backward. The bloody pool rippled and hummed, and on the wind he thought he heard guttural chants.

"Mage portal!" Osriele cried in warning. She raised her hand in preparation for more spell casting.

The black pool trembled, gathering strength before it launched into the air and solidified a foot above the ground. Green flames licked out. Danil rammed his shoulder into Hafryn's belly and sent them both tumbling away with a grunt.

A dark figure stepped through, wearing chainmail beneath a white tabard marked with a peculiar, sharp-edged symbol that Danil had seen before. The large man looked out from under a misshapen helm twisted into the tortured rictus of a dying horse. The trees bracketing the portal trembled and darkened as a putrid wind whirled about them.

The newcomer lifted his helm's visor.

Danil scrambled back, attempting to drag Hafryn with him. His friend lay prone though, his shocked gaze centered on the man that smirked back.

"Hafryn of Eyrie," he purred. "My thanks for freeing me."

Kaul had returned.

17

Danil skidded forward to block Kaul's view of Hafryn, raising his House glyph like a shield. He felt Hafryn shudder behind him, his breath rasping.

The dread lord slid his cold gaze to Danil. "Ah. The traitorous *videre*." He gave a mocking smile. "I have not forgiven your thievery."

The House glyph pulsed in warning. "Kailon will never be yours!"

"And yet you leave it unprotected," Kaul mocked, blue eyes like hard chips of ice. "Many of my magi now traverse its soil and relieve it of its bounty."

But the steady heat rising from his hand was all Danil needed to know that Kailon remained strong and safe. He bared his teeth. "You lie."

Kaul chuckled. "Cling to your defiance, *videre*. You serve me nonetheless."

Scowling, Danil wondered what the dread lord could possibly mean.

Striding forward, Osriele raised both arms, her voice ringing as a barrage of fire struck the dread lord. Kaul was momentarily lost from view, consumed by the heat and flames. Osriele shouted again, and the fire burned hotter still until Danil was finally forced to shield his face.

Laughter burst out from within the fire. Kaul made a negligent sweeping motion with his fist. The flames fell away. "Your efforts are wasted, Osriele of Trudan."

She startled, arms lowering. "How do you know me?"

"There's much to know, blood heir to the throne," Kaul replied, smirking.

Hafryn threw Osriele a suspicious look, a dagger tight in his grip. But Danil wasn't so certain; it would serve the dread lord for them to distrust each other.

Kaul returned his gaze to Hafryn, cruel amusement curling his lips. "And you—how I've hungered for an Amasian under my thumb once again."

"I'm not yours," Hafryn spat, stepping around Danil with his dagger raised so that the tip pointed at the dread lord's throat.

"No?" Kaul raised a mocking brow. "The Harbinger amulet proves otherwise. Here, let me show you."

He snapped his fingers. A crystalline orb formed above his hand, swirling green and brown with pestilence.

Across the amulet, tiny etchings spun and flared as the blue inset stones flickered black. Hafryn flinched, whitening with pain. He gripped the amulet and tugged as if to yank it free.

"It's far too late for that," Kaul observed with a soft tut. He snapped his fingers and the orb shattered like glass.

Hafryn gave a sudden choked cry, trembling as if battling an unseen force. The blade all but rattled in his grip.

"Attend me, wolf," Kaul said, voice thick with triumph.

Against his will, Hafryn took a staggering step toward Kaul.

Ice flooded Danil's veins as he launched after him. "Hafryn!"

Osriele gripped Danil's arm, hissing, "Kaul Mage-Kin can't have you, Danil!"

"Kneel," the dread lord commander.

Hafryn fell to his knees before Kaul, his gaze filled with a mix of terror and hatred.

Kaul clucked his tongue in mock sympathy. "There's no changing your fate, Amasian. It'll go easier if you don't fight it." He laid a hand on Hafryn's shoulder, dipping his clawed fingers into the black blood that stained his shirt. "The rewards will be great, my servant," he purred. He muttered something low under his breath, a spell forming.

A vacant look passed over Hafryn's face as he slowly gathered to his feet. Every muscle quivered as he turned and took a shaky step toward the party. He leaned down, picking up the sword he had discarded earlier.

"Destroy all who are useless to me," Kaul commanded.

Hafryn's gaze fell upon Commander Selen as she stood protectively in front of an unconscious Ruslin. Gethin knelt beside the injured man, having finished tying off a makeshift bandage for his shattered arm. He watched Hafryn warily, hand reaching for his quiver of arrows.

Hafryn's grip on his sword turned white-knuckled. Sweat covered his brow.

"Hafryn, you must fight the compulsion!" Danil yelled.

If he heard, Hafryn gave no indication. Each step brought him closer to the Roldaerian guards.

Danil's vision shifted, revealing a red rope about Hafryn's throat. It pulsed and constricted every time the wolf shifter slowed his feet.

Kaul grinned in delight.

Danil thought desperately of a protective enchantment, fingers weaving. So far from Kailon, he feared it wouldn't be enough against the dread lord, but desperation gave it new strength until it shone iridescent and bright in his mind. The glyph shot outwards to strike the constricting magic.

Hafryn staggered as awareness momentarily returned to his gaze. He hunched, breath heaving with effort.

Danil called forth a new glyph, his palm burning bright.

"Enough, *videre*," Kaul growled. "You cannot fight us all."

The undergrowth shuddered as three new creatures leaped from the redwoods. They skittered to a halt in front of the dread lord, their helms gleaming. Low growls reverberated through the air as they turned shining eyes upon the Roldaerians.

"My bloodthirsty *selasi*," Kaul crooned, sweeping his hands grandly over the snarling creatures. "Children of the blacksward! Feast upon their bones!"

Sword drawn, Commander Selen pulled the shield from her horse and bared her teeth in readiness. Beside her, Gethin drew a bead on the closest creature.

Then blue tipped wings and shimmering air swept over Danil. Sparks of light blinded him moments before Merlias shoved past him, cloak whirling and red hair flying. A barrage of hot-white enchantments shot across the clearing.

The dread lord raised an arm to protect himself.

Danil took the advantage. Heat flared from Kailon's glyph on his palm. Trusting his instincts, he raised it and felt it *pulse.*

Kaul rocked back. The selasi creatures hissed and spat, shredding blindly at the air. One broke rank and fled for the redwoods.

"Custodian! Again!" Merlias yelled as she wove a new enchantment.

Danil called forth the power contained within the House of Kailon, feeling it stretch the distance between them, humming as it traveled through rock and stream. It sang in his ears.

Kaul was blasted back a foot. He roared in outrage. The two remaining creatures scattered.

Merlias stalked closer as she unleashed more glyphs. They battered against Kaul, causing him to snarl from deep in his throat. Beside the enchanter, Osriele shouted and released a pulse of fire that pummeled against the dread lord.

The red rope about Hafryn's throat suddenly loosened. He whirled to face the dread lord. His face was a rictus of a snarl as he raised his sword.

"You die, dread lord!"

Kaul hissed, "Even your defiance serves me." He turned to the black portal and raised both hands. Figures moved in the void, and for a terrifying moment Danil thought he saw Magus Brianna on the other side of the portal. She was dressed in white robes with a circlet on her brow. Ceremonial guards surrounded her.

Kaul snapped his fingers.

The red rope about Hafryn's throat constricted once more. His back arched in pain.

"With me, Harbinger," Kaul commanded.

Sweat formed on Hafryn's brow as he took a halting step toward the portal.

"No!" Merlias cried, throwing her hand out. The earth around Hafryn churned within a series of earth-borne spikes, caging him in place.

Thwarted, Kaul snarled and stalked for the portal. It

surged and crested like waves on the ocean as he stepped through. Danil called again, feeling the heat in his palm as another surge burst forth to snap against the portal, only to have it close with a thunderous clap.

A momentary silence swept over the group before Hafryn collapsed to his knees like a marionette freed of its strings.

The earth-borne cage collapsed, and Danil scrambled to him and gripped him tight. "Hafryn," he gasped, terrified that the wolf shifter remained under Kaul's thrall.

White-faced, Hafryn ran clammy fingers over Danil's cheek. "I'm still here," he rasped, voice desperate to believe it also.

Danil pulled him close, eyes burning.

Sinking into his embrace, Hafryn released a mirthless laugh. "We should have killed Kaul when we had the chance, *fala*."

18

Ruslin cried out as he was lifted into the saddle. Blood seeped through the makeshift bandage covering much of his arm.

"No time for gentleness," Commander Selen muttered in apology. She helped Gethin secure the injured guard to the stirrups with rope. "The dread lord and his creatures may return at any moment."

"I'm going to lose my arm!" Ruslin sobbed, hunching over the saddle. Black lines of sickness already threaded past the shredded sleeve of his tunic.

Swinging up onto his own horse, Danil wove a healing enchantment, feeling it tingle as it shimmered into shape above his fingers.

"Don't!" Ruslin snarled as the glyph drifted over him. He was white-faced and trembling. "You and that cursed wolf have done enough!"

Danil stilled, then blinked in astonishment. "It'll help heal—"

"I said no, traitor!"

Gethin threw a woolen blanket about Ruslin's shoulders, careful of his arm. His mouth tightened as he said, "Do as he says, Danil. Don't make things worse for him."

Cheeks burning, Danil let the floating glyph dissipate in a puff of iridescent light.

Merlias watched the exchange and gave a derisive snort. "You should leave the injured one behind. The selasi have his blood now."

The commander glowered at her. "We're not leaving anyone."

Merlias made a dismissive shrug. "Then you're inviting Kaul to hunt you with his creatures. I won't share your fate."

The air about her shimmered as she leaped upwards, feathers and wings snapping free. The blue-tipped owl took flight and circled over the party once, her cry derisive before she flapped away.

"Who *is* that?" Commander Selen muttered as the Eyrie enchanter disappeared above the tree canopy.

"Merlias, the favored glyph-breaker and assassin of Lord Viren of Eyrie," Hafryn said wearily.

Osriele eyed him coolly. "You have much to explain, Hafryn, about why the enchanter is here."

"Trust me, I have as many questions as you," Hafryn said. He cursed softly as he checked over his mount. A selasi had gotten close enough to rake claws over its trembling flanks. "Danil, any chance you can help the poor beast?"

Danil walked over but a quick look revealed that it was beyond the basic healing glyphs that Elania had taught him. "I'm sorry," he shook his head.

"Mine's gone too," Gethin said, pointing with his chin at the dead animal lying amidst the forest detritus. "Our remaining mounts are too weak to carry double for long, commander."

"We'll have to make do," Selen said. "Gethin, deal with that unfortunate animal. Not you, Hafryn," the woman said as she saw Hafryn draw his blade. "I mean no offense, but you with a blade only adds to our troubles. You already look like a cursed berserker."

Hafryn glanced down at himself in surprise. Black blood spattered his arms and tunic, the stink of it masked only by the putrid corruption rising off the dead selasi only a few feet away.

"Better still, hand over your sword," the commander ordered, her hand outstretched. "If Kaul Mage-Kin returns, I'd prefer he doesn't have the same advantage as before."

Hafryn faltered, gripping the hilt of his blade and turning his body slightly.

Ruslin lurched in the saddle, eyes filled with hate. "The wolf means to attack us again, commander! We need to end them both before they succeed!"

"Again?" Hafryn repeated, startled.

"Shut it, private," Selen barked. She turned grimly to Hafryn, her hand still outstretched. "Your sword."

Danil grimaced. "The amulet had control over you, Hafryn. Kaul did something and then you weren't yourself."

Hafryn's brows shot up. "I don't remember," he admitted.

"You meant to attack us," Commander Selen said, indicating herself and the other guards. "But not Osriele or Danil."

Osriele eyed Hafryn with interest. "I'm rather curious about that, too, but we cannot explore that now. We *must* leave."

Danil nodded. If Kaul returned, there'd be no second chances. The dread lord would take Hafryn through the void and kill whoever stood in his way.

With a pained grimace, Hafryn handed over his sword.

Then he busied himself by removing his pack from behind the saddle of his injured mount. He clambered up behind Danil, pointedly not looking when Gethin slit the lame animal's throat.

Cleaning his blade on his breeches, the corporal gave Selen a grim nod. "I'll mask our trail from the selasi, commander."

"No. If that bird enchanter has the measure of it, such efforts will do no good. Mount up behind Ruslin. We must head for the coast with all haste."

Osriele turned on her horse to address Danil. "You wouldn't happen to know any enchantments that could make our horses more fleet of foot, would you?"

Danil pursed his lips in thought before shaking his head. "Healing requires a balance that I'm not skilled with. I could lay an enchantment that will give the horses a sense of more energy, but I fear that they'd gallop until their hearts failed. I wouldn't risk it until the direst of circumstances."

"And having Kaul breathing down our necks isn't dire enough for you, traitor?" Ruslin snarled.

"We still have a ways to go, and if the horses fall before we reach Isfil, we're doomed." Danil glowered at the guard. "I won't have them die unnecessarily."

"I think Danil has the right of it," Osriele said with a sigh. "Be prepared to use it nonetheless, should the need arise, Danil. I don't think we've seen the last of Kaul or his creatures."

With that, the party pushed their horses as hard as they dared, avoiding the fragmented pockets of forest that increasingly broke up the last relics of marshes. The salty air grew stronger, and in the distance were soft white mounds that indicated sand dunes. Silvers of blue ocean glistened beyond.

Hafryn was a line of tension behind Danil, his grip on Danil's hips almost bruising.

"You're safe," Danil murmured, laying his hand over Hafryn's white-knuckled fingers.

Hafryn shook his head. "I don't understand how Kaul could have broken free. His prison was supposed to be impenetrable."

Danil thought of the shadow fighter who'd mimicked every one of Hafryn's blows. "Perhaps your killing of the selasi gave him additional strength to break the enchantment." He hoped the Amasians tasked with guarding Kaul had escaped injury.

Osriele overheard and drew her tired mount beside them. "I recall references to a magi curse capable of doing what you speak of—a terrible curse buried so deep in our Tower library that the spell itself is lost. I wouldn't have thought any magus could sink so low as to wield it, but..." She gave them a humorless smile. "We know better now."

"What is this curse?" Danil asked, afraid of the answer.

"It feeds murderous energy to the wielder of the spell. With each death, the magus who cast the spell grows in power while also bestowing upon the cursed extraordinary speed and strength. It's a dark magick that inevitably transforms both into beings of terrible evil." Osriele looked Hafryn in sympathy. "You were able to kill two selasi when my fiercest spellworkings couldn't. And you fought like someone with nothing to lose—and we all know that's not true. The amulet must be the channel through which Kaul gains power from the spell."

Hafryn gave a rueful sigh. "Then Selen was right to demand my blade. Killing again will only serve Kaul."

"She has good instincts," Osriele agreed. She hesitated. "Now that the dread lord is free, he'll focus on gathering his loyal servants. We have time to find a way to remove the amulet and return you both to the deadlands."

Hafryn grunted, the tension in his body returning. "This old curse you speak of. Was there anything in your library about it being removed?"

Osriele's gaze grew sorrowful. "Don't lose hope yet, Hafryn. Your unwillingness to bear the curse is a hindrance to Kaul's rising power. If Danil is right, and Isfil holds the answer to defeating the blacksward, then the answer to removing the amulet may lie there as well. I don't believe the two unrelated. The stench of Kaul is all over the blacksward."

He merely nodded, mouth tight, and the conversation grew silent.

They traversed a small, burbling stream as the land became increasingly sandy. Shrubs clung low to the soil as if hunched against regular, buffeting winds.

Danil idly checked the sky but saw no sign of Merlias. A small, startling part of him hoped she would return soon—she'd been unflinching against Kaul, even when it meant rescuing Hafryn.

A mile closer to the coast, Gethin and Ruslin's horse stumbled. Gethin hurriedly dismounted, muttering soothing tones to the animal and brushing its silky nose as it tottered in place. Ruslin was largely unaware of the fuss, slumped forward and gaze listless.

Gethin ran quick hands over the trembling horse's legs. He nodded. "Still sound, commander. She needs a rest, though."

Selen sighed in relief. "A short break, and then we walk the horses from here."

Danil fought down his frustration as he swung from the saddle.

Hafryn wordlessly trudged to the edge of the stream and squatted. Black blood still coated his arms up to his elbows and sleeves. With a sigh, he shucked off his tunic. Bruises showed on his back from his skirmish with the selasi. He dipped his hands into the current to wash off the blood and muck.

"Let me," Danil said, kneeling beside him. He cupped handfuls of cool water and scrubbed Hafryn's arms. He felt the weight of Hafryn's gaze on his skin.

"*Fala*, maybe you shouldn't—"

"Don't," Danil said, not looking up from his task.

"You heard Osriele and the commander. I'm a danger to you."

Danil snorted and worked on the blood trapped under Hafryn's nails. "You didn't flinch when Magus Brianna laid a curse over me for stealing Kaul's journal. What makes you think I won't do the same now, especially when you have my heart?"

Hafryn stared at him, care and regret in his eyes. "*Fala*, this is Kaul we're facing. I felt his mind sweep over me. I fear I could do unspeakable things at his beckoning."

Chilled, Danil thought over what the dread lord had called Hafryn—Harbinger. It wasn't a name idly spoken. Whatever plans Kaul had put in motion, Hafryn was intrinsically bound to play a part.

Danil shook himself and mustered a smile. "We're so close to Isfil now. Let's cling to hope while we have it."

But Hafryn merely hung his head and sighed.

WEARY HORSES FORCED them to stop again late in the night. Moonlight cast a silvery haze atop a line of sand dunes that looked down over the coast. Below them, a burbling stream snaked out from under the dunes and cut across the pebbled beach before being consumed by the foaming waves.

"At least we made the coast," Hafryn said, humorless smile tight.

Gethin helped his injured companion from his horse, grunting as he took Ruslin's weight. Even in the pale moonlight, Ruslin trembled and shivered like a man taken by sickness, muttering to himself as if caught in a fever. The corporal eased him onto a cloak, worry evident on his face as the wounded guard curled into a ball of misery.

"He needs rest, commander," Gethin said, voice low so as not to carry in the ocean breeze. "A few hours at least. This sickness, it's not normal. I fear the creature's bite may carry poison."

Cursing softly, Selen took a quick recon of the dunes. "Tend him as best you can, corporal. No fire," she ordered, her voice low. "An hour is all we can spare."

Gethin nodded grimly and set about replacing Ruslin's bandages. His nosed pinched at the smell as he gently bathed the wound, and even from where Danil stood, he could see thick black lines of foulness spreading up Ruslin's arm.

Danil looked out over the wide bay that stretched for miles in both directions. "We can't be far from Isfil now."

Squinting up at the stars, Commander Selen nodded. "A day's ride. Perhaps two if our pace slows further."

It heartened Danil a little. He traversed the sand to where Hafryn stood looking out over the ocean. Unlike

Ruslin, there was a healthiness to the way Hafryn stood, his eyes bright and skin hale. The amulet was tucked away under his tunic, wrapped in swaddling cloths, though Danil doubted such effort muted the power of its curse.

"I can feel you staring, *fala*," Hafryn said, though he continued to watch the rolling waves.

"You look better."

Hafryn turned and raised an eyebrow. "I suppose I do. The amulet doesn't weigh so heavily on me." He stretched out the knots in his spine.

"Is it because of the fight, do you think? If Kaul gains power every time you kill, he'd find ways to encourage you to do it more."

"And punish me when I don't." Hafryn massaged his eyelids with two fingers. "It makes sense. Time will tell, no?"

That was a forbidding prospect.

The wind shifted slightly and Danil glanced up to see an owl dart along the coast. Merlias landed and transformed in the shadow of the dune. She carried a pack on one shoulder, and Danil wondered where she'd flown to retrieve it.

Hafryn made a low whistle. "What do you think of that?"

Danil shook his head mutely. From the corner of his eye, he saw Osriele watch the enchanter cautiously, hand half-raised as if in readiness to release a spell.

Seemingly unconcerned, the Eyrie enchanter brushed past Commander Selen, who stood with her arms ominously folded, and dropped the pack beside Ruslin.

Gethin threw the commander a questioning look, his hand resting over the hilt of his dagger.

Commander Selen made a quelling, '*wait and see*' gesture.

Fishing out a small packet of wet, crushed herbs,

Merlias said curtly, "Don't just stand about like slack-jawed fools. I need water. Fresh—not that wine-tainted swill you undoubtedly keep in your flagon." She gave Gethin a hard stare.

"Do as the enchanter asks, corporal," Osriele said, her voice mild as she made her way over. "I'm sure Merlias will do her best by Ruslin."

Merlias smiled, baring teeth. "You ride slowly for hunted folk. I flew over your party many times. I imagine Kaul's selasi will find it no less difficult."

Gethin returned from the stream at the base of the sand dune. He handed the enchanter his flagon of water.

Pulling back the fresh bandages, Merlias splashed the wound. The injured guard was too sickly to protest, and Gethin merely sat back on his haunches with a bemused expression as the Eyrie enchanter dabbed the heated skin. Danil saw tiny iridescent flecks of kiandrite as she worked the salve into the wound. A small glyph dropped from Merlias' fingers.

The smell of sickness carried in the air as the kiandrite darkened and died out. The wound looked wholly unchanged. Whatever poison the selasi carried in their fangs, it had truly taken hold of Ruslin.

Merlias bent close and sniffed. "Fascinating."

Hafryn could no longer resist merely watching. "Why are you here, Merlias? Don't feign concern for a Roldaerian guardsman."

She glanced up balefully. "You're blocking my light, exile."

"Exile?" Osriele looked between them. "You know each other, then. Have you been with Danil and Hafryn all this time, Merlias?"

Danil threw Osriele a startled look.

Dusting her hands, Merlias stood. "As a spy, you mean? No. I came for the amulet."

Danil blinked, not expecting her to be so upfront.

"By all means, Merlias, take it." Hafryn spread out his arms.

Lip curling, Merlias said, "I expect only Kaul can remove it. I doubt he'd do so willingly now that he's got a wolf to play with."

"But Hafryn's Amasian," Danil argued. "Kaul hates your people."

Merlias shrugged one shoulder. "It gives the dread lord great pleasure to force an enemy to his will. You should know that by now, custodian."

"Then tell us what you know," Danil pressed. "Kaul called Hafryn a 'Harbinger'. I've never come across it."

"Can't tell you anything about that, I'm afraid." Merlias looked bored and ready to take flight once more.

Danil raised his palm. The House glyph brightened with warmth. "You can't leave, Merlias," he growled. "If we can't remove the amulet, then you must help us destroy Kaul."

Merlias laughed incredulously. "I'll do no such thing!"

"Viren's obligations extend to you, enchanter," Danil said, feeling the truth of it pulse in his hand. "You have to fulfill his promises."

"If you're referring to my lord's quaint vow to keep Hafryn safe, we fulfil ed our obligation in Kailon," Merlias said testily.

Danil shook his head. "You took part in a skirmish. That's scarcely recompense for the return of Eyrie's lost glyphs." Danil squared his jaw when Merlias' eyes turned murderous. "What will your allies think when they discover you quibble over your debts?"

She flared. "Taking on the dread lord far exceeds Lord Viren's obligations—and mine!"

"Then why did you do everything to stop Kaul from forcing Hafryn through the portal?" Danil countered.

Hafryn folded his arms. "He has you there, Merlias. That's also why you've made no attempt to kill me—you're bound to keep Viren's bargain with Danil."

She sneered. "We're a long way from Amas, exile."

"But you're bound all the same."

A light of understanding filled Osriele's eyes. "Oh! Now I see why you sought to heal Ruslin! He's slowing us down. Something follows us, isn't that so, Amasian?"

Merlias glowered at them all, cheeks turning red before she screeched her frustration.

Commander Selen gripped the hilt of her sword in alarm.

Merlias gave them all a murderous look before spitting, "Four of those creatures have found your trail. If you don't kill the injured guard, he'll drag you all to your deaths."

Danil glanced anxiously back at the line of trees in the distance. He had a suspicion the selasi could eat up the distance when they were of a mind to do so.

"Ruslin is our responsibility," Osriele replied mildly.

The enchanter bared her teeth. "You've been warned."

Shimmering light gathered about Merlias before she took to the air. Gethin made a quick warding sign as the owl flapped over his head and swept over the dunes.

They watched until the owl turned into a spec on the horizon.

"Well done, *fala*," Hafryn murmured, clasping Danil's shoulder. "She's furious but she'll stay loyal to Viren. As much as it alarms me, we need her expertise."

Danil blew out a ragged breath. His skin pebbled as if death had brushed by on blue-tipped wings.

Commander Selen studied him with a new light. "You play a dangerous game, Danil," she said, voice admiring. "Very dangerous indeed."

Hopefully, Merlias wouldn't make him regret it.

19

Commander Selen risked ordering an extended break when dawn cast an orange hue over the ocean. Large, serpent-like creatures frolicked just beyond the shore, having kept abreast of the party as they walked the horses towards a rocky outcrop at the far end of the bay. The serpents dove for deeper water only when Merlias flew over them, their raucous whistles piercing the waves.

Danil sank wearily to his knees. He'd managed only a little sleep during the night when he'd taken a short spell atop his horse. Most of the night they'd walked beside the horses, but one too many stumbles had seen Hafryn force him to rest.

"Will you not join us, Merlias?" Osriele called out to the Amasian as she circled the group while Gethin used gathered driftwood to light a small fire. A tripod with a kettle was quickly set over the flames.

Merlias dropped onto the sand beside Commander Selen with a thud, fiery sparks of light spinning about her when she transformed. The commander's horse startled and reared in fright.

"Damned shifters are all the same," Selen muttered under her breath as she stroked the animal's nose until quietened.

Merlias smirked and stepped over Ruslin, who lay feverishly unconscious under a blanket, his hair sweat-slick and clinging to his neck. The enchanter helped herself to a small packet of dried meat and trailbread from the satchel beside him.

Hafryn stood on the opposite side of the fire, measuring the Eyrie enchanter like a lion sizing up prey. Noting him, Merlias tore off a chunk of meat with her teeth, eyes challenging.

Danil shifted his vision to see her blue-tipped owl with its head lowered and wings partially spread. Hafryn's wolf Trueform stalked in front of her, ears flicking when the owl clacked its beak.

"You could be confused for bickering kin," Osriele mused, looking between them and no doubt taking in their matching red hair and green eyes. They were of an age, too, and shared a predatory grace few Roldaerians could aspire to.

Merlias stopped mid-chew and swallowed with a grimace. "You're mistaken, magus. The only blood between us is what can be spilled on the battlefield."

"If only it weren't for your vow," Hafryn said dryly.

The enchanter eyed him with intent, and Danil watched with amusement as her Trueform charged at Hafryn's with a defiant hiss, stopping short when the wolf snapped his jaws in response.

Commander Selen strode over to Danil. She looked fed up and weary. "I need someone on watch. Can I trust you to have a clear head?"

Surprised, Danil replied, "Of course, commander."

Selen nodded and wordlessly pointed to a patch of scrub high up the nearby sand dune.

"Run back if you see anything," Hafryn said, snagging his sleeve. "No heroics."

Danil squeezed Hafryn's arm before setting out above the tide line. The dune looked out over the coast but also afforded him a view of the estuaries and sparse trees inland. A heavy quiet lay over the land, with few birds calling out to welcome the brightening day.

The uneasy silence drew his thoughts toward Kaul. Now that the dread lord was free, he would find a way to bend the Roldaerian army to his will. And with the magi already mostly under his thumb, it would be an easy feat. But Danil stretched his mind towards Kailon and felt its contented murmur. Kaul had yet to draw near the leylines.

A cloaked figure made their way to him from the makeshift beach camp as the sun pitched to early-morning.

To Danil's surprise, it was Merlias who navigated the shifting sand up to him. He threw her a cautious glance when she sat so close to him that their shoulders brushed.

"Relax, custodian, I'm not here to bleed you," the young woman said mildly, her gaze sweeping the distant trees.

"If you mean to criticize Hafryn instead, maybe the sea serpents will care to hear you," Danil said.

She chuckled. "You have a stubborn heart."

Danil couldn't tell if it was an observation or a slight against him. He shuffled uncomfortably, sending a ripple of sand down the dune.

Merlias glanced at Danil's hand. Soft light made the sand glisten about them like jewels. She hummed. "A custodian's glyph grows quiet whenever they leave the territory of their House. Did you know that?"

"I have sentry duty, Merlias," Danil replied, setting his gaze on the ocean.

Merlias continued undeterred. "Custodian powers are dependent upon their proximity to their main lodestone— or wellspring, in your case. Out here, you should be largely useless to us all, Danil. Instead, you defy centuries of knowledge and practice."

Danil turned to stare at her.

The Eyrie enchanter nodded thoughtfully. "Kaul must have plans for you, too."

Cold rushed through Danil. "What do you mean?"

"Kaul would have ordered Hafryn to kill you, otherwise."

The chill in Danil's bones only deepened. Merlias had a point. He'd proven himself as a dangerous adversary when he'd used the leylines of Kailon to imprison Kaul. It made little sense for the dread lord to keep such an enemy alive, unless Danil served a purpose as well.

With an effort, he asked, "Why does my fate matter to you?"

"Perhaps I'm curious about what a human custodian is capable of—especially one chosen on the eve of war against his own homeland. I'd expect such a person to feel rather conflicted."

"I don't," Danil replied, knowing that his heart belonged in Kailon.

"You make a poor showing of it, then," she snorted derisively. "Why are you so far from your wellspring, custodian? What draws you to Isfil?"

Danil desperately wished he had the answer, though he'd hardly tell Merlias even if he did.

"Was it a vision?" she pressed.

He gave her a stony look.

Merlias nodded. "Lord Viren told you of Eyrie's *videre*.

She betrayed us to Kaul in the Great War. No one like her has been born since. But now Kaul's returned, along with a new *videre*."

"I don't see the connection," Danil said as he gazed out over the dune, though his heart began to pound.

She tilted her head. "Don't you?"

Danil sighed, done with her games. "What do you *want*, Merlias?"

"Only to understand where you stand, Danil." She lifted her hand, fingers twitching as a glyph came into being. It looked startlingly like the one she'd thrown in front of Hafryn to break his path into Kaul's portal. "Assassins can make for powerful allies. But only if there's trust."

"I think we're long past that," Danil observed with a scowl. "You've made your animosity to Hafryn and I quite clear."

Merlias laughed. "I think you'll need me before this is done. Both of you."

She snapped her fingers and the enchantment broke apart in a shower of sparks. They landed on Danil's arms like heated darts. He wiped them away.

The Eyrie enchanter rose, dusting her breeches of sand. "Oh, and the Roldaerian commander says it's time to leave. Do come along."

Danil waited for his heart to calm before made his way down the dune and across to Hafryn. The wolf shifter stood beside their horse, his grip loose on the bridle. A distant look crossed Hafryn's face, his head canted as if listening.

Danil followed his gaze along the beach, where hoof prints left a wandering trail in the sand. "What is it?"

Blinking back to awareness, Hafryn frowned. "Selasi," he said. "They're close." He whistled, drawing Commander Selen's attention, before pointing further along the bay.

The commander shaded her eyes, then bellowed at Gethin to get Osriele and Ruslin to their horses. Merlias shot into the air with a burst of light.

"You can sense the selasi now?" Danil asked Hafryn in alarm.

Hafryn's mouth tightened. "It appears so." He swung up into the saddle and leaned down to clasp Danil's forearm to help him up. "Come on. There's still time."

From the corner of Danil's eye, a shadow moved in synchronicity with Hafryn. It sat upon a shadow horse only a few feet away. It turned to stare at Danil, animosity rippling the air.

"Hafryn," Danil said urgently. "Do you sense anything else?"

"I think the selasi are enough, *fala*."

Climbing up behind Hafryn, Danil subtly raised his House glyph toward the shadow figure and its horse. The glyph pulsed.

The figure raised its arm as if suddenly blinded, its horse rearing. The wind kicked up, sand buffeting them all. Hafryn cursed, turned their mount away from the blasting sand. When it calmed again, the shadow figure and its horse were gone.

"What in blazes was that?" Hafryn breathed.

Danil pressed a shaky hand to his friend's side. "Kaul wants you to fight."

"Aye," Hafryn said, steering their mount to the others. "Let's hope I won't need to."

A LOW CHITTER came from somewhere behind the scrub.

On Commander Selen's orders, they walked the horses

close to the waves where the sand was firmer. Rockpools took over the shore as they drew closer to the rocky cliff, and a single sea stack with cawing birdlife stood beyond the jagged outcrop.

Merlias' owl swung over the party and quickly transformed.

Commander Selen raised her fist for the party to stop.

"Five of those creatures—likely more hiding in the rocks at the base of the cliff," Merlias said as twin glyphs circled above her. "It won't be long before they come."

"Do they have our scent?" the commander asked.

Merlias threw Hafryn a glance. "They do, but I doubt it's necessary."

Hafryn scowled at her. "I have no say in what the selasi do."

"True. You're just another of Kaul's pawns now."

Baring his teeth, Hafryn looked ready to launch himself at the Eyrie enchanter.

"Enough," Osriele snapped, surprising Danil when she moved between the two Amasians and scowled at each in turn. "Put aside whatever hatred you have for each other. We've no time for discord."

Both Hafryn and Merlias stepped back, but nothing in their postures indicated they were done. There would be a reckoning between them, Danil knew. With the amulet on Hafryn's side, he may well best the assassin-enchanter. But the battle between them would only serve Kaul.

"The dread lord must suspect our destination," Gethin said, studying the cliff. "Isfil can't be far now. It might even be behind the cliff."

Osriele pursed her lips, eyeing the tired horses. "Now may be the time for your enchantment, Danil. The way things stand, I don't believe we can survive another attack. Racing for the spire our only option."

Danil nodded, already weaving the enchantment in the air. His palm warmed as he pressed it against each horse in turn. Instantly their heads lifted, and even the one who had borne Ruslin for much of the past day gave a full-bodied shake.

"Everyone, mount up," Commander Selen said as she boosted Osriele into the saddle of her horse. "We use the dunes to swing inland and then back on the beach. And hope that Isfil is within reach!"

Danil climbed onto his horse, feeling the comforting heat of Hafryn's hands as the wolf shifter settled behind him.

Commander Selen kicked her horse into the lead. Danil's horse leaped after her, flying across the sand with renewed vigor.

Dark shapes bounded toward them from further up the beach, behind the dunes.

"Selasi!" Hafryn snarled, going rigid.

The commander veered, redirecting everyone close to the shoreline. They thundered along the beach toward the cliff. Selen drew her sword as the selasi gave chase.

Hafryn reached around and took one of Danil's daggers.

"No, Hafryn, you can't!" Danil said, gripping his wrist. "It's what Kaul wants!"

Movement caught Danil's eye, and he had hardly time to cry out before a selasi barreled across the sand and swiped at his galloping horse. The horse neighed shrilly, sidestepping the beast. Hafryn took the advantage and leaped from the saddle.

Danil looked over his shoulder, gasping as Hafryn threw himself at the creature and vaulted upon its back with a snarl. Even with the increasing distance, Danil could see an orange glow in Hafryn's eyes as he plunged his dagger into the selasi's neck.

Danil wrenched on the reins, pulling the horse up and around to gallop back to Hafryn and three more selasi racing down from the dunes to cut him off. There was no way he would leave Hafryn behind.

Merlias' owl dove in front of Danil, transforming as the enchanter flung searing glyphs at the approaching creatures. Danil felt his hand pulse in companionship. He drew a matching glyph and hurled it forward.

The sand in front of the selasi suddenly bucked. Pointed spikes of hard sand blocked their route but the selasi hardly slowed. The creatures struck the barricade headlong, sparks showering from their helms as they were thrust backward. They screeched once before lying still.

Merlias shot Danil an astonished look.

More selasi loped from the dunes, their excited chitters and whistles carrying on the wind.

"Twelve," Gethin counted, blood draining from his face as he drew his horse up beside Danil's.

Danil blinked in surprise, not realizing the other Roldaerians had also turned back to help Hafryn.

Four selasi streaked ahead of the pride. By some unseen agreement, they lowered their helms, barbs flaring, and smashed into the barrier with a thunderous crack.

The barrier exploded in a spray of sand and shells. A sharp stab burst across Danil's palm as the enchantment collapsed and died. The selasi were flung all about, bones crunching as they tumbled head over foot.

The remaining eight selasi leaped over their fallen brethren, unfettered.

"Get behind me, all of you," Osriele ordered. "*Now,* Hafryn!"

Hafryn hesitated, gaze fixed on the selasi but retreated with a curse.

Osriele's ring pulsed darkly as she called on its power. A sparking red barrier formed in front of them, reminding Danil of the one that had initially imprisoned him and Hafryn back in the manor in Aqila.

"It won't hold, magus," Merlias warned, drawing her twin blades. "Not if they strike all at once."

Commander Selen braced her spear in the sand, point facing the approaching creatures.

The sky darkened as Hafryn snatched Ruslin's sword tied behind the injured guard's bedroll.

"*Fala,*" Danil called, struck by the orange flecks that suddenly flashed in Hafryn's eyes. "Don't fight them! You'll only make Kaul stronger!"

A clap of thunder made the horses rear and kick the air. Danil risked a glance over his shoulder at the white-capped waves. The ocean roiled as if a great beast stirred in the depths, frothing and churning.

Mist raced from the horizon at an unnatural pace. It flashed and rumbled, and Danil felt the hairs on his arms rise.

Commander Selen looked at Osriele in surprise.

Eyes wide, Osriele shook her head. "It isn't my doing."

Danil braced.

The mist rolled over them, brushing their skin with a warm burst of energy. It curled up the beach toward the selasi. The creatures hissed and spat, ducking low as if stung. Their scaled hides sizzled, steam rising. Finally, they skittered back with squeals of pain.

Lightning struck the sand with a tremendous crack. The

selasi scattered up the beach, hissing and growling. The lightning landed between them again and the creatures wailed, biting at each other as they bounded up the dunes.

The mist settled, then, curling demurely along the shore. Danil shared astonished glances with his companions.

Then the mist billowed to reveal a glowing figure in pale armor. She strode across the sand, her battle-axe hanging loose in her grip.

Lyria...

"But, how—?" he began.

Striding beside her was an old woman dressed in a simple tawny shroud, her hood drawn up to keep away the damp. Her face was seamed with age, her mouth quick to smile.

"I am Nera Mistborn," the old woman said when they drew close. She motioned to Lyria in bemusement. "The lass insisted I save you."

20

The old woman knew the coast well. She quickly steered the party off the beach and onto a path hidden behind spiky saltbushes that took them behind the rocky cliff. Lyria easily kept pace, appearing more solid as they traveled along. At one point, she strode beside Ruslin's horse and leaned up to sniff the wound. Dark blood seeped through the bandages, the man growing increasingly delirious and weaving in the saddle. The rope tying his legs to the stirrup was all that ensured he didn't fall.

Lyria turned a somber gaze to Nera.

"I have clean beds and healing salves," Nera said to Osriele as if sensing the ghost's concern. "You're welcome to all."

"We're in your debt," Osriele said, struggling to match the old woman's stride. "I fear what would have happened had you not been drawn to rescue us."

Nera waved her hand. "There comes a time when remaining idle proves costly to us all. These parts have been bereft of good folk for a long time."

Danil hung back, watching Nera as she chatted further

with Osriele and the commander. White-haired and her face heavily lined, the old woman appeared innocuous and warm, her gait steady as she led them into the small inlet filled with barnacled rocks and jeering seagulls. But Nera seemed able to see Lyria just as Danil could. He had little idea what that could mean.

Merlias stalked close behind Osriele and Nera, her hands resting distrustfully upon her twin blades.

"How many folk live around here?" Commander Selen asked as she walked her horse around jagged rocks.

"Just myself," Nera replied.

"But I thought—" The commander frowned. "You mentioned a girl."

Nera shrugged amicably and motioned for them to continue on.

Commander Selen looked at her with deepening suspicion.

The opposite side of the inlet ended with a sharp cliff face stretching far into the sea. Waves boomed against it, sending up great sprays of saltwater. Nera took them close to the cliff, and it was only when they were scant feet from the barnacled rocks that Danil could see a split in the cliff's sharp edges. Hidden behind the rock were the makings of a cave.

Lyria stood at the entrance and watched them lead their horses inside. Her gaze fell on Hafryn's Trueform as it trudged at the edge of the party, its tail tucked low. It looked faded somehow, less vibrant. Lyria reached out and stroked its silky ears.

Walking beside Danil, Hafryn suddenly shivered.

"Never had a liking for dark places," the wolf shifter said when Danil threw him a startled look. His Trueform leaned into Lyria's touch, ears pricked. It grew more solid, tongue lolling.

'*Thank you*,' Danil thought to Lyria.

Lyria continued to stroke the wolf's ears.

The cave was scarcely large enough to fit them all. Light streamed in from the other side, where a tiny waterfall tumbled from the rock-face above. The cascading water ran over dark pebbles and into the frothing waves.

"Not far to go now," Nera said, picking up her pace.

Outside the cave was a tiny beach protected from the worst of the changing tides. A black spire shot up from an outcrop of rock surrounded by the sea. Waves washed over the rocky base and funneled up toward arched windows and wide balconies that abruptly reminded Danil of the Amasian spires of Corros. But it looked dreary and unappealing with its black stonework, while the slate roof was domed like the Magi Tower back in Aqila.

"We were close to Isfil after all," Osriele murmured, voice relieved.

Danil studied the spire more closely, but there was nothing he could immediately latch onto to explain why they'd travel so far to reach it.

"Without knowledge of the cave, you'd have spent another three days traversing the cliffs," Nera said to Osriele. "Come along. The tides are unusually high this time of year."

As they walked the shore, a second, smaller spire became visible directly behind the first, attached by a stone gangway. This spire had fallen starkly into ruin, its roof long gone and waves crashing through a large section of broken wall. It appeared to tremble with each passing wave.

"I thought Isfil had just one spire," Hafryn said, squinting to also study the ruins.

Nera took them to the foot of a stone bridge above the high tide line. "No one's used the old tower for centuries," she said as she rested her hand on a stone post heavy with scrollwork. She chuckled. "Keep expecting to wake up one morning and find the stubborn thing has fallen into the sea. Now, put your hand to the greeting post before you cross so that Isfil can welcome you."

Osriele gave the old woman a bemused look but nonetheless touched the post before walking onto the bridge. They all took their turn, Gethin even helping Ruslin reach down from his horse. The stone bridge was slickly wet by the waves, but a few hundred feet on they entered a small courtyard at the base of the main spire. The stones were damp with seafoam, but a stable near the gate proved to be dry and warm with fresh hay and clean stalls awaiting them.

"Were you expecting us?" Danil asked, startled.

"The spire has a habit of providing for every need," Nera said, pausing by the doors.

Osriele bowed. "We're grateful for your hospitality."

The old woman waved it aside. "The old spells are the easiest. There's a tack room to store your gear, then come inside—I have a healing room for your guardsman."

They quickly stripped the weary horses, while Gethin loosened the ropes binding Ruslin to his mount. The injured guard was slumped with his chin on his chest, eyes fever-glazed.

"I'll take him," Hafryn said before easing Ruslin over his shoulder.

Gethin shrugged as he took the saddle into the tack room. "I'll see to all the horses, my lady," he offered.

Osriele nodded gratefully. "Come find us when you're done."

They crossed the courtyard and entered the spire

through an arched doorway. It was surprisingly dry inside despite the smell of salt and brine that lay heavy in the air. Waves boomed against the spire's base like a heartbeat. Resting his hand to the stone, Danil was surprised to find it warm to touch. He gazed up at archways and light streaming in above the curving stairs that led up to the parapet and domed roof. Closed doors lined the inner wall.

Following Nera, they entered a simple room with a raised pallet, chair and long worktable. The room felt freshly aired, the furs on the pallet turned down as if servants had expected their arrival.

Lyria came to stand beside him, arms folded as Hafryn carefully eased Ruslin onto the furs. The wolf shifter grimaced when Ruslin cried out weakly from the jostling.

Nera busied herself with unwinding the bandages. She reared back at the sight of the oozing wound. The rancid smell of decay filled the room. "Oh, my," she breathed, making a warding sign.

Danil grimaced at the deep puncture filled with black pus.

"A selasi bit him yesterday," Osriele explained. "The wound resists every spell I know."

"And Amasian enchantments," Merlias added, arms folded as she leaned against the doorway. She wrinkled her nose at the smell.

If Nera was startled that an Amasian enchanter traveled with the party, she hid it well. "Some people are better suited to tearing and mayhem than healings. He's lucky to still have his arm," the old woman observed before bending close to sniff the wound. "I need a bag of herbs from my rooms." She snapped her fingers and a magelight formed above Hafryn's head. "Be a dear and collect it, would you?"

A bemused look crossed Hafryn's face. "You're rather quick to trust, magus. I'm as much Amasian as Merlias."

"Until you prove to the spire otherwise, you both have run of the place just like anyone else." Nera made a shooing gesture. "I do need those herbs, however."

With a soft, amused huff, Hafryn gave the back of Danil's neck a gentle squeeze and then trailed after the magelight.

Nera's gaze settled on Danil. "You look spry enough, young man. You can help me. As for the rest of you, there'll be food in the dining hall."

Osriele bowed. "My thanks, Magus Nera. Your hospitality is a blessing."

The old woman waved her hand. "I go by Nera. There are no airs out here."

Osriele inclined her head. She and the commander made their way out of the room, their footsteps fading in the corridor outside.

Arms folded, Merlias lingered long enough to give Nera a narrow look before stalking out of the room.

The old woman chuckled under her breath.

Behind her, the air rippled before a steaming bowl of fragrant water and dry cloths came to sit on the table. Nera wordlessly dipped one of the cloths before wiping the raised edges of Ruslin's wound.

Danil quirked an eyebrow. "Why not have the herbs brought here the same way?"

Nera smiled slightly, not looking up from her work. "You're a curious young man," she said. "You're Roldaerian, no? I can hear it in your words."

Danil said nothing, his throat suddenly tight. If he'd stayed true to Roldaer, Hafryn wouldn't be under Kaul's thumb now.

"Yes, Roldaerian for certain, but your heart belongs to the Amasian."

"Hafryn, yes," Danil whispered. He searched her lined face to measure her thoughts.

She dipped the cloth back into the water. "There's a darkness over him. You know this, yes?"

His throat closed over. If only he'd stopped Hafryn from donning the amulet. It was such a stupid, innocent mistake that would surely cost them dearly.

"Was it Lady Osriele? Is that why you're in her company?" Nera asked sharply.

Danil startled. "No, I—we came together to stop the blacksward."

"Together, you say." She sat back. Her eyes crinkled as she smiled. "How unexpected." Nera set aside the dirty cloth and took up a fresh one. The acrid stench of Ruslin's injury eased slightly. "I didn't think there was anyone capable of pushing back the blacksward. Stars know I've tried to stop the poison, too. Frightening the selasi is the best I can offer."

Danil's heart sank. "I couldn't stop it, either. I'd hoped —" He gazed about the room. "Our quest brought us here."

"To Isfil? On purpose?"

Danil nodded.

"Whatever for?" Nera asked, a perplexed frown deepening the lines of her brow. "Isfil has been so long removed from the machinations of Roldaer that I'm surprised there are folk who even remember its existence."

Danil glanced at the ghost standing in a corner of the room, her arms folded. "It was Lyria who insisted we come."

Nera followed his gaze, her expression startled. "*Lyria?*"

Hafryn arrived then with a leather sack slung over one shoulder. He dropped it beside the pallet, sweating slightly.

"Ah!" Nera took the bag with a satisfied grunt. "No trouble retrieving it, I see."

Hafryn quirked an eyebrow at her. "Sounds like you expected otherwise, magus."

"Only if you're an enemy of the spire," Nera said mildly while undoing the ties.

Danil gaped at her. "You sent Hafryn to your workroom as a test?"

She pulled out packets of dried herbs and flowers and spread them out beside Ruslin's sweaty arm. "And he passed, darkness and all. Be grateful," she said mildly.

Hafryn gave her a black look. Danil noticed he still carried Ruslin's sword.

"Don't flash your fangs at me, Amasian. I'm hardly your enemy," Nera said, wetting the tip of one finger and dipping into a sachet filled with purple seeds. "Now, off with you both. Food's waiting, and the spire has rooms ready."

"We won't be getting comfortable," Hafryn said lowly.

Nera shrugged. "Suit yourself, wolf." She appeared set on ignoring them both as she slathered the unguent over the puncture wound. Ruslin's skin sizzled.

Hafryn muttered something under his breath about meddlesome magi. He tugged Danil's sleeve.

Danil trailed after him, wariness sinking into his bones as the last of Nera's words sank in. Somehow, the old woman knew Hafryn's Trueform was a wolf.

Despite having never seen Hafryn shift.

21

The curved stairwell led them up a series of levels high above the booming waves. Pale stone archways with fine scrollwork marked the entrance to each new floor and were a stark contrast to the austerity Danil recalled of the Magi Tower in Aqila. Sconces in the walls housed glittering balls of magelight.

Danila and Hafryn strode past tapestries that were worn and faded with age. A magelight danced in front of them, guiding them toward the sound of voices beyond the curve of the corridor.

Rounding the corner, Danil felt his gaze suddenly drawn to an old tapestry of the two spires. Standing on the stony beach was a young woman in pale armor, her battle-axe shining as if studded with kiandrite. Sigils painted her forehead and cheeks.

Danil suddenly gripped his friend's arm. "Hafryn," he hissed. "It's her! Lyria!"

Startled, Hafryn drew close and examined the tapestry. In the background, the broken spire looked freshly ruined, with fingers of smoke curling out of shattered windows.

Lyria gripped her axe as if she were responsible for the destruction.

Hafryn shook his head. "It can't be her, *fala*. The tapestry has to be nearly as old as Isfil." He touched a frayed corner, grimacing as fibers fell away.

"She looks exactly like Lyria's ghost, battle armor and all," Danil insisted.

Hafryn eyed the tapestry mistrustfully. "Could this woman be an ancient kinswoman? Perhaps she spent time here at the spire."

"It's possible," Danil allowed. "But why would Lyria's ghost look just like her?"

"Why indeed?" Hafryn murmured. He stepped away from the tapestry, expression thoughtful.

"Nera can see Lyria, too," Danil reminded him.

"All things considered, I'm not sure I trust Nera to speak honestly." Hafryn shook his head. "Regardless, we won't find our answers standing here."

The magelight waited for them further along the corridor. It led them to a brightly-lit dining hall with a single, long table and crackling hearth. Osriele sat at the end of the table with a veritable feast spread out before her of roasted meats, root vegetables and gravy. A cabinet opposite her held various decanters of wine, which Commander Selen was idly sampling. Tapestries of the Fens lined the walls behind Gethin, who sat further along the table with a plate piled high.

Osriele waved them over. "Join us, my friends."

Danil sat opposite her, eyeing the food with astonishment. "This isn't what I thought Nera meant when she said the spire provides for every need."

"Truly, Isfil is a wonder," Osriele agreed. "Not even the Magi Tower holds such power."

"Then why is the spire practically abandoned?" Danil asked.

"Distance, I expect," Commander Selen said with a shrug. "What purpose would a magus have in taking such an arduous journey when there's little to do here other than be waited upon?"

"The magi can enjoy that easily enough in Aqila," Hafryn said dryly, dropping into a chair beside Gethin. The corporal nudged a plate of herb-stuffed fish toward him.

"Indeed so, Hafryn," Osriele said with a slight smile. "Although I'm sure Nera prefers the solitude."

Danil folded his arms. "She notices a lot for someone who chooses to avoid company."

Commander Selen gave him a curious look, turning fully away from the row of decanters. "How so?"

Danil told them of Nera's earlier slip of the tongue while she tended Ruslin.

"I'm not sure I see your concern, Danil," Osriele said. "If Nera indeed knows Hafryn's a wolf, it's because he has a certain air about him."

"Trueforms aren't a reflection of an Amasian's nature," Danil argued. "I've seen fearsome enchanters turn into tiny scrub-wrens and warriors become voles."

Hafryn speared a neatly cut square of fish. "He's right, Osriele. Entire Amasian Houses can hide their Trueforms from the rest of Amas. Just looking at me isn't enough to know my wolf."

Osriele folded her hands in her lap. "Nera could have left us at the mercy of the selasi. Instead, she risked her life and spent tremendous energy to save us. I doubt she means us harm."

Danil fought not to scowl. It was clear Osriele still struggled to view her fellow magi as potential enemies, even with evidence of them poisoning Roldaer. He worried the edge of his thumb with his teeth. "But the spire's supposed to be abandoned. Why would Nera be out here alone?"

"Not every mage craves the honor of residing in Aqila, though Magus Nera would enjoy quite a following in the royal city. That lightning spell was no small feat."

"Can't fault Magus Nera's hospitality, either," Selen observed as she turned a goblet in her hand. Beads of condensation showed on the glass. The commander settled into a chair, her spear leaning against the wall behind her. It was the most relaxed she'd appeared since they'd left the royal city.

Gethin merely grunted his agreement around a mouthful of food, gravy dripping off his knife.

Looking down the length of the table, Danil noted it was more food than they could all possibly consume. It reminded him a little of the great feasts in Corros, and he glanced at the walls, half-expecting to see iridescent glyphs and kiandrite embedded in the stone.

Selen gave Danil a terse look. "Why are you so fretful, Danil? Lady Osriele has risked everything to bring you to Isfil. Will you finally explain why, or are we still unworthy?"

Danil resisted a grimace. "I don't know yet," he admitted.

A moment of astonished silence settled over the room.

Commander Selen set her goblet down with a thud. "Say again?"

Danil thought over the tapestry, wondering if it was somehow tied to Lyria's insistence that they travel to Isfil. But all it did was raise more questions.

The commander looked between him and Hafryn as the silence stretched. Her jaw hardened. "I knew this was a ruse —an Amasian ploy to draw Osriele from the royal city!" She shot out of her chair and planted her fists on the table in front of Danil. "Well, now that we're in Isfil, what will you dare to do next, traitor?"

"I don't know why we're in Isfil," Danil admitted. "But there has to be something." He could hear the desperation in his voice.

"You don't *know?*" she snarled.

Gethin slowly lowered his hand under the table to the hilt of his sword.

Danil growled in frustration. "I'm not your enemy, commander! It wasn't me who came to the border looking for war!"

"So, it's vengeance you want, then! A rogue magus kills a few folk and you take it as evidence that all of Roldaer is evil."

Osriele slapped her palm on the table. "Enough of this foolishness! We are allies! We don't turn on each other! I expect better of you, commander, at least."

Commander Selen looked at Osriele in surprised offense before her face congealed into a mask. She bowed stiffly to Danil. "Forgive my rudeness, Danil. I spoke out of turn."

Danil knew he dared not walk the floors of Isfil alone. He sighed, shoulders dropping as frustration and exhaustion pulled him low. "I understand why you don't trust me, Selen. A few months ago, my greatest concern was how to survive the deadland ice floes. Now I find myself standing between Roldaer and Amas—and trying to save both. If you think I don't know what I'm doing, you'd be right. But for whatever reason, I'm here when others who you no doubt deem more loyal and capable are not. And I *will* do everything to save Roldaer. I give you my word."

The commander studied him intently, mouth thin. She

eventually gave him a short nod. Gethin's hand fell away from his sword.

"What should we do, then, Danil?" Commander Selen asked, tension still underscoring her voice. "I'm not the sort to be comfortably idle."

He ran a hand through his hair. "Nera hasn't said we can't explore the spire. There must be something—a strange symbol or relic, perhaps. Or knowledge we can use to stop the blacksward, since all spellwork has failed."

Selen slowly nodded. "How will we know if we've found such an item?"

Danil resisted the urge to shrug. He hardly knew what to look for, either.

"I've found it's important to trust your instincts in these things," Hafryn said mildly, rocking back in his chair.

Danil threw him a grateful look.

The commander folded her arms, dubious but nonetheless resolved to do her part. "I suppose our search is to include the broken spire, too?"

"I haven't found a way across," Gethin said.

"The walkway still exists. We saw it from the beach," Hafryn pointed out. "Though likely it was sealed off years ago."

The commander glanced at Osriele. "Odd that we had no idea the second spire existed."

"It is rather strange," Osriele agreed. "Isfil has long been out of favor, but I have no recollection of it being described any differently than as a single spire."

Gethin looked toward the door. "Speaking of strange—where's the enchanter?"

Danil froze, suddenly realizing Merlias wasn't in the hall. Hafryn straightened, hand falling to Ruslin's blade at his hip.

"She'll be in her quarters, I expect. A magelight guided her," Osriele said, looking unconcerned.

"And you expected her to follow it?" Hafryn exclaimed with both eyebrows raised.

Commander Selen stilled, her brow furrowing. "Gethin."

With a sigh, the corporal quickly shoved in a mouthful of bread before pushing away his plate. He strode from the hall, his sword bouncing jauntily at his hip.

"I appreciate your caution, Hafryn, but Merlias doesn't appear as problematic as you expected," Osriele observed, her expression mild.

Hafryn snorted, poking at his food with little enthusiasm. "You don't share our history. She's little more than spite and enchantments."

Danil recalled the first time he'd met Merlias in the hold of Viren's skiff. She'd gleefully tortured Hafryn in order to secure their compliance. That she'd somehow become an ally sat uneasily with him, and probably always would.

Gethin quickly returned to the hall and placed a fist over his chest. "Found the enchanter on the battlements," he said. He motioned over his shoulder. "You'll want to see for yourself, commander."

Cursing under his breath, Hafryn scraped back his chair and rose with the others.

They all took the winding stairs up to the very height of the spire. Damp covered much of the stone, with one corner of the parapet covered in brown algae. It was already mid-afternoon, with clear skies turning the waves a welcoming blue.

Merlias crouched atop the battlement like a predator in search of the unwary. "They followed us through the cave."

Looking down, Danil spied movement on the shore.

Sunlight flashed off multiple helms and scaled hides. The spit and snarl of selasi carried over the crashing waves. There had to be dozens of them.

Hafryn's mouth tightened. "We're trapped."

EVENING SAW Merlias return from a long flight over the coast and nearby marshes. Danil watched her arrival from the parapet where it was his turn to observe the selasi below. The moon had yet to rise over the ocean, but starlight was strong enough to shine off various helms and armored spines. He suspected even more selasi had arrived since nightfall.

Merlias eyed him as she stepped from the battlements and threw her woolen cloak about her shoulders. Torchlight made her curls fiery red. "You shouldn't be unattended, custodian. Kaul's horrors aren't limited to animals with overlong teeth."

Danil fell in step with her, a magelight bobbing above his head. "I'd ask what you know, but you enjoy your secrets too much."

Merlias looked at him sidelong and smirked as they took the winding stairs down to the main level. "You must think I'm rather petty to be nursing a grudge when Roldaer's forces march for Amas."

He didn't respond, thinking her actions were plain to everyone.

The door of Ruslin's healing room sat open as they strode past. A low stench of sickness wafted into the corridor from the bed where the guard lay swaddled in blankets. Gethin sat slouched uncomfortably in the chair, boots resting on the edge of the pallet. He looked bored and sleepy but his blue eyes steadily tracked Danil and Merlias as they passed.

Merlias' amusement only deepened. "Hafryn does indeed irk me, but the reasons are not as personal as you think. My House may not be kind, Danil, but we've been the shield of Amas for centuries. There are consequences when one of our own betrays their duty."

"Hafryn was never going to be an Eyrie assassin," Danil muttered softly, not wanting his voice to carry. "You had no need of him."

Merlias sighed as if already weary of the conversation. She raised a finger. "He crossed the Northern Reaches as a child—alone—and befriended the great Dragon Prince." She lifted a second finger. "When few Amasians could safely patrol the deadlands, Hafryn volunteered and thrived." With a third finger raised, she added, "And when the magi first encroached the border, many expected he'd lead the Amasian army across the deadlands and remind those scum that we've been playing nice for centuries."

Danil slowed to stare. Her words were far more generous than he ever thought possible.

The Eyrie enchanter's nostrils flared. "Hafryn had potential, custodian. But he's too proud and willful, and he chose you over his duty to Amas. While history may show that he chose right, and that joining the House of Kailon ensures the protection of our people, I still think he abandoned Amas."

"And you think withholding what you know about the amulet is a fitting punishment?" Danil countered angrily. "You saw how Kaul controlled him. The dread lord is our enemy, not each other!"

Merlias clenched her teeth and looked away. She was silent for a time before she finally admitted in a soft voice,

"Truth, Danil, I scarcely know more than you do about the damn thing."

Danil's eyes narrowed. "I don't believe you."

She shrugged, turning back to him. "You're right that Viren sent me to find the amulet. I don't know why and it's not my place to question his reasoning. But Viren did give me one warning—do not wear it. To do so would open a path to darkness not known since the Great War." She sighed. "And then you two idiots came along."

Danil folded his arms. "But you couldn't enter the burial mound anyway."

"The amulet chose Hafryn." Merlias nodded in agreement.

Cold flooded his innards. "*Why?*"

"You care for him, yes?"

"Of course," Danil said, a little thrown by the question.

"You're pliable when your heart is threatened, Danil. Maybe Kaul knows that, too. For whatever reason, he still wants you alive."

Swallowing hard, Danil asked desperately, "Did Viren say anything about removing the amulet? Surely he must know."

"He never said, but you must think. It was found in a burial mound—perhaps of the last person to wear it. Hafryn may never be able to remove the amulet himself."

"We'll kill Kaul," Danil growled. "It's clearly one of his relics."

Merlias made a slow study of him, a smile forming on her face. "You make ridiculous proclamations about the impossible, and yet the world still falls to your will." She raised her chin in resolve. "Very well, custodian. I'll see this through with you."

Danil blinked, not sure what had just happened. "Does this mean you'll be fair to Hafryn?"

She laughed gaily and continued along the corridor. "Now you ask too much!"

They found Osriele seated in a small reception room with the commander. An alcove on the far side of the room had a well-used air, with plump couches and warm chairs set in front of shelves brimming with books and scrolls. Hafryn had left off to sleep some hours ago, with his turn at sentry duty to begin in the early hours.

Commander Selen rose. "What have you to report, enchanter?"

"I'd say every creature within fifty miles is making its way here—there'll be close to forty selasi on the beach by midday tomorrow," Merlias said as she threw herself onto an ornate divan.

Danil sat on a footstool, scraps of parchment stretched out in front of him. He'd earlier hoped to discover a spell to break Hafryn's amulet, but Nera's recommended readings on curses offered little more than potions for mischievous spells and common rashes.

Commander Selen swore under her breath. "We can barely hold our own against one selasi, much less those already on the beach."

"Nera assures me that no selasi may enter the spire without her knowing," Osriele said, sitting in an overstuffed chair with her boots stretched toward the hearth fire. "Isfil will hold."

Merlias snorted.

Osriele raised an eyebrow. "You don't believe our host?"

"I'm doubtful of anyone who's as powerful as she is and chooses to hide in a place like this. She's played least in sight since we got here, too."

Osriele set aside the scroll she was perusing to study her more closely.

To Danil's surprise, Commander Selen grunted and said, "I agree with the enchanter to an extent. We've searched every room on this level, and most are without so much as a cobweb. I've yet to find anything more useful against the selasi than a dinner knife."

Osriele gave an eloquent shrug. "Apparently, then, weapons aren't necessary."

Merlias chuckled sourly as she slouched deeper into the couch. "Now you sound as wishful as the custodian."

Danil glowered at her. It appeared their alliance would do little to soften Merlias' attitude toward him, too.

Osriele shook her head. "You've called Danil a custodian a few times, Merlias. What does it mean?"

Lips curling, Merlias said, "It means more power than you can possibly imagine, magus. But you wouldn't enjoy it —too many demands and restrictions. Too many eyes watching every enchantment you create. Custodians are bound as much to the people of their House as they are to their kiandrite."

"Magi were once so bound." Osriele nodded.

"Believe me, magus. You were not."

"If you're so against my kind, why are you here?" Osriele asked, leaning forward intently. "Our quest is to save Roldaer."

Merlias smiled coldly. "That may be your quest, but it's certainly not mine. Now, if you'll excuse me, I've been on the wing for most of the day. Do wake me when the selasi inevitably break in."

They watched Merlias stride out of the hall, her red curls bouncing.

"That woman," Commander Selen said under her breath. She sounded both infuriated and admiring.

Osriele eyed her commander with amusement. "I believe it's my turn at sentry duty. Commander, if you'll join me?"

The commander made a lazy salute before offering the magus her arm.

Danil had little doubt they wanted to speak about Merlias in private. He wasn't sure how he felt about that, now that he and Merlias had reached some measure of agreement.

"Good night, Danil," Osriele said mildly.

"And to you both," Danil replied, gathering his stack of parchments and rising also.

He followed them from the main hall, idly noticing how the hearth snuffed itself out behind him. The main floor had a number of rooms lining the inner wall, and Danil made for one with twin sconces lit outside.

Easing the door open, he was unsurprised to see Hafryn already sprawled asleep on the pallet, his clothes in a messy pile on the floor. Evidently, s the spire didn't think they needed clean tunics and breeches.

Drawing closer, Danil saw lines of sweat on Hafryn's throat and arms, his breathing short and rapid. His fingers raked the furs as a frown marred his face.

A dark, human-shaped shadow stood at the edge of the pallet and watched as Hafryn squirmed.

Hairs rising, Danil realized the shadowy fighter had returned. He made a warding enchantment and threw it toward the figure. "Get away from him!" he hissed.

The shadow looked at him balefully.

Danil raised his House glyph, heat flaring. "I said *away!*" The glyph roared.

Thrown backward, the shadow dropped low and disappeared through the wall.

Hafryn stirred and drew in a deep, rasping breath. He sat up, flecks of orange fading from his green eyes. "*Fala?*"

Danil collapsed onto the pallet beside him, unease coiling in his belly. "Are you well?"

"I dreamt of fighting," Hafryn murmured, rubbing his chest above the amulet. His bare arms were trembling and cold to touch.

Danil grabbed the blanket at the foot of the pallet and threw it over them both, snuggling close.

"Cursed amulet," Hafryn muttered, mouth pulling down.

"I'm not done with searching Nera's books," Danil said, resting his hand on Hafryn's chest.

Hafryn grunted. "According to Nera, Isfil should provide us with everything we need. If the knowledge is here, you'd have already found it."

"Same with a counter curse for the blacksward, do you think?" Danil bit his lip.

"Let's hope not."

Danil felt a familiar rush of uncertainty but resolved to force it aside. They were too far from Kailon to be wrong.

He pressed his mouth to Hafryn's collarbone.

Hafryn quirked an eyebrow at him. "What's this?"

"The sooner we find out why Lyria brought us to Isfil, the better," Danil grumbled against Hafryn's throat. "But that doesn't mean we can't take advantage of a bit of privacy."

"I like your thinking." But Hafryn did no more than hold him close and press his lips to Danil's brow.

Danil lay quiet for a moment, thinking. "That dream—did you see Kaul?"

Hafryn pulled back slightly with a questioning look. "No, though my limbs ache as if I've been battling all the selasi in the world."

Kaul had to be steering Hafryn's dreams and feeding off every kill, no matter if they were real or imagined. It worried Danil what would happen if the shadow fighter managed to take control of Hafryn. But Hafryn seemed not to know the shadow fighter was there at all.

"Let's forget our worries for a night, *fala*," Hafryn said, voice soft. He abruptly rolled, tumbling Danil onto the pallet beneath him. "I think I know of a better way to make my limbs ache."

"You *think*?" Danil wrapped Hafryn's red braid around his fingers.

"Hmn." Hafryn ran his gaze over Danil, green eyes mirthful. "It *has* been a while."

Grinning, Danil pulled him down and reminded him.

22

Danil lay awake with Hafryn's warm length pressed against his side. Sweat still clung to the wolf shifter's skin, his breathing deep and restful. Winding a curl of Hafryn's loose red hair about his fingers, Danil had to admit he felt little of the usual contentment and ease that came from their lovemaking. There'd been a fevered edge to Hafryn's mouth, a desperation that made it clear where Hafryn's thoughts lay.

The amulet was almost dazzling in the dim magelight and even the crack at the bottom couldn't detract from its strange beauty. The symbols etched into the gold surface reminded Danil of both Roldaerian and Amasian magic. It made sense now, knowing who commanded the curse. Kaul reveled in twisting everything to his will.

Hafryn murmured something against Danil shoulder, a frown gathering on his face. Danil idly stroked above his eyebrow, but the tension remained.

A heartbeat later, Hafryn woke with a jolt. He sat upright, a wordless snarl caught in his throat. He gazed about the room, his green eyes glassy.

Danil carefully gripped his shoulder. "Hafryn."

Hafryn whirled, but recognition flooded his face a moment later. His shoulders sagged. "*Fala*, I—" He stopped, swallowing carefully.

"Bad dream?" Danil asked.

Hafryn shook his head, wariness returning. "I thought I sensed...fury. Like being trapped in the cold and dark."

Danil sat up beside him, bushing back Hafryn's loose red waves to study him more closely. His friend radiated confusion. "Could it be the selasi on the beach?"

Hafryn rubbed his chest above the amulet. "It feels closer than that. Almost like it's within the spire itself."

Cold flooded Danil's veins. "They've breached Isfil?" He threw back the covers.

But Hafryn made no rush to move. "Not quite, but it makes me nervous all the same. There must be rooms far below us." He slid off the pallet and trotted across the stone floor to where their clothes lay together in a haphazard pile. Hafryn fished out his breeches, expression determined.

Danil joined him. "You're not due for sentry duty for a few hours yet—time enough to see if anything's amiss."

Hafryn gave him a grateful look. "Bring your sword."

Dressed, they checked the corridor before traipsing down the stone stairs opposite Ruslin's room. Magelights set into wall sconces lit the way, reminding Danil once more of Corros and the way the great citadel sparkled at night. An ache grew in Danil's throat as he wondered if Kailon would ever be home to such a stronghold. Likely not in his lifetime, if at all.

They continued down the winding stairwell. Unlike the upper levels, the damp and cold seeped up from the depths of the spire. The magelights grew flickering and scarce, but

Hafryn removed a sconce from the wall to light their way. The booming waves grew muted.

Tilting his head, Hafryn said, "We must be beneath the surface."

Danil glanced uneasily at the damp walls. "The water can't get in." He threw a sharp look at Hafryn. "Can it?"

Hafryn grimaced. "I daresay magic is holding Isfil together. Still, I wouldn't want to be here during a storm."

With that drumming in Danil's mind, they continued until the stairs came to an abrupt stop at the base of an uneven, rough-hewn floor of dark rock.

Hafryn lifted the torch above his head, squinting into the gloom to reveal a wooden door heavily seamed with iron. "Whatever's drawing me here lies beyond the door."

"Careful, then," Danil murmured, fingers twitching in readiness.

Nudging open the door, they entered a stone room that looked emptied and long abandoned. A section of the floor had fallen away, revealing a jagged pit that dropped far into shadows. Water dripped somewhere below.

Peering over the edge, Danil spied something dark and scaled stalking through the gloom. A low growl emanated from the darkness. The hairs on the back of his neck rose.

"Selasi!" Hafryn hissed.

Danil jumped back from the edge. "Gods! How did it end up down there?"

In the flickering light, he watched the creature pace agitatedly. A growl reverberated off the stone. Leaning back on its hunches, it leaped up, powerful talons ripping the air below where they stood.

"It can't reach us." Hafryn raised the torch high. A segment of the ceiling was missing directly over the pit. Air whistled in the cavity. "Must have fallen through."

"But from where?" Danil wondered, arching his neck to get a better glimpse. The cavity spanned far higher than he expected. "Nera said Isfil would stop the selasi from entering."

"The broken spire may be another matter entirely. Perhaps this adventurous fellow decided to swim for it."

"That's a worrying thought," Danil said.

"We'll need to investigate."

Danil was hardly eager to search a tower that looked heartbeats from collapse, but he knew Hafryn was right. He eyed the selasi's thick scaled hide and ominously large fangs. Bereft of its helm, it looked more like a giant feline. Its orange eyes were unnaturally bright in the flickering light.

"This is what woke you?" Danil asked.

"It makes sense, sort of, since it's also one of Kaul's creatures," Hafryn reasoned.

Danil glared at his lover. "You are not a creature of Kaul, Hafryn! I won't let you think like that."

Hafryn bit his lip, his hands clenching and unclenching unconsciously. "I feel different. Not right. I think his grip on me is getting stronger. I can't stop it." He looked directly at Danil, taking up his hands and holding tightly. "I need you to promise me something. Promise me that if I go dark, if he takes me, that you'll kill me."

"What? No!" Danil shook his head, trying to wrench his hands free.

"You must! If I become what he wants, this *Harbinger*," he spat. "Then every time I kill, it will make him stronger. And who do you think I'll be killing?" He growled low, and Danil felt his heart stutter when flecks of orange showed in Hafryn's eyes, brought about by the mere thought of killing. "It'll be Amasians, Danil. I'll be killing my own people. I can't...I won't be that monster. Please, you have to, *fala*!"

Danil shook his head again. "There's still time, Hafryn. We can find a way to get that blasted amulet off you."

"You and I both know that's a false hope." Hafryn pursed his lips. "If you don't give me your promise, then I'll ask it of Merlias. We both know she won't hesitate."

"But she'll also take the smallest excuse to kill you!"

"And you will take the last, and perhaps doom us all," he countered. "But when that time comes, I need to know that I can rely on you, that you will not falter. Too much is at stake, *fala*. I need your blade to strike true."

Danil stared at him, unable to say the words even to himself.

The selasi leaped once more, raking the air a scant few feet from where they stood and startling them apart. Danil nervously backed to the wall.

Scowling, Hafryn walked along the edge of the pit. "Settle down," he snapped.

The creature dropped low and quavered. It settled onto its belly, fangs tucked behind its lips.

Danil glanced at Hafryn in alarm. "You're commanding it now?"

"Looks like it," Hafryn replied grimly.

"The amulet is glowing," Danil noted. It cast a faint brightness against Hafryn's tunic.

"It probably wants me to kill yon selasi. Let's check the other spire before we discover ourselves overrun," Hafryn said, backing away from the pit with another dark look.

DANIL TRAILED AFTER HIM, lost in thought as they left the room and climbed the stairs. Their conversation had added a new tension between them, one Danil was desperate to ignore.

"We'll need Nera to show us where to access the walkway."

Hafryn snorted. "If she cares to show herself."

The old magus had kept herself scarce since their arrival, claiming to be busy in her workroom. Danil wondered if she actively avoided the party or was merely a recluse befitting the spire.

A spark of light drew his gaze upwards to where Lyria stood at the top of the stairwell, waiting.

"Hafryn," he whispered, gripping his sleeve.

Hafryn slowed, gaze wary.

Danil approached her with caution now that he was no longer certain who or what she was. But when they drew close, Lyria retreated to a wall and seamlessly disappeared through it.

Frowning, Danil pressed his hand to the smooth stone. There was nothing of note on the wall—no marks or strange etchings caught his attention. "She's gone."

Drawing closer, Hafryn studied the wall. He ran nimble fingers along the grooves and ruts in the stone. "A hidden passage, perhaps?"

Danil quirked an eyebrow at him. "Maybe Lyria wants to help. We could certainly do with some right about now."

They searched in earnest until Hafryn crouched to study a bit of crumbled rock near his boot. He pushed against it. A low grating sound echoed about them before the wall began to slide away. A small dark passage opened before them, the air heavy with damp.

Hafryn peered in. "It must lead to the other spire," he murmured. "Careful—the floor might not be sound."

Danil eyed the passageway nervously. From the outside,

the broken spire seemed ready to collapse at any moment. The air within the corridor stirred. "There aren't any cobwebs," he noted.

Hafryn grunted. "Something's been through here recently."

Danil took the first steps into the dark hallway. Jagged rocks covered the floor from where part of the passage had collapsed sometime over the past centuries. Raising his hand, Danil let the iridescent light of Kailon brighten the way. A few feet ahead, a large hole lay hidden amidst the rocks. Claw marks raked the side of the void before disappearing into the darkness.

Hafryn jumped over the hole with nimble grace. "Come on, *fala*."

The booming crash of waves against rocks grew louder as they navigated the gangway, and Danil had the discomforting image of them walking directly over the frothing water. The passageway spilled out into the broken spire. The interior was worse than Danil expected. Large sections of the outer wall facing the ocean were gone. The heady smell of seafoam and spray was thick about them, with the floor submerged under at least three feet of ocean. Stars and a few low, scudding clouds were visible overhead where the roof once sat.

Unlike the surviving spire, this one was bereft of levels. An uneven staircase lead to a solitary platform where two columns of black stone stood on either side of a circular window. The main floor below was stripped bare of everything but a few barnacled statues and foundation rocks.

"What a mess," Hafryn said with his hands on his hips as he took stock. "There's no more selasi, at least. Our best option is to enchant the secret passageway closed."

Danil nodded, stepping down into the frigid water. He waded to the far side of the tower where waves lapped against the broken stone. He leaned out to study the starlit ocean. This far from the beach, he could no longer hear the hiss and fighting of selasi grown bored with waiting. The rolling waves revealed no creature swimming out to attempt another ingress into Isfil.

Straightening, Danil eyed the stairs only a few feet away that lead up to the platform. He tested the first few steps, careful of the slick algae. "Come on, Hafryn."

Sighing, Hafryn waded over to him. The staircase groaned warningly, bits of stone splashing into the water below.

"Careful, *fala*."

Reaching the platform, Danil was disappointed to find it devoid of interest. The two black columns framing the empty window were plainly wrought, the floor pitted and marked with age. Whatever purpose the platform once served had long been stripped away.

Leaning against the casement, Danil fought off his rising frustration. He had to face the grim reality that his insistence that they ride for Isfil proved to be foolish. With selasi guarding the beach, they were trapped even as Roldaer's army marched closer and closer to Kailon.

"Danil," Hafryn hissed from the stairs.

He turned to see the columns beside him aglow. Veins of light streamed across the black stone. Danil stroked it, glimpsing images of sparkling water filled with laughing children cutting through stone archways and dense green forest. Danil stepped back with a smile. "It's kiandrite from Altonas before it was ravaged. But why is it here?" He backed further away, looking between the two columns. He gasped when understanding hit him. "It's a magi portal."

But it glimmered iridescent rather than tortured red, meaning that no magi had forced the kiandrite to do their bidding. Located so deep within Roldaer, Danil wondered how it was possible.

The air between the two pillars abruptly shimmered, and for a heartbeat Danil saw a new region within the Fens. Still water and dead trees spread far into the misty horizon, the place devoid of life as if the blacksward had swept through long ago. A granite hill stood in the distance. Something glimmered.

Then the image swirled, and he was back within the broken spire. But the walls and foundation were now strong and whole, the air warm and almost fragrant with a coming spring storm. Startled, Danil walked across a woven rug to the new stone banister and looked down. Interwoven dark and light stone formed an eight-pointed star across the main floor. A stone workbench sat in the center, with a large wooden bowl resting atop it. A half-dozen robed magi standing in a ring around it.

Danil crouched out of sight.

A magus clasped a large kiandrite crystal, which she raised high. It flooded the tower with iridescent light, singing of leylines that danced along the shoreline and meandered up rivers into ponds and lakes and groves where trees grew large and sprawling. With a rush of understanding, Danil realized he was looking upon a Roldaerian lodestone.

But how...?

As one, the magi began to chant. The tower grew cold as darkness pressed upon the crystal. It flickered as if confused, its song stuttering. A red-laced spell formed above it. The kiandrite turned sickly green, and Danil felt its rising fear.

The chanting increased in fervor until the magi all but shrieked. The magus holding the crystal slammed it onto the table. Blinding red light flooded the tower. A thunderous crack rocked the foundations as the iridescent light of the crystal blasted free.

Danil hunched, blocking his ears as a section of wall thundered into the sea.

The magi scattered, screaming. Large portions of roof tumbled inwards, crushing those too slow to dive out of the way.

Blinking, Danil saw that the kiandrite crystal was no more. Instead, the wooden bowl was brimming with iridescent dust. Swallowing a rush of bile, Danil realized he was somehow watching the first time the magi had created their mage-crystal tea. So desperate were they for personal power, the magi had destroyed their own lodestone and set in motion the eventual ruin of Roldaer itself.

But Danil felt his gaze drawn to a new figure cleaving to the damaged wall. The young woman glowed as if made iridescent dust, her face marked by strange sigils. Rising, she gazed about in horrified confusion, then looked down at her shining robes and arms as if startled by her own form.

"Lyria," Danil breathed in recognition.

Gaze snapping up, she pinned him with a look.

Danil froze.

As if recognizing him, Lyria straightened. *'Custodian. Fulfill your duty. Do not fail the leylines, lest the fate of Roldaer be shared by all.'*

Danil could only stare, confused, as she turned her attention to the surviving magi. Her robes shifted and reformed into the battle armor that he knew her by as she stalked forward. A battle-axe materialized in one fist she stalked toward the first mage who was attempting to scramble back, screaming.

Then the vision wavered and was gone.

Staggering away from the portal, Danil stumbled to the edge of the platform, his ears ringing.

Hafryn urgently gripped his shoulder, "Easy, I have you, *fala*."

Danil sucked in a ragged lungful of air, startled once more by the stark ruin of the tower around them. "I know what happened here," he rasped before sharing all he had seen.

Hafryn's lips parted in consternation. "What is Lyria, then, if not a ghost? And why would she be in your vision?"

Danil shook his head, hardly knowing the answers himself.

Splashing came from main floor below.

Danil twisted, startled to see Nera at the foot of the staircase. At the old woman's side, Lyria gripped her large axe as if ready for battle once more.

"So, she chose a Roldaerian in the end," Nera said. She looked between Danil and Lyria. "How unexpected."

23

"How is it you can see Lyria, magus?" Hafryn asked, stalking down the stairwell. "She died at the border."

Nera smiled, unconcerned by his approach. "You assume much, Hafryn Wolfkind. I don't know this Lyria you speak of."

Danil glanced quizzically at Lyria as he took the slippery steps. The ghost idly strolled atop the broken wall, looking out over the ocean as waves lapped at her boots.

Nera followed his gaze. "That is Marama who you see, Danil. Her name means 'light' in Roldaerian Old Tongue."

Knowing what he did now, it made a lot of sense. Danil's heart ached. "I thought she was a magus who'd died trying to warn us. Lyria—she'd been badly burned; I thought Marama was her ghost." The truth was somehow worse. He took in the ruin of the tower. "The magi destroyed the lodestone of Isfil."

Nera tilted her head, surprise and curiosity in her eyes. "They did. It was the first of a dozen lodestones lost across Roldaer. And so began the magi's path to war. Although..."

She hesitated. "I don't understand how you could know this, Danil."

She looked curiously at Marama, who appeared intent on ignoring her.

Hafryn folded his arms. "When a lodestone is destroyed, its leylines wither and die. That's why there's no more Roldaerian kiandrite."

Nera nodded. "The magi were too slow to realize their mistake. In their hunger to steal power directly from the lodestones, they took little notice of how mage-crystals no longer formed in lakes and streams or pushed themselves up out of the earth."

Hafryn's eyes narrowed. "You understand a lot about kiandrite for a magus, Nera."

Nera smiled slightly. "One doesn't get to my age without coming upon knowledge that changes them."

Danil asked, "Are there others like Ly—like Marama?" It had looked as if she'd been wrested from the lodestone itself.

"If so, they've never revealed themselves to me," Nera said with a shrug. "As I understand it, Isfil was the first to have its lodestone destroyed. Marama's existence may well be an accident."

Danil shook his head. "But what is she?" He'd spent so long believing Lyria's ghost had latched onto him that anything else felt strange.

"She's the protector of Roldaer—or what's left of it. If she's turned to you, Danil, it means you have a task to fulfil."

Hafryn grunted. "That's why we came to Isfil in the first place. But I don't see how knowing what the ghost is can change anything."

Nera grunted, eyeing the ruins about them. "Let's not

speak of it here," she murmured. "Some days the darkness of what happened lingers more strongly."

She navigated her way back to the walkway, water sloshing about her.

They left the broken tower to find warmth and dry clothing in Nera's workroom. A lifetime of study was evident in the room, from scrolls spilling out of bookcases to oddments held in cases and trunks. A well-used day bed sat in one corner, and Danil imagined the old woman often drowsed midway through her research.

Marama strode the length of the shelves, fingers drifting but not quite touching any of Nera's possessions.

Glancing uneasily at the door, Danil asked, "What about the selasi? We have to block the walkway and steps to the lower levels."

"Isfil is aware of its misstep now. We're quite safe," Nera said dismissively, bending to light the hearth fire.

Hafryn loitered in the doorway and eyed the mess of scrolls and gems strewn across the worktable. "What have you been up to in here these past few days, magus? Not avoiding us, I think."

Nera straightened, bones creaking. She chuckled at his distrusting regard. "When Marama sent me to rescue your party, I initially believed you were just unlucky travelers. But then I saw what you carry, Hafryn. The Harbinger amulet of Kaul Mage-Kin is a difficult taskmaster."

Hafryn paled and made an aborted move to grip the amulet.

"You know what it is, then!" Danil gasped. "Do you know how to remove it?"

Nera's face turned somber. "It hasn't been used since Kaul last walked among us. But I suspect you already know this."

Danil nodded, throat closing over.

"Things aren't so different now from the time of the Great War," Nera murmured, fussing over some parchment on the edge of her worktable. "Back then, there were three acolytes who, by virtue of their actions, gave Kaul great power."

Hafryn folded his arms. "Kaul had many allies amongst the magi, but I've never heard of three acolytes."

She smiled slightly. "Much about the Great War is lost— some of it purposefully so. The magi pine for old glory."

"And yet knowledge of the three acolytes resides here in a magi spire," Hafryn said, tone dubious.

Tapping the side of her head, Nera said, "Perhaps I'm older than I appear, wolf."

Hafryn snorted testily. "You'd have to be older than the Great War. That was centuries ago!"

Nera raised an eyebrow. "Isfil provides what is needed, yes?"

Danil looked her over. It seemed impossible that anyone could live that long, much less do so without going mad.

"If Isfil is truly as you say, it hasn't shown us how to remove the amulet," Hafryn said.

She nodded, suddenly sympathetic. "You have the hardest battle ahead, wolf. I've spent these last days trying to understand what happened to the last Harbinger. After the downfall of Kaul, the Harbinger lost some of his power, but none of his desire to kill. Many were slaughtered, Roldaerian and Amasian both. Eventually, he was lured into a warded room, and enchanters tried to destroy the amulet. I understand the attempt failed." She reached out and squeezed his hand. "It was ill-fate that you found the amulet, Hafryn, and worse that you chose to wear it. The amulet will increase your need to fight and kill until you desire nothing else. And yet, if Marama has indeed chosen Danil as her protector, then all can't be lost. You must fight Kaul's power over you, wolf."

Pale-faced, Hafryn said, "I'm no enchanter, magus. I don't know how to fight Kaul."

"I'd have thought it obvious, dear boy." The old woman smiled. "With your heart. Kaul only ever saw love as a weakness, and therein lies our chance. Until the High Priestess and *Videre* emerge to serve as Kaul's other acolytes, we have time to prevent the dread lord from regaining his power."

Both Danil and Hafryn flinched.

Dry-mouthed, Danil recalled his old vision of the *videre* who'd used her unique ability to see beyond to help Kaul bury the glyphs of Eyrie. But he was nothing like her. He'd never aid Kaul.

Hafryn gripped Danil's wrist and gently squeezed in comfort.

"What is it?" Nera said sharply, noticing. "You recognize my words."

Swallowing, Danil said, "I'm the custodian and *videre* of Kailon."

"*Videre!*" Nera gasped. She whitened. "Kaul's *videre!*"

"Never Kaul's," Danil snarled.

A desperate light showed in Nera's eyes. "There has only ever one *videre*. And like the Harbinger, they are bound to the dread lord." She shook her head. "But Marama should not have attached herself to you, Danil. That's quite impossible!" She paced, muttering under her breath.

Chest tight, Danil said, "Please, we don't understand."

"Perhaps the High Priestess knows," Nera continued unabated. "Which among your party is she?"

Danil and Hafryn exchanged startled looks.

"In the Great War, the three acolytes of Kaul always walked together," Nera insisted. "The Priestess was Kaul's closest adviser and ally."

"There's no one like that among us," Danil said, shaking his head. "We're here to stop Kaul."

"Are you so certain?" Nera asked. "Being wrong will cost not only your life, but the lives of everyone in Roldaer and Amas."

"We're certain," Hafryn said firmly.

She tapped her lips in thought.

Shouts came from the corridor, along with running footsteps. Hafryn stepped back to peer outside.

Commander Selen and Gethin sprinted past the doorway.

"What's happening?" Hafryn called after them as the pair climbed the stairs leading to the parapet.

Gethin glanced over his shoulder, shouting, "Strangers approach from the beach!"

Hafryn threw Danil and Nera a startled look before taking off after the two Roldaerians.

Merlias and Osriele were already atop the parapet, leaning on the battlements as they looked to the shore. The breeze buffeted against Danil as he turned to see that the selasi had retreated to above the high tide line.

A few feet from the hissing waves stood two people. Footprints showed they'd come from the cave at the end of the inlet. One stranger was a young man, his hair dark and loose about him. He wore only a simple shift that offered little protection from the bitter wind. His companion placed a hand on his shoulder until he knelt on the damp, pebbled beach. He trembled, hugging his arms about his middle.

His companion was a dark shadow beneath robes and a hood. A red symbol was emblazoned on the cloak as it rustled in the wind. More, unfamiliar markings were scorched black into the stones around the pair, no doubt the outcome of some curse.

"Show yourself, stranger!" Osriele shouted down.

The stranger pulled back their hood. Dark, greying hair was held in place by a circlet over the woman's brow. She was delicate featured and thin lipped. She smirked up at them and waved.

Danil sucked in a breath. "Magus Brianna."

"No. *That's impossible!*" Hafryn hissed.

Beside him, Merlias stared at the magus with a mixture of intrigue and chagrin.

Hafryn rounded on her. "Viren swore the Eyrie would deal with Brianna and her cronies captured in Farin," he growled.

Merlias lifted her gaze. "How do you think we learned of your amulet, Hafryn?" she said somberly. "We may have miscalculated by letting her go."

"You think?" Hafryn snarled, eyes starting to glow.

Her nostrils flared. "Your custodian had stripped her of her power, and finished matters by stripping her will. I have no answer to why she's here now."

But Danil feared he did. From the corner of his eye, he saw Nera make a warding sign.

Below them, Magus Brianna raised her arms, her lips moving. The air grew cold as the clouds drew close. Pebbles vibrated at her feet.

"What spell is that?" Commander Selen asked.

Osriele wordlessly shook her head.

Magus Brianna chanted, her voice snatched away by the wind and distance. She grabbed a fistful of the kneeling man's hair and triumphantly wrenched his head back to bare his throat. A blade flashed in her fist.

Movement on the sand caught Danil's gaze. His vision changed, and suddenly he saw a small vole beside the young man. It moved frantically, pushing against an unseen barrier as if trying to escape.

He lurched forward to grip the stone parapet. "He's Amasian!"

Hafryn stiffened before roaring his outrage into the wind.

Danil raised his hand, too late to form an enchantment.

Magus Brianna struck downwards.

"No!" Danil cried out as the blade bit deep.

Blood sprayed across the shore. The young man slumped to the side with scarcely a gurgle, while the vole collapsed beside him before winking out. Low bellows and triumphant hisses rang out from the selasi.

Magus Brianna laughed in delight and raised her arms once more. The blood quickly turned black and tar-like on the shore. It quickly lurched up the beach and toward the water, slamming up against the waves. Acrid, fetid air rolled over the spire.

"Blacksward!" Commander Selen shouted. She yanked Osriele away from the parapet, pushing her toward Gethin and the stairs.

Danil's pulse danced wildly as the blacksward gnashed at the waves. He thought back to Fens and the small bird that the male magus had also killed to create blacksward.

The magi didn't slaughter animals to create the blacksward—they needed more powerful creatures to activate the death curse.

"They're sacrificing Amasians," he whispered.

THE BLACKSWARD SLITHERED across the beach and enveloped the first rocks of the bridge.

Merlias turned on Osriele and blocked her retreat. "How many?" she hissed. "How many of my people lie slaughtered to feed the blacksward?"

Osriele shook her head tearfully. "I swear to you, I didn't know."

The enchanter's eyes turned contemptuous. "Your kind have captured and enslaved my people for years! All in preparation for *this*?"

Hafryn trembled beside her, his face a rictus of rage.

Osriele wordlessly shook her head again.

Commander Selen pushed her way between them. "The blacksward approaches. Nera, can Isfil stand against it?"

Nera watched the churning blackness with fascinated revulsion. "Not without aid."

"Have you no boat to allow us to escape, then?" Selen pressed.

She shook her head.

Cursing, the commander said, "Then we prepare ourselves. Barricade the entrance as best we can." She motioned for everyone to follow her.

Both Hafryn and Merlias ignored her. They gazed murderously at Magus Brianna standing untouched by the blacksward, and for a moment Danil thought the pair could be mistaken for twins with matching red hair and blazing green eyes.

Magus Brianna strode up the beach toward the waiting selasi. The dead Amasian lay discarded like driftwood on the beach.

Jaw clenched, Hafryn banged his fist against the stone parapet. "Merlias," he hissed.

The Eyrie enchanter met his gaze, cold.

Some sort of understanding passed between the two Amasians.

Merlias wove a new glyph. It flared brightly with concentric circles and tiny florets much like the Eyre House glyph. She pressed it to her breast. The air sparked around her, and suddenly a massive owl stretched its blue-tipped wings. It was almost as tall as Danil, its beak sharp and gleaming.

Before Danil could blink, Hafryn leaped atop the parapet and threw himself over the edge. The giant owl rocketed down as Hafryn fell.

No!" Danil screamed, reaching desperately for him.

Merlias caught Hafryn by the shoulders with powerful talons. They flew over the restless water and headed straight for the magus.

Magus Brianna sensed their approach, her expression delighted.

Merlias released her grip, and Hafryn rolled at speed before clambering to his feet directly in front of Brianna. Merlias' twin blades flashed in his fists.

Brianna clapped her hands like a child at a puppet show, her words lost in the wind.

Roaring, Hafryn attacked.

Danil swore and pushed himself away from the parapet. He sprinted down the stairs, ignoring Nera when she called out to him.

He made for the courtyard. The cloying stench of death rose up more strongly than he imagined possible, almost as if the damp stones had already turned into poisonous blacksward. Covering his mouth with his sleeve, Danil ran for the gate. His hand barely touched wood before something slashed the air behind him.

Whirling, Danil barely had time to roll out of the way

before Ruslin drove a sword deep into the door. The guard yanked the blade free and stalked after him. Black lines of infection were replaced by sallow skin and red sores covering much of his hands and face. Flies buzz about him. A crazed look burned in the man's eyes.

"What are you doing?" Danil cried.

Ruslin ignored him, striking the air where Danil stood heartbeats earlier. A horrid stench emanated off the guard, almost as if he was already long dead. The dreadful wound on his arm no longer hampered him. A terrible strength urged Ruslin onwards.

"We're allies, Ruslin!" Danil said, ducking under a sweeping blow. He gripped his dagger, not wishing to cause the man harm. "Don't do this!"

Ruslin bared yellow teeth, his tongue so swollen he released a gurgling shriek when he raced after Danil.

A sword suddenly struck up against Ruslin's blade. Danil dove away, peering up in grateful astonishment at Commander Selen. The woman was grim-faced as she shoved Ruslin away.

"He's fever-addled," Danil warned.

"No, he's not." The commander followed after Ruslin as he staggered upright. "Put aside your sword, guardsmen," she ordered.

But Ruslin ignored her as surely as he had Danil, cackling as he launched at Selen. The pair exchanged rapid blows, far faster than Danil thought possible when one combatant was so grievously injured. But Commander Selen held her ground, exchanging strikes and parries until Ruslin was on the retreat.

Backed up against the courtyard wall, Selen suddenly drove her blade deep into the guardsman's belly. Ruslin hardly flinched, instead continuing his maniacal cackle. The commander wrenched her blade loose and struck the guard's heart.

Ruslin slumped to his knees, blood pouring from of his mouth.

She leaped out of range of his sword.

The guard crawled after Selen, attempting to strike the woman even as weakness took him. Commander Selen skirted wide and then pressed a boot to his shoulder, forcing him flat. Grim-faced, she drove her blade through his throat.

Ruslin shuddered and finally grew still.

Expression closed, Selen cleaned her sword on the edge of his cloak.

Danil edged cautiously toward her. "Forgive me, commander. I didn't want to fight him."

But she shook her head. "We'd already lost him to the poison during the night. This was something else."

Danil stared uneasily at the body.

"Go on, Danil. Go save your wolf," the commander said softly, her gaze still on the body of her former comrade.

Startled, he gave her a nod and then hurried for the gates.

Magus Brianna waited for him at the end of the bridge. She spotted him and spread her hands expansively. "Come, now, *videre!*" she called. "We have our Great Lord's work to do!"

Danil desperately looked past her, searching for Hafryn. The clang of steel rang out behind the blacksward where the selasi formed a ring around their opponent. A dark shadow danced in time with Hafryn, cutting and slashing and drawing so close that for a heartbeat Danil feared that Hafryn and the shadow fighter were one.

Yelling, Danil ran the length of the bridge toward Magus Brianna.

She laughed gaily and raised her hands, spitting out harsh, guttural words. Repulsive red light swirled around her, glowing in increasing brightness as he neared.

Danil wondered how she'd regained her power after having been stripped of it by the wellspring in Kailon. He formed a blocking glyph and hurled it at the foul woman. It streaked across the bridge and Danil grinned in satisfaction as the flagstones bucked, large boulders and rocks wrenching upwards like a wall.

Magus Brianna nimbly jumped over the obstacle. Blacksward oozed after her.

"The Harbinger will cleave out your companions' hearts and leave the selasi to feast upon their bones," she promised.

"Never going to happen," Danil snarled as he began to form another enchantment.

The magus laughed. "Your companions are turning against you, *videre*. Kaul Mage-Kin is your one solace."

Danil shook his head. "Hafryn and I will never be his acolytes!"

Brianna widened her gaze mockingly. "Someone's been telling you stories, *videre*. There's no choice for you or the wolf. Plans have been in motion for years."

"Is that why you lost control of Kailon?" Danil snapped. "The leylines defy you and your puppet master."

She flared, face reddening. "Your mistake is thinking you were victorious by becoming custodian of the deadlands. You still stand before me with no options or hope," she spat. "I need only bend you to my will and the leylines shall fall with you."

Clenching his teeth, Danil said, "Try it. Failure is something you know well."

Face congealing, Magus Brianna snarled out a new

curse. Danil ducked as it careened toward him. The House glyph woke with a searing burst of light.

Feather-light fingers brushed Danil's shoulders. He whirled.

Marama strode past him, axe whirling to cut the curse in two. Iridescent light reflected like a beacon off the slick rocks and surrounding waves. The blacksward shirked back.

"Enough of that, relic," Magus Brianna said. Her hands pulsed with red fire. It snapped out, licking and biting before suddenly wrapping around Marama's waist. "Time to end your meddling."

Magus Brianna pulled out a pouch from her waist, quickly throwing out a handful of red, tortured kiandrite dust to cover Marama.

The spirit stilled, arms pinned to her side. The blacksward swarmed around Brianna and edged forward in anticipation.

Brianna's lip curled in triumph. She made a reeling motion and dragged Marama toward the blacksward. The oily darkness leaped up, crawling up her legs. Marama threw back her head and silently screamed.

"Marama!" Widening his stance, Danil threw out an enchantment, bolstering it with the blinding light of the House of Kailon.

But Marama flickered, her skin pulsating as the blacksward began to slowly eat through the light. More blacksward flowed over her back and forced her to her knees.

Danil rushed forward, hand glowing, but Brianna beat him to it. With a harsh snarl she threw another curse, red fire curling around Marama's throat and propelling her face-forward into the blacksward.

The blacksward swallowed her in a final, quenching spark of light.

"No! You murderous bitch!" Danil snarled, eyes burning. "You've destroyed her twice!"

Magus Brianna smiled. She snapped her fingers at the blacksward. "Take him."

The blacksward roared.

24

D anil leaped from the bridge.

Frigid, bitterly cold water closed over him and dragged him down. He flailed, tangled in his cloak before he kicked up to the surface. He gulped a lungful of air, coughing.

Laughter rang out.

"You only hasten your doom, *videre!*" Brianna shouted, gripping the edge of the bridge. The blacksward pooled under her fingers.

A wave crashed over him, tumbling him end over end. The weight of his boots pulled him down. He kicked up again and made for the shore. A new wave shoved him deeper.Someone grabbed a fistful of his tunic and hauled him to the surface.

"*Idiot!*" Merlias hissed furiously. She kicked them toward the shore.

Danil's knees hit the stony beach, stumbling as a wave crashed over him. He choked on saltwater.

Merlias thumped him on the back. "Why'd you jump, you idiot! I nearly had her!"

Breath heaving, Danil rasped, "Sorry?"

The Eyrie enchanter glowered. "You were a decent distraction until you went haring off into the water where you can't swim!"

"I can," he protested, coughing. He looked up toward the bridge but saw Magus Brianna was gone. "She killed Marama." His throat closed over.

"Who?" Merlias swore vehemently. "Get out of the water before a sea serpent has you!"

Danil ignored her, gaze drawn up the beach where the hisses and snarls of the selasi grew loudest. Hafryn continued to fend them off with his blades, eyes glowing vibrant orange and the shadow fighter mimicking his every move. Between Hafryn and Danil was a mass of boiling, slithery blacksward.

"We have to save Hafryn," Danil said. "Brianna won't let him escape."

But before Merlias could curse at him once more, a tremendous roar rocked the beach, causing them both to duck in fear.

A silver dragon rocketed into the sky from behind the spire. Mighty wings stretched wide as it released another raucous bellow across the beach. The dragon swooped low and spat fire atop the blacksward. It bubbled and hissed, delivering a fresh wave of rotting stench. A wave of fierce heat rolled over Danil.

Arching his neck to watch the silver dragon, Danil wondered how he could have been so blind. There was only one person at the spire who could possibly be the ferocious creature.

"That devious woman," Merlias said, voice admiring as she came to the same conclusion.

Nera wheeled overhead, chest widening she drew in air

for another flaming blast. Selasi scattered in fright, bolting for the cave. Hafryn suddenly stood alone on the beach.

Danil raised his fist and cheered, eyes tearing in relief.

But the powerful flames did little more than burn a thin path through the þlacksward. The beach steamed with the acrid stench of decay, and Danil gagged, coughing. Throat stinging from the smoke, he sprinted through the burned path up to Hafryn.

His friend was blank-faced, the whites of his eyes almost entirely consumed by the orange glow as he heaved in great breaths. Black blood dripped from his blades, a handful of selasi lying dead around him.

"*Fala?*" Danil said carefully, not quite brave enough to touch him this time.

The shadow fighter watched with an air of smug satisfaction.

Snarling, Danil raised his hand, but the shadow fighter danced away before the light could reach it.

Hafryn let out a convulsive breath. Lifting his hands, he gazed at the blades as if they were strange to him. He shuddered, the twin swords falling to the stony beach with a twang.

"Show respect for my blades, exile," Merlias snarled as she snatched them up.

"Not now, Merlias," Danil warned. Glancing over his shoulder, he saw the dragon glide low once more. Flames pummeled the blacksward, slowing its progress across the sand. He gripped Hafryn's arm and ushered him down the charred path toward the beach.

Hafryn abruptly fell to his knees and let out a wretched sob.

The young, vole shifter's body lay sprawled atop the pebbles before them, the rising waves lapping against naked legs. His sightless eyes still contained the terror of his last moments.

"It's Talis," Hafryn choked out, shoulders shaking.

The name sounded vaguely familiar to Danil. In a rush of memory, he realized Talis was the captured shifter taken by Magus Ronan in the forests outside Altonas before Kailon had begun to heal.

"Curse them," Hafryn said harshly, trembling. "Curse every magus ever born."

Merlias clenched her teeth, glyphs buzzing about her head.

Danil knelt and called forth the House glyph's warmth. He gently closed the young man's eyes. *May you return to the mountains of Amas and find peace,* he thought.

"We can't help him now," Merlias muttered coldly, though tears glittered. She shoved at Danil brusquely. "Move it, custodian!"

She threw Hafryn's arm about her shoulders and lurched him upright, muttering something lost in the roaring flames.

As if sensing their distraction, the blacksward charged toward them once more.

"Merlias, you have to fly him out of here," Danil said desperately, fearing what would happen to Hafryn should the blacksward touch him. "I won't lose him to Kaul!"

"I'm not a pack mule," Merlias snapped. "I can't simply take flight with a man in my talons! Either of you would be too heavy."

Looking about desperately, Danil said, "Then we swim for it." The blacksward had previously slowed when fetching up against water in the Fens. He hoped the same would be true now.

Cursing him for an idiot once more, Merlias cupped

both hands and yelled, "Nera!"

To Danil's surprise, the silver dragon landed in the tiny margin of space separating them from the blacksward.

"Get on!" Merlias shouted, clambering up Nera's hind leg onto her back. She gripped one of the dragon's bristling spines and leaned down to grasp Hafryn's arm. With Danil shoving from behind, they got him up. Danil pressed him against a spine and held tight, feeling him tremble with barely suppressed rage and grief.

Nera craned her neck to see them securely holding on before launching upwards with a powerful beat of her wings. Danil's stomach lurched at the sudden speed of it. They pitched over the oily shore before reeling toward the spire.

The silver dragon landed in the courtyard, pressing flat to the stone as Merlias and Danil swung Hafryn off. To Danil's surprise, he saw Osriele and her guards partway across the bridge, armed and preparing to battle the oily blackness writhing near the spire.

Danil whistled frantically for them to return. Sliding from Nera's shoulder, he quickly shielded his eyes from the blasting wind when Nera launched upwards once more. "Nera, wait!"

The silver dragon streaked back to the shore, her seething cry making the hairs on Danil's arms rise.

Osriele hurried over to them, her expression tight and haunted. "She can't stop the blacksward. No one can."

Danil set his jaw. "Get everyone inside," he said before running into the spire and up the winding stairs to the parapet. The wind felt even colder against his skin. Danil leaned against the parapet and cupped his hands. "Nera! Come back!" He didn't think she could hear beyond the blistering flames and the harshness of the cold wind. "*Nera!*"

But she wheeled over the spire, her silver scales flashing against the clouds. Powerful talons clawed deep into the stone parapet as Nera landed. She flapped once against the wind before she transformed.

Nera gave him a determined look. "Isfil is mine to protect, young custodian. Do not ask me to abandon it."

Danil noted the steel in her gaze. "The magi will kill you now that they know what you are—that's if Isfil isn't overrun by the blacksward."

She gave him a hard smile. "Not even a *videre* sees everything."

He frowned.

"I'll be fine, Danil of Roldaer and Amas. Make our kingdoms safe again. Both are worthy and deserve to thrive."

Danil's throat closed over as he thought of Marama and Talis and the suffering of so many people across both kingdoms. "How can you say that?" he choked out. "Look what Kaul and Magus Brianna have done!"

"Things can't continue as they are," Nera agreed. "You'll know what to do when the time is upon you. Now, head for the broken spire. Its portal will take you where you most need to go."

But he didn't know how to work it.

"Marama chose you for a reason, Danil." The old woman's eyes moistened at mentioning the spirit's name, and Danil knew the dragon shifter had lost the one most dear to her.

Nera gave him a considered nod, gripping his shoulder in farewell before taking to her dragon form once more. Stepping back as the wind snapped around him, Danil realized she was larger than even Sonnen. She shone like glory as she launched back off the turret.

Silently wishing her well, Danil hurried back down the

stairs, determined to ensure that his fight to stop Kaul and his magi didn't end at a lonely spire on the sea.

The Roldaerians waited for him on the first level, sweating and worried. If they were angry at him for what had happened to Ruslin, they showed no sign of it.

Hafryn slouched against the wall, shoulders hunched as if the weight of three lands lay upon him. He stared at his hands as if they had betrayed him.

Danil eased him upright, searching his eyes for green and feeling a small measure of relief that some still remained.

Hafryn gave him a weak smile, knowing his thoughts. "I'm still here, *fala*."

Danil hugged him close, trembling. "Don't do that again," he whispered.

Hafryn brought his arms about Danil and sighed into his neck. "Stay with me. Don't let me go into the dark."

"I've got you," he murmured, pressing his lips to Hafryn's forehead. "We'll be back in Kailon before we know it. We'll go swimming. It'll be cold with the first meltwaters of Amas, but we'll warm in the sun afterwards. You can even hunt us down a coney, and I'll make that stew you favor with the honeyfrost flowers."

Hafryn didn't reply, but his grip tightened around Danil.

Clearing her throat, Commander Selen said, "The spire is about to be overrun."

Regretfully, Danil pulled away. "We can escape through the broken spire," he said. "Hafryn and I know a way across."

Motioning them to follow, he ushered them along the corridor and nudged the stone that opened up access to the other tower. Surprised murmurs came from the Roldaerians.

Danil peered cautiously into the darkness, hoping more selasi hadn't swum into the broken spire and now lay in wait.

Hafryn noticed his hesitation and shook his head minutely. "It's clear."

Taking a deep breath, Danil warned of the gaping hole in the floor before they entered the broken tower. The powerful tide thundered over the rocks and sent shallow, foaming waves across the floor.

"It's upstairs," Danil said, wading to the stairwell. "Hurry!"

The stone columns pulsed soft blue and green in greeting when Danil reached them. He touched the stone, hearing the fleeting laughter of children swirl around him.

"It's a portal," Osriele breathed in shock. "But how? We'd have known of its existence back at the Magi Tower."

"I don't think this one was created by the magi," Danil said, knowing that it hadn't been present at the spire's destruction.

"Let me awaken it," she said, pressing her ring to the stone. The kiandrite flickered and then bristled with spikes of light. She snatched her hand back with a gasp.

Merlias snorted. "Kiandrite doesn't like to be forced, magus. I'd have thought the custodian would have taught you that by now."

Osriele's cheeks turned pink. "But Roldaer's pillars have always ceded to my will."

"Let the custodian try," Gethin said.

Danil and Osriele threw him an astonished look.

The corporal gave a terse shrug. "I care not whose magic gets us out of here—just make it done."

Turning, Danil looked over the pillars, unsure how to go about it. He returned his hand to the stone and closed his eyes. Tendrils of light brushed over his knuckles. '*If you know Marama's will, please, take us there,*" he thought.

The air about him crackled like static before a storm. It coalesced into a dazzling wall of shimmering white, silver and green. The kiandrite embedded in the pillars sang joyfully in his mind.

"Impossible." Osriele stretched her hand over the luminous portal. "You shouldn't be able to do this, Danil. It takes years of training to command the portals."

"That's why you don't deserve that ring on your finger." Merlias shook her head in disgust. "You don't *command*, Osriele, you ask. Should the kiandrite say no, you don't then force it to your will."

Osriele frowned.

"I have very little innate magic," Danil admitted. "It's my connection to the leylines and my desire to do good by them that allows me to enchant."

The lines on Osriele's brow deepened.

"Where does this portal lead, Danil?" Commander Selen asked, unsheathing her sword as she eyed the shimmering vortex.

"Not here, at least," Gethin said. Lowering his helm, he strode through without a backward glance.

The commander blinked at his audacity, but then she and Osriele followed.

"One day, that smart mouth of yours is going to see you cursed," Hafryn observed to Merlias.

"What are you talking about, wolf? I'm delightful." Merlias raised an eyebrow and motioned her hand forward. "Unless you intend on opening a new portal that sends us home, lead on, custodian."

Danil grimaced at the enchanter, but took Hafryn's hand and guided them through.

25

D anil stumbled over a desiccated tree root. Misshapen trees twisted around them, tortured branches stretching towards the sky like bony fingers. Fouled water cut between mounds of burned soil and shriveled reeds. Bloated remnants of moldering animals floated in the murky water.

"Still in the Fens, I see," Commander Selen muttered, nose crinkling as she trod in something furred and oozing. "The blacksward has touched here, too."

Osriele covered her mouth and nose with the stained edge of her cloak. Gethin was already a few hundred feet ahead, bow ready as he surveyed the area from a hummock of reeds.

Merlias stumbled on animal bones and cursed. "You couldn't portal us somewhere useful, Danil? Or are you not done playing hero for Roldaer?"

Danil forced back an angry reply, knowing there was grief underlying the enchanter's snarking. The magnitude of their discovery lay like a heavy stone in his heart, too. It was impossible to know how many Amasians had been slaughtered to unleash the blacksward. But it was clear now that Kaul was the progenitor of the curse—the dread lord took sick pleasure in using the blood of his enemies to spread ruin.

"I asked the kiandrite to take us where we needed to go," Danil said. He gazed at the pale granite hills breaking up the flatlands in the distance. Their gentle, distant curves were startlingly familiar, and it took him a moment to realize he'd seen them in the heartbeats before Marama had steered his vision to her cataclysmic past. "We head that way."

Commander Selen eyed the granite hills. "We're gravely exposed should the selasi come upon us—especially now that we're without horses. At the very least, we should camp on higher ground tonight."

Osriele nodded her agreement. "Lead on, commander."

The party strode the treacherous marshes and sucking mud.

Beside Danil, Hafryn edged around soiled pools where not even toads or snakes resided. The amulet radiated a constant, surly glow. As if sensing Danil's regard, Hafryn said, "I won't apologize for trying to kill Brianna, *fala*."

Acid fury burned Danil's throat. "I want her dead, too. Just—don't go doing it without me."

Hafryn gave him an echo of a smile. "I think we can safely assume that Brianna is Kaul's High Priestess."

Heartsore, Danil managed a nod. It made a grim sort of sense, considering Brianna had first attempted to control Kailon's leylines for her master all those months ago. "But I don't understand how the Eyrie didn't know. Brianna was their prisoner in Farin for a time."

"And they let her go," Hafryn murmured.

Merlias thrust her way between them. "I, too, want to

know why she was released. Had I known, I'd have gutted her myself."

Danil believed her. Merlias was nothing if not thorough with those she deemed her enemy. "Perhaps she bargained information for her life."

"It appears Brianna withheld some pertinent details," Hafryn said. With exhaustion lining his shoulders, he told Merlias what they'd uncovered about the three acolytes of Kaul.

"Brianna likely wanted an Amasian to find the amulet, knowing it would please her master," Danil added once Hafryn was done.

"Then I'm in your debt, Hafryn," Merlias mused, studying him a new light. "Brianna's words brought me to the Fens. It could well be me wearing that amulet."

"Kaul would dearly love to enslave an enchanter," Hafryn said. "The damage you'd have wrought would be cataclysmic, Merlias."

Merlias quirked an eyebrow. "Flattery, Hafryn?"

"You've an odd way of seeing things," he replied dryly.

They pushed on, squelching through the mud to reach the rest of the party.

Gethin slowed to trudge beside them. "What do you suppose your dragon friend will do?" he asked. "Her lair won't survive the blacksward."

"Don't call it a lair," Merlias said. "Isfil is Nera's home, not some hole in the rocks used by an animal."

The corporal bowed slightly, color on his cheeks. "I know that, enchanter. I meant no disrespect."

She gave him a dark look but didn't so much as spin a glyph threateningly over him. "She'll take to the wind once she accepts Isfil is lost. Be grateful she sought to help us first —dragons don't always care for smaller folk."

Gethin nodded, mouth downturned. "Her help wouldn't go astray right about now."

"If Nera's anything like the dragons I know, she'll be focused on retribution," Hafryn said.

The terrain slowly changed to a mix of shallow wetlands and dry stretches of brush, all devastated by the blacksward. Much of the powdery scorching had been blown away, leaving charred reeds, blackened soil and brackish water that stung like nettles on exposed skin.

But the granite hills stood in stark relief against the devastated land, with softly rounded boulders and curved stone reaching for the sky. Danil imagined many creatures had taken to the rocks and crevices to hide from the spreading poison.

Commander Selen pointed to a stack of boulders atop one rocky hill. "Our best vantage by far." A ledge of rock jutted out below the boulders, wide enough to offer protection from the elements. "I suggest we spend the night there."

Gethin ran an assessing gaze over the dead brush and reeds around them. "There's sufficient materials hereabouts to make snares. Should make the selasi hesitate if they reach us during the night."

Selen nodded and motioned him away. The corporal took off at a trot.

The rest of the party searched for a way up onto the ledge. Small animal trails marked with droppings indicated rock hoppers and rodents still lived amidst the boulders. Turquoise butterflies and singing crickets clung to the rocks to bask in the afternoon sunlight.

"Not everything falls to the blacksward, then," Osriele observed as startled finches took flight.

Walking in the shadow of an overhang, Danil spied a

small dot of light imbedded in the rock high above. He squinted as his companions moved on. The House glyph on his palm grew warm as if in greeting.

"I think there's kiandrite up there," Danil blurted out, his voice starling the crickets into silence.

Hafryn strode back and ran his gaze along the overhang. "I don't see it."

"It's very small," Danil admitted. He pointed to the glimmering niche of rock. "See?"

The rest of the party either shook their heads or gave bemused shrugs.

"I could take wing," Merlias mused. "But I sense no kiandrite, custodian."

Eyeing the stained rocks, Danil supposed the blacksward would have consumed any crystals in its path. All the same, he knew what he saw. He used small footholds to clamber his way up a channel carved out by centuries of rainfall. The glitter was tiny, mostly buried under the rock. Danil reached for it, his hand pressing against momentary resistance.

The crystal suddenly leaped into his hand.

Startled, Danil almost fell. He cleaved to the rock and opened his hand. Scarcely larger than his fingernail, the crystal sparkled gold and green and dusky pink. The glyph on Danil's hand swirled in matching colors.

Jumping down, he held it to the light. Soft whispers told of marshes and fresh-flowing estuaries, of long-legged storks and croaking frogs and beavers making dams throughout the Fens.

"It's Roldaerian," Danil realized.

Osriele's eyes widened as she pushed in close. "Impossible!"

Danil ran his forefinger along its edge as the whispers

transformed into songs of wide plains and vibrant hills, of farmers and four-legged folk trammeling across the earth. Underneath was a lingering echo of lines of power hidden deep below the surface.

"Oh, glory," he breathed. "It's still connected to the leylines of Roldaer."

Hafryn and Merlias shared astonished glances.

Understanding rushed over Danil. "This is why the blacksward is in the Fens. Kaul must know that kiandrite still exists here!"

It was what Marama had been so desperate for Danil to discover. This small, fragile crystal was the very last bastion of the Roldaerian leylines.

"I don't get it. What's so important about a Roldaerian crystal?" Selen asked, frowning.

"Kiandrite doesn't merely sprout from leylines," Merlias explained, her excitement rising. "They serve as protectors and nurturers. The more kiandrite, the stronger and better defended the leylines are."

"But Roldaer has no leylines," Osriele argued.

Merlias shook her head. "Just because they're empty doesn't mean they no longer exist."

"Kaul must intend to poison the leylines with blacksward—but he needs this crystal to gain access. The blacksward will be impossible to stop should he succeed," Hafryn said. The rainbow light from the crystal danced across his cheek.

"Poison one leyline, you poison them all," Danil murmured in understanding.

Hafryn nodded. "We should have realized long ago that Roldaerian kiandrite still existed. That's why the kingdom's leylines still run untouched despite the blacksward." He gazed at the crystal in wonder. "I can't believe that one small shard is enough to stop Kaul from taking over the leylines. He must sense the crystal's resistance."

"And Marama," Danil added. "She's protected Roldaer ever since the magi turned her lodestone to dust."

Mouth tightening, Hafryn nodded. "And Marama."

But now she was gone, and it was their duty to protect the Roldaerian leylines. Her words began to make sense.

Danil said, "If the dread lord takes this crystal, there'll be no stopping him. The leylines will be breached, and the blacksward will spread into Kailon and Amas as well."

"Then we'll protect the crystal at all costs," Osriele said. She went to touch the crystal and suddenly snatched her hand back when a spot of black slashed across its surface. She smothered a gasp.

"Careful, magus," Merlias said, amusement thick in her voice. "The last crystal of Roldaer is quite done with magi."

Chin raised, Osriele said, "I seek only to protect it."

"Your kiandrite ring speaks against you," the owl shifter snorted.

Osriele flared. "Then you take it, enchanter, if you're so pure."

"I'm not so willfully blind. The crystal has obviously chosen Danil as its protector. I dare not touch it."

"Why him?" Commander Selen asked.

"He's both custodian and Roldaerian." Merlias looked Danil over casually. "I imagine the crystal is rather surprised such a human exists."

Danil gave her a determined look. "Even so, you should take it. You can fly it to safety in Amas."

Merlias asked curiously, "You'd trust me with such a task, Danil? I have no care for Roldaer."

"Our goals are the same. We seek to protect the people and lands we love."

She raised an eyebrow, mouth curling a little. "We understand each other after all, custodian." But the crystal darkened warningly the moment she reached for it. She sniffed. "Though it looks like even this little piece of Roldaer doesn't know what's best for it."

Frustrated, Danil pushed his mind toward the crystal and urged it to go with Merlias. It flickered mulishly, telling him of sun-warmed rocks and ancient stone going deep underground that had kept it secret for eons.

"It wants to stay here," Danil said.

"Best not to force it otherwise," Hafryn cautioned.

Commander Selen sighed gustily. "Then we make camp and decide our next steps."

Danil held the crystal close and hoped its stubbornness wouldn't cost them all.

MOONLIGHT AFFORDED them a sprawling view of the Fens from atop the boulder stack. The tainted marshes brightened to silvery streaks of water interspersed by droopy reeds and scraggly trees. The party risked a fire in the bowl-shaped curve of the boulders where the wind couldn't reach them. A somber quiet held over them, with little conversation beyond the sharing of a brace of coneys that Gethin had caught and roasted that afternoon.

Seated beside Hafryn on a slab of rock, Danil ate with little intent and noticed that Hafryn's meal sat untouched. The wolf shifter instead thumbed the deep crack running across the bottom of the amulet, his expression contemplative. The dark gems around the edge of the medallion swallowed the moonlight.

"Where do you think Nera will go now that Isfil's fallen?" Danil asked quietly.

Stirring, Hafryn tucked the amulet under his tunic and sighed. "Who can say? She's avoiding Amas for a reason. I expect Nera isn't even her real name."

Danil looked at him curiously.

"Only ancient dragons turn silver, *fala*. It's possible she even fought in the Great War."

Danil couldn't imagine being so old and weary. "That's how she knew about Kaul's acolytes," he surmised.

"I suppose so," Hafryn replied. "It was a bleak time for both kingdoms. Countless scores of Amasians were killed. When Kaul made the deadlands, it happened mid-battle. He didn't care that his own fighters were caught in the maelstrom." A haunted look passed over his face. "It'll be no different this time."

"There won't be another deadlands," Danil swore. "And he made a mistake thinking we'd be his acolytes."

Hafryn squinted at the distant marshes. "He could rob you of that choice as surely as he has mine. You're already doing exactly what he wants."

Danil looked at him sharply.

Shrugging, Hafryn said, "You used your *videre* abilities to find the Roldaerian crystal when the blacksward failed to do so. Kaul will know we found the crystal. He'll come for it soon."

Danil rubbed his arms. "How can you be so certain?"

Hafryn tapped his temple, smile wry. "He's like a dark shadow on the edge of my vision. I'm sure he can sense me as surely as I can him."

Instinctively, Danil searched the surrounding granite for the shadow fighter but saw nothing in the wavering firelight. Tension gripped his spine. "Can you sense the selasi, too?"

"They're a long way off," Hafryn said. He sighed and rubbed his eyes. "I'm a risk to Kailon, too, *fala*."

Danil turned back to him, startled. "We're in this together, Hafryn. If you sense Kaul, we'll use it to our benefit."

Hafryn nodded, but nothing in the line of his mouth said that he believed it. "Don't forget that you're a custodian first."

Uncertain of what he meant, Danil turned his gaze to the rest of the party. Merlias had yet to return from her patrol, and with Commander Selen perched in the shadow of a boulder as sentry, there was only Osriele and Gethin sharing the fire. Osriele cut a forlorn figure, her expression pensive as she ate.

Following his gaze, Hafryn said, "There was a time when we thought Brianna was a rogue magus acting in secret. We underestimated how much the Magi Council supports her."

Osriele heard the comment. "You could simply ask me what I know, Hafryn," she said mildly, her expression shadowed.

He leaned forward, arms braced on his knees. "I've always thought slaughtering an entire village is excessive even by magi standards—at least before the blacksward. Brianna should have been punished for what happened in Farin, and instead she regained her power."

Danil wondered at that. The wellspring at Kailon had stripped Brianna of both her memory and mage abilities, but now she was even more powerful than before.

"It wasn't the Magi Council who pardoned her," Osriele said. "King Liam heard of her plight and was moved by her desire to secure kiandrite for the benefit of Roldaer."

"And you believed that drivel?" Hafryn asked, eyebrows shooting up.

Osriele grimaced. "My cousin has always been a fair king—decent, even, though he's unwisely frustrated the Magi Council in the past. Admittedly, his demeanor changed these past years, but we were never close enough for him to speak why."

"You didn't think it remarkable that he allowed Brianna to kill dozens of villagers without consequences?" Hafryn pressed.

"The blacksward had already begun its incursion by then. The lands of Trudan were among the first to fall." Osriele lifted her shoulders and sighed. "I was distracted by my own losses." She glanced at Danil. "I'm sorry, Danil."

Old grief sat like a ball in his throat. With an effort, he asked, "What of Amasians like Talis? He was taken months ago—you must know where they're kept prisoner."

"I couldn't say, Danil, truly."

"Brianna knows," Hafryn growled. "She slaughtered Talis on that beach because she knew how much it would hurt us."

The magus had judged correctly. By stoking Hafryn's grief and rage, she'd drawn him onto the shore to fight, thereby feeding Kaul more power.

"Were you and Talis close, Hafryn?" Osriele asked gently.

Hafryn's throat worked. "Talis was barely man-grown. He meant to do good." He shook his head and abruptly leaped to his feet. "I'm going to check the snares," he said.

Danil bit his lip, watching Hafryn navigate the uneven stone until he dropped out of sight. In the tense silence, he turned back to Osriele. "Talis traveled with us for a time. A magus captured him during an ambush."

Osriele nodded. "There's much the magi must atone for."

But Danil didn't believe they were deserving of the opportunity. If Roldaer was to endure, it had to be without the magi.

Sighing, Osriele said, "How are we to survive this, Danil? We are but a rock surrounded by poison."

"The crystal is the last thing that stands between Kaul and the destruction of all the leylines. It doesn't matter that Brianna is his High Priestess—he'll want the last crystal of Roldaer for himself. When he comes, we can destroy him."

Disbelief and astonishment flashed in Osriele's eyes.

"We'll use Gethin's snares," Danil continued, straightening as the idea took him. "If we overlay them with glyphs and spells, they'll slow him enough that we can take the advantage."

"Kaul is a dread lord," Osriele argued. "He'll come with more magi and selasi than we can reckon with."

Danil nodded. "Then we leave enough traps to make them falter. We need only the smallest opportunity. Kaul's been defeated before."

Though that was when Danil had the might of Kailon under his feet, and the steady courage of many Amasians around him. The odds were sharply against them, this time.

Osriele released a soft, astonished laugh. "Is this how you've rallied Amasians to your cause, Danil? By sheer audacity and blind trust?"

Danil shrugged. "What else should we do, Osriele? Kaul is coming regardless. I won't cower in some hole and hope he spares us while our lands fall to him."

She studied him with a mix of resignation and acceptance. "You have a habit of challenging folk beyond their comforts." She nodded. "I look forward to discovering what we can do together with these snares."

"We start at first light, then," Danil said, relieved.

"Hafryn believes Kaul is still some distance away, and we will need all the rest we can get."

Osriele smiled her agreement. "As you say, Danil."

They returned to their meals, and Danil made sure to eat well, knowing he'd need all his reserves for the upcoming task. He hoped Merlias would set some Eyrie traps when she reappeared, too.

Night grew deeper around them. In the quiet, Danil pulled the Roldaerian crystal from his pouch to study it. The iridescent light was like a balm to his heart. The crystal was so tiny he wondered how it and Marama could have possibly fended off the blacksward when it swept over the hills. Now that Marama was gone, it was even more vulnerable.

Holding the crystal close, he whispered, "I won't let Kaul have you."

As if acknowledging his words, it flickered soft pink. More colors swirled in its depths. Danil left himself be drawn into its comforting light. Whispers floated about him, so soft that he had to tilt his head to hear. Individual voices melded and separated from the pooling light until he heard one that was low and rumbling, reminding him abruptly of Sonnen.

"Danil."

Jerking back into awareness, Danil looked up at Gethin. Osriele was curled up in her cloak on the other side of the fire, though Hafryn was still nowhere to be seen. The moon had drifted from its position to the north and now sat directly overhead.

"Sorry, I was...somewhere else," Danil murmured. "What is it?"

"Sentry duty. It's your turn to relieve the commander."

Nodding, Danil tucked the crystal back in his pouch and scrambled to his feet.

Gethin gripped his sleeve. "Stay a moment, Danil."

Danil looked at him expectantly.

The corporal glanced at where Osriele slept, her kiandrite ring a red dot in the darkness. His voice dropped low. "Lady Osriele plucked me from the Aqila's city guard when I was scarcely older than you."

Danil blinked, surprised the man would share such details about himself. "Oh," he managed.

Gethin's mouth twisted. "I've seen many strange things in her company, but none so unexplainable as her faith in you."

Danil resisted the urge to fold his arms in discomfort.

The corporal measured him, blue eyes unreadable. "I don't question your heart, Danil, though I fear you've ridden us into a corner. Osriele will likely use the last of her magical reserves tomorrow to set those protective traps—then she'll be defenseless. Unlike enchanters, the magi can only do so many spells before the magic fails them."

Danil suddenly realized that he hadn't seen the magus drink any kiandrite-infused tea in days. Her stores must be long gone.

"My bow won't stop a magi attack," Gethin continued. "If you're indeed the salvation she craves, you damn well better prove it soon or I'll carry her from here whether she wills it or not." Gethin drew closer in warning. "I can no longer afford to give you the benefit of the doubt."

Resisting the urge to step back, Danil appreciated then why Commander Selen had chosen Gethin to join their small party. The man was so fiercely loyal to Osriele that he'd defy her orders to keep her safe. Strangely, it made him trust the corporal more.

"I understand," Danil said.

The Roldaerian studied him for long heartbeats before he stepped back. "Good."

"Gethin," Danil called as the man withdrew to the far side of the ledge. "We won't fail."

The man merely nodded, then disappeared into the darkness.

We can't fail.

The alternative was too devastating to contemplate.

26

Danil squatted over a snare half-hidden under a thorny bush. His fingers weaved and released a biting glyph that settled atop the snare. The enchantment shimmered before disappearing from view.

Done, he stood with a groan and cricked his aching neck. Gethin moved in steady outward circles amidst the rushes and scraggly brush, laying down more physical traps under the steady gaze of Commander Selen, who stood on the highest point of the hill as lookout.

Danil idly scanned the sky. A few eagles rode the spirals, but no oversized owls soared nearby.

Hafryn lounged beside him in his wolf Trueform, panting in the noonday sun. To Danil's eye, the wolf appeared bigger than usual, his paws wider than dish plates. The amulet hung from his neck, its chain elongated to accommodate the wolf's size.

Danil bent and scratched behind its ears until its eyes rolled in pleasure. "Time to move on to the next snare." He smiled fondly at his friend. "Coming?"

Hafryn stretched and shook the dust from his russet coat.

Osriele broke off her work nearby. "A few more should be enough," she said. "I dare not drain my ring to nothing."

Danil nodded and wondered if Gethin had spoken to her. "I'll keep going a bit longer."

Osriele eyed him contemplatively. "Portalling us here should have drained you beyond all reckoning, Danil, and yet you show no sign of tiring. You truly do have an enchanter's power. It seems quite incomprehensible considering your Roldaerian heritage."

Danil couldn't explain it. Being so far from Kailon, he'd expected his ability to create enchantments to be on the wane. But his House glyph glowed as brightly now as it did when he dipped his hand into the kiandrite wellspring.

Osriele gazed out over the distant marshes. "I admit I've fought your words, Danil. Our teas and tinctures are what have fed the magi for centuries. It's difficult to change simply because a companion wishes it so."

Danil eyed her curiously. "What do you wish for Roldaer, then?" Despite how Osriele had risked everything to protect the kingdom, he wasn't going to help her return things to how they once were.

She laughed suddenly. "I wish for fewer peasants so intent on turning the kingdom on its head!" She shook her head, smiling. "No, in truth, I know the magi have lost the right to stand at King Liam's side—and Roldaer's as well. When all this is done, should I survive, I'll speak to my cousin and see to it that the Magi Council is no more."

The air suddenly shimmered as Hafryn transformed. His green eyes held dark shadows of grief, but something close to hope shone there as well. "You'd really do that, Osriele?"

Her smile grew heavy. "I must. Those who support Kaul reside in the highest echelons of the Magi Council. I won't hear tales of them being coerced to the dread lord's will— not when I've seen for myself what true coercion looks like." Her gaze fell meaningfully to the amulet. "And yet you still resist him, Hafryn."

Hafryn swallowed, paling slightly. "I try."

"What of your need for kiandrite?" Danil asked the magus.

"We can't all take Amasian lovers, Danil," Osriele said with a playful smile.

Danil suddenly laughed. "Hafryn has many desirable qualities, but he's no enchanter. If you truly wish to be done with forcing kiandrite for your spells, Sonnen may be willing to help."

"The dragon prince?" Osriele blinked. "Why would he take such a risk?"

"Roldaer's leylines need safeguarding if kiandrite is to ever thrive here again," Danil said. "Sonnen can give you access to the great libraries of Corros and help your people defend and nurture the land once again."

"Do you really think mage-crystals can return to Roldaer?"

Danil felt the weight of his pouch. "They never left, Osriele."

She nodded, expression contemplative. Then her gaze lifted. "Ah, Merlias has returned."

The blue-tipped owl glided over the still waters of the marshes before transforming mid-flight. Merlias landed with a rolling flourish.

"Show off," Hafryn muttered.

The Eyrie enchanter ignored him and straightened her

tunic. "You've all been busy. I could smell enchantments on the wind for miles."

Startled, Danil said, "Will Kaul realize what we're doing?"

"Perhaps, or he'll assume we're desperate—which we are," Merlias added with a humorless curl of her lips.

"Seen Kaul, have you?" Osriele asked.

Merlias nodded, her mouth tightening. "At the head of the Roldaerian army, no less. They'd already passed the crossroad outside Camrin by the time I spotted it."

"The army is coming *here*?" Osriele lowered the snare she held in shock.

Danil's stomach dropped.

"Unnecessary, in my view. A few selasi would be enough to overrun us," Merlias said. "Kaul must think Nera is with us. He'll have learned in the Great War to never underestimate a raging dragon."

Blood draining from his face, Danil asked, "How long do we have?"

"A day at most before the front battalions are here. Magi have spelled the soldiers to march without rest."

Osriele cursed softly under her breath.

"We can't expect any chance of help," Merlias continued. "The nearest village is three days on horseback, and they don't look the sort to be interested in fighting a dread lord."

Hafryn folded his arms. "If we flee, we'll be overrun."

Osriele shook her head. "Danil's plan still holds true. At least we can control how Kaul and his creatures' approach."

Unspoken was the reality that they were all unlikely to survive.

Sighing, Osriele added, "I'd best tell Selen. She's mostly accepted our decision to hold fast here, but the news will be a blow all the same."

They watched her stride for the hill and use an animal trail to climb between the rocks.

Turning to Merlias, Danil said, "Thank you for warning us. I don't expect you to stay and share our fate."

"You actually mean it, don't you?" She laughed. "You don't wish to see me dead."

Danil shrugged and gave the enchanter a half smile. "Not recently, at least."

It was true, he realized. Over the trials of the past few days, he'd come to see her as more than someone who exchanged poisonous barbs and enchantments designed to inflict suffering.

Merlias suddenly clasped his hand. The House glyph of Kailon grew warm between them. She grinned sharply. "I like you, too, custodian."

"Thanks, I think," Danil uttered, wondering if she were somehow sun-crazed or exhausted from her travels.

Smirking, Merlias withdrew her hand. A momentary imprint of the Kailon House glyph showed on her palm before it faded. Seeing that Danil had noticed, she winked and took flight, fluttering so close that both Danil and Hafryn had to duck.

Heart thundering, Danil watched the owl wheel back toward the hill. "What just happened?"

Hafryn shook his head bemusedly. "I have no idea."

FOR THE REST of the day, they made preparations. Danil took his turn checking the glyphs and spells that formed a net around the hill to ensnare anything that would sneak up on them. He often had company on his walks, with either Hafryn or Gethin at his side. To his surprise, Gethin showed him how to twist long reeds together into string for the snares, and in return the corporal sat back and quietly watched when Danil strengthened his work with tiny glyphs inscribed onto dirt and sticks. Long lines of twine became sharp enough to cut skin, while patches of ground turned to taffy. Other snares were bright fireballs waiting to explode. Danil hoped it would all be enough.

When he asked about whether they should use pits or trenches, Gethin shrugged.

"Save your enchantments," the corporal said patiently. "Protecting the camp is the best we can do. But you should also find a place to hide your crystal—somewhere no one else can be forced to speak of under torture."

He chilled at Gethin's calm demeanor.

The Roldaerian crystal murmured in the back of his mind, curious about his activities. Its steady mumblings were an ancient, brassy note, so unlike the frolicking nature of Kailon's leylines. By habit, Danil felt his gaze pulled west towards Kailon. Relief burned through him now that Kaul's army had turned toward him instead, but he knew that Kailon's reprieve would be only temporary.

Danil scrubbed a hand over his scalp in frustration.

A low whistle made him glance up. Hafryn took his turn atop the tallest boulder, his body a dark outline against the sun. He pointed north.

Danil squinted. Black dust plumed in the distance. "Is that the army?"

Gethin nudged his shoulder and said tersely, "Let's get back to camp."

They clambered up the water-smoothed side of the outcrop, following the trail made by rock hoppers. From the better vantage point, Danil could see something large moving amidst the black dust.

"It's not the army," Commander Selen said, taking up her spear. "Or selasi."

Gethin clambered atop a boulder with his bow in hand. "It's damn big, commander."

It ate up the distance separating them. Danil caught flashes of hard, spiked quills and reptilian skin rising out of the dust. Then a terrible roar echoed across the marshes.

"It'll be on us in short order," Hafryn said as he slid off the tallest boulder to stand beside Danil.

"Prepare yourselves," Selen ordered as she unsheathed her sword.

The creature was easily five times taller than any man, its scaled girth rivaling that of Sonnen in his dragon form. Blue-black, pebbled skin looked impossibly hard to penetrate. As it opened its powerful, reptilian maw to release a guttural roar, Danil saw teeth so massive they could easily bite a person in half.

"Holy gods," Hafryn gasped.

It hit the first line of snares, clawed feet stomping. Fiery columns of dirt flew into the air, spearing the reptile. Dirt rained across the boulders with a hiss, making everyone duck low.

The creature staggered only a few steps and released a weird, rasping sort of cackle.

"It's laughing," Gethin noted, perturbed.

Hafryn cursed. "I've brought Kaul's creature straight to us."

"You can't know that," Danil snapped. "It likely senses the Roldaerian crystal."

Hafryn seemed not to hear him, gaze grimly fixed upon the massive, reptilian creature.

Merlias' blue-tipped owl twirled and spun over the creature and dropped a wave of glyphs. They struck its scaled brow with puffs of flaming light, but did little more than make the reptile shake its head in irritation. It swiped the air, barely missing Merlias. She spun low, whirling free wide of its grasping claws.

"Its hide is too thick," Gethin said as he hefted his bow and drew a bead on the reptile. "The snares won't hold it back for long."

"Its purpose must be to clear the way for Kaul," Osriele agreed grimly.

A sprawling line of darkness spread out across the horizon.

Kaul's army, Danil realized.

"Time to retreat," Commander Selen said, motioning to Gethin.

Hafryn shook his head. "Retreat to where, commander? We can't outrun the creature. And even if we could, do we abandon the last crystal of Roldaer?"

Danil fished the crystal from his pouch. It was soft pink in his hands but turned an uncertain yellow when it spied the creature.

A greedy bellow reached them. The reptile tore through another line of enchantments, uncaring at how they spat and tore at its legs and underbelly.

Merlias reeled overhead, glyphs falling from above. The reptile lashed its tail and hurled spiked quills into the sky. Merlias dove, wings tucked close to her body as she twisted away from the first quill but scored a slicing blow from another.

She plummeted.

"*No!*" Hafryn cried when Merlias crashed to the ground in the shadow of the reptile's leg. She lay still, wing visibly askew.

"Come on, wolf," Commander Selen said.

She skittered down the smooth rocks and boulders with Hafryn close on her heels.

The reptile watched their approach with beady, hungry eyes.

Cursing, Danil raced to the far side of the boulders and skidded down the side trail, coming out under the overhang. He raised the crystal high. Light from his House glyph refracted through it.

"Over here!" he yelled.

The massive reptile let out a frenzied roar and thundered toward him. Hafryn and Selen dove out of the way.

Danil turned and ran. The ground bucked and shivered as the reptile gave chase. His lungs burned and legs pumped as he leaped over a series of boulders and splashed across shallow water pooling at the base of the rocks. The reptile tramped after him, hissing.

Danil raised the crystal and *pushed*. Blinding light rocketed upwards.

The reptile lurched back with a shrill cry and scratched at its eyes.

Danil sprinted, breath rattling. He dove behind a hummock of reeds and hid amidst the wilted blades. Cold mud seeped through his tunic and breeches.

The reptile straightened, head upraised to sniff the air.

Holding his breath, Danil waited to see if the creature sensed the Roldaerian crystal in his fist, half submerged in the mud.

It stomped closer. The reeds shivered.

In the sky above its thorny shoulder, a speck of darkness formed and steadily grew larger. More specks joined the first.

No... Danil's heart thundered.

They couldn't fight off the reptile much less whatever new hell flew towards them.

Atop the hill, Osriele shouted and pointed.

Then Danil spotted it—*wings!*

They shone wide and luminous in the sunlight. One set flashed gold.

Danil half-rose, gaping as hope warred with disbelief.

Sonnen...

Five dragons shot toward them, each carrying large, square boxes. From experience, Danil knew each box would hold dozens of Amasians.

Hafryn's red wolf suddenly barreled into Danil, sending him tumbling across the reedbed. Dirty water sprayed over them as the reptile stomped where Danil crouched only heartbeats before.

Hafryn transformed and bodily heaved him to his feet. "*Run, damn you!*"

Lurching out of the mud, Danil sprinted back toward the granite boulders. The reptile's shadow spread over them, followed by a roar so loud that it stabbed bright pain through Danil's ears. Hafryn spun and leaped, swords cutting through the air. The blows scarcely marked the creature's scaled flesh, though it howled as if mortally stuck.

Fire suddenly roiled across its back in a heady plume. The reptile turned to face the new threat, only for twin fireballs to strike its chest and shoulder with staggering force.

Golden scales filled Danil's vision before he was swept off his feet with Hafryn and lifted up by powerful talons. The ground rapidly dropped away, and Danil cheered as Sonnen flew them to the hill.

The golden dragon deposited them on the rock and transformed.

"Stay here," Sonnen barked, golden eyes blazing. He swept past Osriele, who stood frozen in shock, and launched off the edge amidst sparks of golden light.

A battalion of Amasian enchanters spilled out of large carrying crates set down by the other dragons. Large cats, wolves and bears sprinted unflinchingly toward the reptile as gold, green and blue dragons pummeled it from above. Owls and eagles ducked and weaved, offering additional defense to the boars, snakes and badgers that set up a ring around Danil and his companions.

Bombarded by dragon fire and enchantments, the reptile recoiled with a shriek. It reeled about and lumbered for the marshes leading to the blackening horizon.

Landing atop it, Sonnen's golden dragon unleashed a jarring roar, white fire exploding. Heat prickled Danil's skin as the scorching blaze pierced the reptile's skin and burned deep.

It squealed, staggering wildly. Sonnen's powerful talons wrenched its head back and mercilessly ripped open its scaly throat.

Putrid black blood gushed across the soil. The golden dragon flew free with a powerful flap of its wings.

In the sudden quiet, Danil nearly staggered in relief.

A large hand gripped his shoulder and steadied him.

"Easy, custodian," Blutark said behind him. "You're with friends now."

With a cry, Danil whirled and hugged the bear shifter. Blutark chuckled in his ear and returned his grasp before reaching out to clutch Hafryn's arm in greeting.

"Gods, are we glad to see you!" Hafryn blurted, laughing.

Running up the animal trail, Elania grinned so brightly that the snow leopard Trueform slinking beside her practically glowed iridescent. "I knew if we followed Kailon's little trail of kiandrite energy it would lead to you both! A custodian is always connected to their House. Should have realized the Roldaerian army would be on your heels as well."

Danil embraced her, relief so powerful it lumped in his throat.

Sonnen's golden dragon landed close by amidst whirling dust. He transformed and took in the milieu below. Sour, rancid air already floated up from the reptile's oozing corpse. Gaze sweeping across to take in Gethin standing warily in front of a white-faced Osriele, the dragon prince shook his head at Danil.

"What have you gotten us into this time, custodian?" he rumbled.

27

By nightfall, the steady beat of drums officially announced the presence of the Roldaerian army. Sentries returned with reports of the army setting camp on the horizon, with campfires producing dots of light across the horizon.

The unrelenting drumbeats served as a counterpoint to the incessant buzzing of flies on the reptile's carcass a few hundred feet from camp. The breeze swept its putrid stink over the tallest boulders until an enchanter set up a shielding wall to block out the worst of the smell. Others set about fixing tents amidst the boulders and the dry expanse of ground directly in front of the hills.

Danil found Merlias in the healer's tent with Elania by her side. Iridescent glyphs floated over the Eyrie enchanter, showering flecks of healing light over her shattered bones and grazed skin. She appeared fragile in a way Danil struggled to reconcile with the fierce woman he knew her to be. The reptile had very nearly killed her, and Danil supposed it was only dumb luck she still lived.

As if sensing his stare, Merlias opened baleful eyes. "I'm not dead yet, custodian."

Her surly words sent a jolt of relief through him. Settling on his knees beside her pallet, he asked Elania, "She'll make it, then?"

Elania smiled benignly. "A full recovery if Merlias refrains from transforming for a few days."

Merlias rolled her eyes. "There's an army that plans to swarm right over this hill. I intend to deliver the reckoning the magi so richly deserve."

Giving Danil a wink, Elania said, "Bedrest for today, at least, Merlias. Your ribs were nearly crushed."

The Eyrie enchanter muttered something under her breath but settled deeper into the pillows. Her mouth tightened with pain, but she glowered with hostility. "What were you thinking, trying to lure that monster from me? That foolishness could have cost us everything."

Startled, Danil said, "I couldn't just stand by and let the creature kill you."

But Merlias said harshly, "Now Kaul knows you'll risk losing the crystal if given the right incentive. He'll use it against you."

Danil resisted folding his arms. "Maybe so, but it also tells him that I'll do everything in my power to protect those important to me."

"Myself included, custodian?" Merlias gave him a withering look. "Sweet talk doesn't suit you."

Danil huffed a sigh.

"I'm burning with questions but I dare not ask," Elania said as she looked between them. The last time Danil had mentioned Merlias to her, it hadn't been with affection. "Sonnen will merely have you retell it."

"Then have him come in here, by all means," Merlias

replied curtly. "As Councilor Viren's representative, I won't be sidelined because of a few scratches."

Amusement tilting her mouth, Elania stood. "I'll go fetch him, then, before the sedative in your drinking water wears off."

Merlias sniffed and made a shooing motion.

Watching Elania leave the tent, Danil said, "That was rude. Elania's a powerful healer and enchanter in her own right—and my friend."

"People from the House of Corros irk me," Merlias muttered, fussing with her blankets.

"Too pure and earnest for you, Eyrie?"

Merlias gave him a flat look. "Fairly gives me a rash."

Danil chuckled.

The tent flap pulled back as Elania returned with Sonnen, Hafryn and Blutark. To Danil's surprised, Osriele, Selen and Gethin also joined them.

Blutark enchanted a ring of seating around Merlias, then poked his head out of the tent and called for tea. Commander Selen and Gethin remained standing behind Osriele, who wore fresh robes no doubt given to her by one of the enchanters outside. Osriele's face firmed with determination as she settled in her chair.

"We've been out setting up a new perimeter around camp," Hafryn said, sitting beside Danil. "How goes it here?"

Danil raised an eyebrow meaningfully at Merlias. "As can be expected."

The Eyrie enchanter pointedly ignored them, her gaze on Sonnen. "Councilor Viren sends his greetings, Dragon Prince Sonnen," she said formally.

Sonnen gave her a steady look. "I'm certain he does, considering I saw him in Kailon only days ago. I left him to oversee matters there," he rumbled.

Danil looked up in surprise. The Eyrie Councilor had earned a lifetime of distrust from both Danil and Hafryn, but much must have happened in their absence for Sonnen to expose Kailon to Viren's slippery intrigues.

If Merlias was similarly surprised, she hid it well. "Then my lord told you of my task in Roldaer."

"He did." Sonnen's eyes blazed. "Viren's arrogance almost cost you dearly, Merlias. I am saddened to see that the burden was placed on Hafryn's shoulders instead."

Merlias grimaced before she stated, "I had my orders, my lord."

Danil glanced at the amulet resting on Hafryn's chest. It was largely quiescent at the moment and seemed to scarcely weigh upon Hafryn at all.

Folding her hands in her lap, Osriele said, "If we are to make plans, perhaps Hafryn should not hear them, given that he's tied to the dread lord now."

Hafryn threw her a startled look. The Amasians in the tent shared scowls and irritated looks.

"I'm sorry Hafryn," Osriele continued. "The amulet quite possibly drew the creature to us. Kaul may well use the amulet for other tasks—he could be listening in right now."

Sonnen gave her a steady, assessing look. "I appreciate your caution, Magus Osriele. We've all had to deal with startling revelations of late. Were it not for the likes of the two magi we left in Corros, much of Amas would not have a clear understanding of what is at stake."

Osriele leaned forward excitedly. "You speak of Magus Bornil and his apprentice."

Sonnen nodded. "They survived the attack on the border. It was their knowledge of the blacksward that finally mobilized the Houses of Amas to join the war effort." He paused, golden eyes turning heavy. "Although, it is clear your Roldaerian friends did not reveal everything about the blacksward."

Raising her chin, Osriele said, "My quest is to destroy the blacksward. That hasn't changed even though I've made some difficult discoveries."

"The perfidy of your fellow mages is no surprise to enemies of the Magi Council, Princess Osriele," Sonnen rumbled. "But I am curious about how much you knew of the method used to create the curse."

"I swear to you, Prince Sonnen, I didn't know that the magi were the ones guilty of spreading the blacksward," Osriele declared. "In truth, I thought it Amasian in nature at first."

Merlias pushed herself upright, cheeks coloring. "It's always Roldaer who destroys that which it doesn't own or deserve! It was with the support of Roldaer that Kaul first destroyed Kailon, and it was Roldaer again who stole from the deadlands even after you befouled it. It'd be fitting for your destruction to be at our hands, but there's no need."

"Enough, Merlias." Sonnen laid a hand upon her shoulder. "Your defense of your new House becomes you, but now is not the time for it."

Merlias glanced at Sonnen in shock before looking at the lightly glowing glyph upon her palm. She clenched her fist.

Sonnen returned his hard gaze to Osriele. "We have learned how the blacksward is created. Many Amasians have suffered a terrible fate. I must know—did you partake in the kidnapping and imprisonment of my people?"

"I—never!" Osriele glanced about hesitatingly, grimacing as she admitted, "Such activities were merely rumors over the years."

"But it is an odd rumor," Sonnen rumbled. "What magus would capture an Amasian if not to kill them?"

"It's possible some private holdings make use of slaves," Osriele admitted. "But, again, it's only rumor. I never thought to look into it."

Gethin glanced at her with obvious dismay.

"Amasian slaves," Hafryn growled. "Because having a frightened and cowed peasantry of your own wasn't enough."

Danil caught his sleeve, sliding his grip down to squeeze Hafryn's hand.

Osriele nodded, mouth tightening. "I have said it before, Hafryn Wolfkind. Magi are deeply flawed. If we survive this, I will do all I can to make amends. I'll see to it that the magi are no more."

Hafryn glowered at her, unappeased, even as Elania and Blutark looked startled by Osriele's declaration.

Sonnen raised a hand. "There will be a reckoning, Hafryn, but it cannot be today. Lady Osriele, your words speak well of you, though we are not done with this conversation. Not every Amasian captive can be accounted for, even with the spread of the blacksward."

"Truly, I'm sorry. I never saw an Amasian slave myself," Osriele said. "But I'll give you every aid possible, Dragon Prince," she vowed.

Sonnen gave a satisfied rumble.

Blowing out an angry huff, Hafryn stood, his cheeks dark. "I need fresh air," he muttered.

Half-rising, Danil said, "Hafryn..."

But Hafryn stalked to the entrance, pulling the flap back with an audible snap.

"Let him be, custodian," Sonnen murmured, tone troubled. "He will return when his distress is not so sharp."

An uncomfortable silence settled over the tent.

Sonnen clapped his hands and turned back to Danil. "I don't believe Elania has had the chance to look you over yet. Are you well, custodian?"

Surprised, Danil nodded. "Better for all of you being here. We were at our luck's end before you came upon us."

Sonnen released a pleased rumble. "You can imagine my surprise when I heard your voice through one of Elania's magelights, Danil. Seeing what you carry now, I believe you used the Roldaerian kiandrite."

Startled, Danil pulled the thumb-sized crystal from his pouch. It blazed a contented mix of greens and pinks. "I didn't know," he murmured.

"That was rather apparent," Sonnen continued, voice meditative. "The conversation I heard was between yourself and another. Something about faith and doubt, I believe." The dragon's golden eyes flicked momentarily to Gethin.

Gethin held the dragon's gaze, unflinching.

A faint smile curved Sonnen's lips. "Be at ease, Corporal Gethin. We share a common desire to protect those in our care."

Danil thought to the previous night and how he'd held the Roldaerian crystal close and promised to keep it safe. Holding the crystal tightly once more, he told Sonnen and the others of what had befallen them since passing through the portal into Aqila. Elania exclaimed in astonishment when he spoke of Nera, while Sonnen shook his head and admitted he had no knowledge of a silver dragon. Continuing, Danil felt his heart ache when he mentioned what Magus Brianna had done to Marama.

"To have endured so much, only to fall at the final hour," Blutark murmured.

"Marama must have been all that remained of the Isfil lodestone," Elania added sadly.

Sonnen rubbed his chin. "It is extraordinary that a remnant of a lodestone could exist in such a form and for so long. Marama must have expended great energy to find you, Danil."

"I'm still unsure why," Danil admitted. "How could she have known where the last Roldaerian crystal was?"

"Her leylines extend deep into the Fens," Elania supposed. "Marama likely kept her last kiandrite hidden for centuries, only for the blacksward to sweep through. She must have been so desperate."

"Probably more desperate than we can imagine, considering Marama did not seek another envoy once Hafryn became ensnared by the amulet," Sonnen rumbled thoughtfully.

Danil felt his frustration rise. "But if all of this stems back to the Great War, how can we know so little about the amulet or Kaul's three acolytes?"

Sonnen placed his hands on his thighs and leaned forward. "Kaul used his *videre* in the Great War to conceal the fighting glyphs of Eyrie. It is possible knowledge of the acolytes was likewise hidden."

Danil straightened excitedly. "If such knowledge exists, we may find something to use against Kaul."

"It depends on how the information was buried," Sonnen said. "All references to the acolytes may well be lost forever." He glanced thoughtfully at Merlias. "However, Viren has admitted that Kaul's former *videre* was an Eyrie. Her knowledge of the amulet may well lie within the Eyrie archives."

Elania nodded, realization brightening her eyes. "And since Danil returned the lost glyphs of Eyrie, he might have unknowingly uncovered lost information regarding the Great War, too."

Danil glanced at the Eyrie enchanter with sharp hope.

Merlias tilted her head. "Our archivists have kept busy with new finds since Danil visited to our lands," she conceded.

"*Visited?*" Danil blurted, unable to help himself.

Merlias smiled a little. "Now that we know what to look for, it's possible the archivists may find something of use."

"Will you join with Elania and send a message to your archivists?" Sonnen asked. "We will need every detail you can spare."

The enchanter nodded. "I prefer to have Hafryn free, also." Noticing everyone's stares, she added with an eyeroll, "It obviously doesn't serve us to have him as Kaul's pawn."

Sonnen took that as agreement. "Elania, please see if you can reach the Eyrie tonight."

Nodding, Elania withdrew from her chair and took to a quiet corner of the tent. She cupped her hands, light filtering up as she whispered.

Watching her for a moment, Osriele turned back to Sonnen. "I admit I don't understand. Why would Kaul seek to repeat certain features of the Great War when he lost?"

Sonnen shook his head. "Kaul was defeated only because of a miscalculation he made regarding the kiandrite lodestone he attempted to enslave. When it rejected him, the deadlands were made and he was believed killed."

Blutark stroked his chin. "But now Kaul's going after the leylines themselves."

"With only a tiny crystal remaining in Roldaer, there's hardly anything left to resist him," Osriele said.

"Except us," Danil said determinedly.

Sonnen smiled. "Except us, custodian."

BUOYED with hope that they may yet free Hafryn of the amulet, Danil made his way to the tent set aside for them both. It was close to a wall of rock offering protection from the wind but still afforded them a view of the approaching army. In the past hours, more flickering lights had come to line the horizon.

Danil paused outside the tent. The dragons had brought in close to a hundred enchanters, and while it heartened him to see so many, he knew staying would surely lead to everyone's deaths. But no amount of cajoling, even by Sonnen, would move the crystal. It seemed determined to live and die within the Fens.

Studying the flickering lights of the Roldaerian army once more, he thought, *We're really in for it this time.*

Stepping into the tent, he froze. The interior was in disarray, the brazier toppled and hot coals hissing on the rocky ground. A small trunk was shattered as if cleaved in half by a blade, the pallet kicked apart.

Hafryn lay slackly unconscious amidst the mess, blood streaming across his face and his sword flung from his grip.

Standing over him was a large, armored man wearing a horned helm and a cloak so dark it sucked in the light. A pestilent-green portal slowly whirled at his side.

Kaul...

The dread lord snapped his gauntleted fingers. Hafryn floated upwards and then toward the green portal.

"No!" Danil cried, leaping.

A solid wall of shadow rippled and struck Danil, sending him flying. He crashed against the central tent pole and collapsed, winded. The shadow fighter braced its feet, ready to pounce once more.

Kaul turned, blue eyes delighted. "My traitorous *videre*! How I grow bored of waiting."

Feeling heat stream into his glyph, Danil pulled himself up to his feet and growled, "Let Hafryn go, Kaul."

Hafryn drifted only a few feet from the portal, his hair floating about his face as if he were submerged in water.

The dread lord laughed. "I think not. There's far too much fun to be had yet!"

Danil raised his hand. "I'm not asking."

Pouting mockingly, the dread lord said, "My last *videre* wasn't nearly so insubordinate. Perhaps I should have made two amulets."

"You'll pay for that mistake," Danil promised.

"I don't think so," Kaul taunted. "I have your beloved, and you'll come for him willingly when the time arises."

The dread lord flicked his hand. Hafryn drifted closer to the green-flamed portal.

Yelling, Danil threw himself after Hafryn. From the corner of his eye he saw the shadow fighter leap into action. But this time Danil was ready. Iridescent light pulsed from his outstretched hand and burned through the shadow. Shrieking filled the tent.

Danil leaped toward the portal and rammed his shoulder into Hafryn's side, tumbling them both free.

But the dread lord was on him in a heartbeat. He gripped Danil's tunic and wrenched him up off his feet. Powerful hands clenched about Danil's throat.

Danil felt the burn of an unfamiliar sigil against his skin. Hot, fetid breath brushed his cheek.

"Show me what I desire, *videre*."

Bright, hot agony pulsed through him. Danil gasped, flailing, and pressed his House glyph to Kaul's wrist.

"The crystal, *videre*." Kaul tightened his grip, choking the air from Danil's lungs. He shook. "Reveal its presence to me!"

A wall of light suddenly exploded between them. Flung back, Danil tumbled across the tent. The light traveled with him, burning bright from his hip where the Roldaerian crystal lay in his pouch.

Snarling, Kaul reached for him.

Outside, shouts of alarm drew close, and the flap of the tent burst apart to reveal Blutark and Sonnen.

Blutark threw one of his enchanted blades with a yell. It struck Kaul in the shoulder, but the dread lord continued with a snarl.

The dread lord threw a glyph to the ground. Black smoke roiled out, rapidly filling the tent.

Danil's nose and throat burned. He coughed, staggering.

"Get back!" Sonnen warned.

In the haze, Danil saw Kaul raise Hafryn's unconscious form off the ground.

"Hafryn!" he choked out dizzily. He lurched after the dread lord as the black smoke thickened until the glowing green portal grew lost in the darkness.

An iridescent glyph landed at Danil's feet. Air whooshed about him, sucking up the sickening smoke. The tent cleared.

The green portal shrank, ready to collapse to nothing. Kaul stood beside it, smirking.

"No!"

Danil desperately threw himself at the dread lord but missed when Kaul stepped into the portal.

Taking Hafryn with him.

28

"Danil, you must wait," Elania pleaded, following him about the tent.

Ignoring her, Danil finished strapping a leather bracer onto his forearm before tucking a dagger into each boot. Blutark watched somberly from his perch on the edge of a chest, hands clasped between his knees. His bear Trueform stood on its hind legs, body a long line of tension. The only person whose presence was a surprise to Danil was Gethin. The Roldaerian corporal wore a mottled tunic and breeches similar to those the protectors of Altonas usually wore. He was cleanshaven with his dark hair woven into a braid at the nape of his neck.

"Custodian!"

Danil gave Elania a hard look. "Don't ask me to do nothing, Elania."

"I would never," Elania replied, hands placating. "But rushing to face Kaul is exactly what he wants."

"He'll do something to Hafryn. I know it."

Elania nodded. "Hafryn shall fight with all of his will.

And he'll take comfort in knowing we're coming for him. But rushing in without a plan will only get us all killed."

Danil swallowed heavily, pulling on his cloak. "You haven't seen what Kaul can do. Hafryn—the amulet steals his resistance and forces him to fight. I've watched him lose more of himself each time. I can't let him face that again!"

Gethin leaned against the central tent pole, his arms folded. "Haring off isn't what Hafryn would want, Danil."

Danil looked at him sourly. "What are you even doing here, Gethin? Hafryn's fate isn't your concern."

Pushing off the pole, Gethin said amiably, "The wolf and I enjoy mutual respect. Unexpected, I must say, but true all the same."

"I'm happy for you," Danil muttered. He shouldered his pack. "Now, don't step in my way."

The tent entrance furled open and Sonnen entered. The dragon prince took in the tense air, pausing only at seeing Gethin among them. He motioned for everyone to leave.

Elania drew close and pressed a quick, comforting kiss to Danil's brow. "We *will* get him back," she promised in his ear.

Danil noted her Trueform watched him, bright lines of iridescence glowing amongst the fur, before she followed Blutark and Gethin out.

Sonnen waited for the sound of footsteps to fade. He clasped his hands behind his back. "Forgive me, Danil. I should have anticipated that Kaul would come for Hafryn."

A hard lump formed in Danil's throat.

"There is no news yet from Eyrie about the amulet. But you should take heed of Elania's words, custodian. Hafryn's love for you burns brightly—brighter than any darkness an enchantment can inflict. Hold onto that."

Exhaustion tugged on Danil's bones. "If it hadn't been

for me, Marama's crystal would still be hidden and Hafryn would never have ended up in the Fens to find the amulet. This is all my fault."

"I do not believe so, Danil of Roldaer and Amas." Sonnen studied him contemplatively. "You have acted admirably for someone whose fate has not been of their own choosing."

Danil looked at him bleakly.

"Both custodian and *videre* were thrust upon your inexperienced shoulders. Perhaps you are indeed Kaul's *videre* like you fear, but you became the custodian of Kailon first. That counts for something, I think."

"What use is it against Kaul?" Danil asked. "He's too powerful."

"Like you, Kaul is of both Roldaer and Amas, although his connection is through his parentage rather than his heart. He hates Amas with every fiber of his being, and finds no belonging with Roldaer unless it is reshaped to his liking. That is weakness, Danil." Flames showed in Sonnen's eyes. "You, however, are the protector and custodian of Kailon. You stand between our two kingdoms."

Danil didn't see how that could possibly matter when they were so far from Kailon now. "But how—?"

A familiar tinkling sound made them turn as a glass orb forced its way through the tent entrance. It was unaffected by protective glyphs snapping at it, and instead floated to where Danil and Sonnen stood in the firelight. Alarmed shouts came from outside.

"It's a glory sphere," Danil said in recognition as it slowed to a halt before him. "Magi use them to communicate with each other."

Sonnen said, "I have seen such spells before."

Two enchanters rushed into the tent, their hands weaving iridescent glyphs.

Sonnen made a calming motion. "All is well, my friends. We shall deal with our unexpected visitor."

The enchanters eyed the glass orb suspiciously but backed outside.

Reaching out, Danil touched the cold glass. It shattered into fragments that fell about his boots. But instead of a rolled parchment like Danil expected, a dot of light floated in front of him, carrying a voice that stretched out across the distance.

"*Videre*," Magus Brianna cooed. "You know what our lord demands."

Glaring at the bobbing light, Danil growled, "I'm going to kill you, Brianna."

Her disembodied laughter filled the tent. "An empty threat from a pawn fast ending his usefulness! The same can't be said for your wolf lover, however."

Cold threaded his veins. "What are you doing to him? I swear, if you hurt him—" Danil snarled, unable to stop himself.

"Bring the Roldaerian crystal to us, or witness what happens when Kaul makes blacksward from his Harbinger."

Dread coiled within Danil.

"Begin your march now—I'm sure you can find us," Brianna said gaily. "Our Great Lord has waited a long time, *videre*, and he is fast out of patience."

Sonnen drew close, his lip curling. "Set Hafryn free first, magus."

Brianna laughed again. "I thought I saw the dragon prince fly over us! I'll wear your skin for slippers, Sonnen. There are no flames or enchantments strong enough to protect you."

"You are welcome to try," Sonnen growled.

"Then I'll see you tomorrow, also," Brianna said gaily.

The point of light dropped to the ground and sputtered out.

Danil fought not to tremble. "They're going to kill Hafryn."

Sonnen shook his head. "Brianna might wish it, but Kaul is not nearly so done with him. There is hope yet."

"How can you know that?" A desperate rage filled him. Marama had entrusted him with her final crystal, and yet Danil could well lose everything if he fulfilled her task. But was no world worth living in without Hafryn.

"Take heart, Danil. Kaul fears you."

Danil released a disbelieving snort.

"You have entrapped him once before and become that which he could never be—a true enchanter of Roldaer and Amas. The leylines speak to you in a way I've not seen before. Kaul is right to be afraid. Use that against him."

He had no idea how to do that, and they were fast out of time. Swallowing, Danil gathered his resolve. "They both die, Sonnen. Kaul and Brianna cannot live."

"I will help you, Danil," Sonnen vowed, raising the House glyph of Corros on his palm. It brightened with the strength of his words. "And we will not go alone."

29

Dawn cast orange and pink light across the marshlands as large felines, bears, horses and grouse marched toward the Roldaerian army. Danil strode among the Amasians who stayed in their human forms, together with Osriele, the commander and Gethin. The air hummed with enchantments.

Scarcely a mile separated them from the Roldaerian army now. This close, Danil could make out the individual battalions of soldiers. Robed magi corralled nervous conscripts in mismatched armor to the head of the army, clearly preparing to send them in early against the Amasians.

Danil released a slow, pent up breath.

He saw no sign of Hafryn or his captors.

The Amasians paused on a strip of flat mud between large hummocks of sedges and grasses. Battle on such terrain would be dangerous, but there was no other choice. Merlias, having stubbornly ignored Elania's protests that she needed to rest, flew overhead with a squad of eagles.

She stood out palely amidst the darker birds, and Danil was strangely relieved to see her.

"We make our stand here," Sonnen said, raising his fist. Both human and Trueform enchanters spread out, iridescent glyphs flitting through the air.

Commander Selen planted her spear into the mud in front of Osriele and drew her sword.

The magus looked pale as she gazed across at the waiting Roldaerian army. "I recognize some faces, Prince Sonnen. The firemages won't have much success in the marshes, but the cursethrowers are another matter."

Sonnen motioned to his archers to get ready. Among them was Gethin with an Amasian wayfarer bow in his grip. Tiny inscribed glyphs glowed across the polished wood. Danil had watched him practice with a handful of enchanters the night before—in every melee they'd experienced together, he'd not had time to appreciate the corporal's unwavering manner but was glad of it now.

"I still don't see Hafryn," Blutark said. "Nor Kaul and his bitch High Priestess."

Danil glanced past the quailing rows of conscripts to the main army. Thousands of trained soldiers stood in ready formation. An eager air of anticipation hung over them, and Danil could easily understand why when he glanced about at the meager hundred or so Amasians standing with him. On account of sheer numbers, he and his companions would be quickly overrun.

Cupping her hands, Elania released a ball of light. It bobbed and dipped over to Danil.

Danil steeled himself and strode into the puddles beyond the line of Amasians. "Kaul!" His voice rang out far louder than normal. "Show yourself!"

The Roldaerian army grew quiet for a moment before

taking up jeers and battle cries, their boots stomping the mud and dirty water. Only the ragged conscripts showed little fervor, instead huddling close together.

Undaunted, Danil continued to stride toward the army, the light bobbing after him. "The leylines will never be yours! If I am your *videre*, then all I see is your doom!"

The battle cries reached a new, fevered pitch.

Coming to a halt between the two opposing forces, Danil removed Marama's crystal from his pouch and held it up high. Light from his House glyph flooded through it like a beacon.

"If you want this, Kaul, come pry it from my dead fingers!"

The shouts fell away to low murmurs as iridescent light reached the Roldaerians. Some raised their hands as if to touch the changing rays.

But then the ragged conscripts shuffled apart, making room for a new creature.

Danil's heart stuttered.

Adorned in black battle armor with spikes planted along his shoulders and arm guards, Kaul rode languidly atop a massive, helmed creature. Growls reverberated through the space between them. At Kaul's signal, the creature loped toward Danil, the full whites of its eyes supplemented by a glowing feral orange. It took Danil a moment to recognize the russet fur and long snout. A golden amulet with blue gems hung from the giant animal's neck.

Hafryn...

Hot fury flooded Danil. His fist clenched over the crystal, blocking out its light.

Stopping in front of him, Kaul patted the red wolf's neck and smirked. "I agree to your terms, *videre*."

30

The giant red wolf growled deep in its throat and drew closer to Danil. Nothing in its eyes said Hafryn recognized him.

Danil took a careful step back.

"You can defy me no longer, *videre*," Kaul observed. "Give me the stone and I will spare you the indignity of dying under your beloved's fangs."

Ignoring the dread lord, Danil showed the wolf his House glyph. "You know me, Hafryn," he entreated softly. "Come back to me."

Under the dark helm, the wolf's low, ferocious growl continued unabated.

Kaul grinned. "Sentimentality only hastens your fate." He set his fingers to his lips and whistled.

Robed figures shoved their way through the Roldaerian conscripts, their voices deep and guttural as chanted spells took shape. Danil sensed movement behind him as enchanters pressed forward. Glyphs shot overhead.

Ducking low, Danil's gaze was drawn once more to Marama's crystal. He didn't understand why Kaul didn't simply take it. His gaze narrowed. "You know it will reject you," he realized, gaze snapping back to the dread lord. "You hate Amas, but it's Roldaer who rejects you—down to the very last crystal!"

Kaul's face convulsed. "It cannot defy me when you are dead." He drove his fist into Hafryn's side.

The giant red wolf charged across the mud toward Danil, eyes glowing with unfathomable hate.

Danil skidded, ducking under a powerful swipe. He got tangled in a stand of reeds but scrambled to his feet once more.

Kaul laughed uproariously and patted Hafryn's neck. "It's impolite to play with your food, Harbinger!" he chortled. "Retrieve the crystal first, at least!"

Danil refused to draw his blade. Somewhere within the giant wolf, Hafryn still remained. The amulet was bitterly bright, the blue gems afire as the wolf loped after him.

Splashing through muddy water, Danil spared a quick glance at the surrounding fighting. Dragons screamed fire at the army from overhead, holding back the main force while magi ducked through the flames to engage with Amasian enchanters. Osriele was in the thick of it, beating back former colleagues with a barrage of curses. Danil pitied the woman then, understanding the turmoil that she must feel at fighting against her own people.

Powerful claws raked across Danil's back. He cried out and stumbled into the water.

A heavy weight pounced atop him and drove him beneath the surface.

Danil gouged his fingers into the mud, desperate to heave the wolf off but was unable to budge an inch. Choking on gritty water, Danil flailed but only sunk deeper. Terrified, he realized he'd drown.

Suddenly dragged out of the water, he skidded across a reedbed before coming to a halt in the mud.

The monstrous red wolf stood a few feet away, furiously shaking its head as if confused.

Kaul rolled to his feet, having been bucked free of the black saddle. Wrath coiled around him like a cloak.

Merlias stood behind the oversized wolf, her hand still raised. An iridescent symbol blazed on Hafryn's red fur in the shape of the Kailon House glyph. The Eyrie enchanter met Danil's gaze and nodded grimly before taking to the sky.

More of the Roldaerian army joined in the fray. Blutark, Elania and a handful of enchanters rushed past, hands weaving as they met a new wave of magi. The air shimmered as one enchanter transformed mid-step into a massive green dragon. Fireballs cleared a path all the way back to the cowering conscripts.

A flash of irritation crossed Kaul's face. He hissed something unintelligible and thrust it upon Hafryn. The wolf shuddered, letting out a pained whine as it pawed at the amulet about its neck.

"Obey me, Harbinger," Kaul growled and cast a new curse.

The internal struggle drained from the red wolf's body. He straightened, slitted eyes fixed on Danil.

Before Danil could stagger away, the wolf was on him once more. A giant paw stomped on his chest and belly. Danil cried out under the crushing weight. Hot breath brushed his cheek and Danil blinked up into glowing eyes bereft of green.

"Hafryn," he rasped out, struggling to wedge him off.

"Take the crystal, Harbinger," Kaul commanded, hand outstretched. "Bring it to me!"

Fire suddenly struck the dread lord from behind. It consumed his cloak in a roar of flames, but Kaul quelled it with a slashing motion and then turned to face the new threat.

Osriele braced her feet, teeth bared. "Your reign over my people ends, dread lord!" She shouted a new spell and flung it.

With a negligent swipe, Kaul sent the spell spinning into the nearby fighters. Cries of pain came from amidst the flames. The dread lord unleashed another curse, turning his full attention on Osriele.

Red cords of agony wrapped around Osriele. She cried out and fell to her knees. Her fingers convulsed as she tried to form a spell.

Gethin pressed desperately through the melee to reach her, unaware of the firemage stalking behind him. But then Elania's snow leopard leaped over him and tore open the firemage's throat. Commander Selene was on her heels, spear driving through another enemy.

Kaul stalked to where Osriele knelt trembling. He crouched, his smile oily as he gripped her hand. He twisted, bones crunching as he wrenched the rubied kiandrite ring from her finger. "Thank you for your aid, princess."

Osriele gasped, eyes watering from the pain, and tried desperately to wrench free of the binding spell.

Done with her, Kaul rose. "Attend me, High Priestess."

Boots tramped in front of Danil's vision before he saw a red cloak and grey-streaked dark hair. Magus Brianna muttered a few strange words, hands weaving. Shadows burst free and whirled around Kaul before settling over the ring.

Smirking, Kaul donned the ring.

Danil's vision flickered. Tendrils of reddened shadow

and iridescent light coiled around the dread lord, twisting and shivering in a tortured dance. It reminded Danil of kiandrite and blacksward warring with each other, of Amas and Roldaer at odds for centuries. As a halfbreed, Kaul embodied the people of both kingdoms.

But so do I, Danil reminded himself.

He suddenly understood what Sonnen meant the evening before. Roldaer and Amas might be in conflict, but it didn't have to be so. Beneath the surface of each kingdom was the one thing that united them all.

Leylines...

One needed only to connect them.

Kaul strode toward him, the red kiandrite ring glittering darkly. "You finally see my purpose, *videre*. The lands will be united again." He raised the ring. "I need only bind a crystal of Amas with the last crystal of Roldaer."

But the Amasian kiandrite of Osriele's ring had become so tortured by centuries of magi coercion that it would irreparably taint Marama's crystal. That taint would travel through the empty leylines of Roldaer and spill into Kailon and Amas, poisoning them all.

Danil couldn't let that happen. He had no crystal of Amas, but he did have Kailon. Perhaps he could—

Searing pain rocked through his side as talons clawed the pouch from his belt. Marama's crystal tumbled free.

"No!" Danil cried. He thrashed, fingers raking out toward it.

Fangs snapped the air inches from his arm.

Kaul laughed. "Excellent, Hafryn!" He scooped up the crystal and held it aloft. It quailed dull orange in his grip. "You may bear witness, *videre*."

Throwing back his head, Kaul shouted out a terrible curse and slammed the two crystals together. Hot red malevolence spewed over Marama's crystal, consuming all light.

Enchanters and magi alike fell back with cries of alarm.

Shrieks and tortured screams filled Danil's mind. Desperation tightened his throat. He needed to be free to stop the unfolding disaster.

Desperate, Danil reached up and blindly grabbed the amulet chained about Hafryn's throat. Burning agony seared through him. He screamed out but refused to let go. The Kailon glyph on his palm brightened like the sun, sending forth tendrils of iridescent light.

In his hand, the amulet shuddered, the crack in the bottom widening to reveal an unexpected shimmer of iridescence.

Kiandrite!

In Kaul's arrogance, he had created the amulet with the one thing that Danil could call upon for help. Hidden behind layers of curses and yet protected from the amulet itself, the crystal sang a greeting to Danil.

Help us! Danil cried desperately.

The crystal oscillated pink and determined dark blue. *You must be the bridge*, it whispered back. *Reconnect that which was torn apart.*

Suddenly, Danil knew what to do.

The wolf attempted to pull away, but this time the strength was all Danil's. He felt his fingers punch through the amulet, shattering it to pieces as his hand clenched around the kiandrite. His other hand found russet fur and warm skin. He gripped tight. The tendrils of light curled about them both, pulsing and spreading like roots of a tree.

Amas, Kailon and Roldaer joined as one.

The iridescent light speared into the dirt and from there spread rapidly. Danil felt himself and Hafryn shunted across the miles, through damp soil and desert sand, pushing up between rocks and mountains, skimming under lakes and basking in dappled sunlight. The youthful song of Kailon swelled around them then, together with the ancient murmurs of Corros and Eyrie. The poisoned shadows of Altonas pulled them further, drawing him and Hafryn to the grieving crystal of Aqila and beneath the blacksward chewing through Isfil.

Danil and Hafryn whirled within it all. Contained within the light, they seared through the shadowed poison, stitching together fragmented pockets of radiance until all the lands melded together in a tangled, luminous thread. Danil felt the moment the last tendrils connected, unified once more.

A clarion tolled and called them back.

Opening his eyes, Danil saw only verdant green. Blinking, he found Hafryn atop him, eyes wide and wondering.

"*Fala,*" Hafryn breathed, pressing their foreheads together.

Danil wrapped his arms around him, eyes watering in relief.

The amulet lay shattered on the ground beside them, smoldering. A few feet away, Kaul held aloft the merged crystal of Amas and Roldaer. He turned his face from the joyful, iridescent light as if it burned him. The tortured red of the Amasian crystal was no more, replaced with the gentle trills of kiandrite reconnected with its homeland.

Kaul's fist shook. He threw the merge crystal aside with a snarl, skin blistered.

The dread lord took a step back, diminished somehow. He commanded a curse, flinging it at the merged crystal but it was unfettered by the attack, intent instead on the leylines unfurling deep below the mud.

Enchanters, sensing his new weakness, stalked toward the dread lord. Magus Brianna flung herself in front of the bewildered halfbreed and drew up a pestilent-green shield.

Sonnen's golden dragon landed in a billow of wind before he transformed. "Do not interfere," he ordered the enchanters. "The leylines have chosen their avatars."

Danil felt iridescent power flood through him. Sparks cascaded from his fingers. Hafryn rose bemusedly beside him, arms folded while his wolf Trueform was immersed in pure light.

Snarling, Kaul said, "You are my acolytes. Mine to command!"

"You are wrong, dread lord," Sonnen said. "They are what you could never be—the bridge between Amas and Roldaer. The lines of power between our lands are intertwined once more."

Kaul sneered over the pestilent shield. "All the easier to corrupt, then."

"They are forever closed to you now, Kaul Mage-Kin," Sonnen stated.

With a snarling grin, Kaul said, "We shall see, dragon. Priestess, now!" he yelled before Brianna jumped in front of him, arms spread wide. A foul green light formed around her and the dread lord. A blast of wind rocked everyone back.

Danil lowered his arm to see the pair gone.

Not this time!

He called to the leylines about him, letting power sing through him. The world had endured enough of the dread lord and his dark priestess.

"Danil, wait!" Hafryn yelled.

The leylines whirled around Danil like a thousand dancing torches.

'*Let's end this,*' he said to them.

'*Agreed,*' the leylines belled.

He immersed himself in their will and was carried away.

CRUMBLING rock fell all about him. Danil instinctively crouched as the groan of collapsing buildings made him look skyward.

The Magi Tower lurched dangerously from side to side. Its recognizable red dome was already gone, together with a significant portion of the upper levels. Thick blocks of stone lay strewn across the courtyard, with more falling in a roar of dust and clattering debris. The place looked hurriedly abandoned by guards, with swords and spears cast aside.

Shadows moved at the corner of his eye, and Danil whirled to see Kaul and Magus Brianna take the dangerous journey between the falling stones toward the columned portal at the far end of the courtyard.

"Kaul!"

Kaul whirled, snarling. "Meddlesome *videre!* You should not have come alone." He stalked toward Danil, snapping out curses that brushed over Danil as if they were nothing but gossamer silk.

"My Lord, we must flee!" Magus Brianna yelled, looking between Kaul and the quiet pillars.

"Attend me, High Priestess." Pale lips curling, Kaul snapped his fingers.

Brianna stiffened like a marionette and took rigid steps toward them. Dark tendrils corded between Kaul and Brianna, feeding power between them.

"So that's how your abilities returned," Danil said to Brianna in realization. "He gave you some of his power! The leylines continue to deny you their magic!"

Magus Brianna sweated, gritting out, "A blessing from the Great Lord to his High Priestess."

But with the magic of the leylines thrumming within him, Danil could sense that both the dread lord and his acolyte were vastly drained of their former strength. At any moment, he knew Kaul would use the cord to steal back the last remnants of Brianna's power.

Danil mentally reached for the darkness tethering the pair together and *twisted*. The tendril snapped like a dried twig.

Brianna shrieked in outraged pain, hand outstretched as if to clasp the destroyed tendril. She looked to Kaul for succor.

But the dread lord ignored her, teeth bared as he rounded the last stone block separating him from Danil. "You dare to steal from me. The leylines are *mine*." He snarled a curse.

Raging red spears battered against Danil, lashing his skin.

But the leylines immediately washed over him like a cool, healing balm. Iridescent light burst through the cracked stone about their boots.

Danil smiled in welcome before returning his gaze to the halfbreed. "You can't own something that is part of us all, Kaul. The leylines will not be controlled, and there are consequences for those who attempt to use them by force."

The leylines swelled through the cracks, rising like a wave and rushing over the courtyard to where Kaul stood.

The dread lord stepped back, mouth dropping.

The wave blasted over him, burning and eating through the

shadows. Kaul shielded his face, unleashing a terrible howl. The light burned through him, pushing through the darkness. In desperation, the dread lord raised his hand, attempting to pull the tortured crystals of the Magi Tower's portal stones to him. They flickered though, and in the surging light of the leylines reverted to their iridescent nature and rebuffed him.

The dread lord cried out, fear in his eyes as his power was stripped from him. The leylines seared beyond his flesh and bones, burning so brightly that Danil was forced to look away.

In a crack of light, Kaul, dread lord of Roldaer and Amas, was no more.

The leylines back eased with a gentle hum of satisfaction, seeping into the cracks like a receding tide.

Danil sucked in sun-sweetened air, his mind filled with the melodic hum of freed kiandrite in the walls and stone all about him.

Magus Brianna stumbled over a block of rubble and wailed in despair. "Curse you, thief!" she shrieked, tears streaming. "I should have killed you with the rest of your pathetic village!"

Danil watched her stagger to where Kaul had last stood. "You and your fellow magi have turned the world upside down in your quest to control the leylines. Now, the leylines will decide your fate."

Iridescent light stirred beneath the soil once more. It spread, seeking out the Roldaerian individuals whose bellies contained the tortured red kiandrite. Finding them, the light sliced through like a blade.

Brianna paled as if sensing what was happening. "No," she gasped. "No!"

"You've robbed Roldaer of both land and comfort," Danil

said. "You would've reduced it to nothing in your quest for power. Now, you and every mage have nothing. You *are* nothing."

The leylines pulsed severed free all connection to the magi of Roldaer. The hot sparks of red kiandrite in the back of Danil's mind fizzled out amidst the anguished cries from the magi.

Never again would the magi be able to use kiandrite. The magi were no more.

Roldaer was finally free.

Brianna screamed in despair and suddenly launched herself at him. "You die, thief!" A blade flashed in her fist.

Danil stumbled back in surprised pain as the blade sank deep into his side. Hot blood splashed down his side. He fetched up against a block of stone, gasping.

"You've been a burr in my shoe for too long, thief. I will have my vengeance!" Brianna hissed, a manic light in her eyes as she slashed the blade once more.

Danil rolled clumsily, stumbling when his boot caught on loose rubble.

A loud crack sounded behind Danil as he fell backward and away from Brianna's next wild swing.

Overhead, the Magi Tower shuddered and leaned dangerously as if yanked about by a powerful force. Silver flashed.

Brianna tilted her head back and gaped.

The massive tower suddenly collapsed. Big blocks of stone thudded and crashed across the courtyard. Spears of rock splintered and shot in all directions. Danil hunched, covering his head as a massive block roared over him, close enough to scrape his knuckles.

Brianna wasn't so swift. She scarcely drew breath to

scream before a large portion of the wall fell atop her. Her outcry was abruptly cut short.

Danil kept low, gripping his side as the last remnants of the Magi Tower tumbled down the hill toward the royal city.

Dust and quiet settled over the rubble.

Danil painfully raised his head. Blood streamed between his fingers when he gripped his side. Bright pain flooded his innards. He felt his lifeblood spilling, and with dismay, Danil thought of Hafryn waiting for him back in the Fens.

The leylines called out, badgering and cajoling him to act, but he felt weakness grip tight.

Silver flashed, reaching for him, and then Danil fell into deep, dark silence.

31

The bustle and noise of a large camp dragged Danil awake. He opened his eyes to find himself in a tent filled with soft furnishings and gentle light from a warming brazier. An oversized, ghostly wolf Trueform sprawled at the end of his sleeping pallet, its nose tucked under its paws and powerful lungs steadily rising and falling in sleep. Iridescent light streamed through its fur.

Murmured voices drifted in from outside in an amiable mix of Roldaerian and Amasian accents. He idly wondered at that, but then the tent entrance peeled open and Hafryn ambled in, dragging cold night air in with him.

Green eyes brightened at seeing Danil. "Awake at last, *fala*," Hafryn said with a soft smile. He settled on the edge of the pallet. The iridescent wolf flicked its ears with awareness. "You've slept almost an entire day."

Danil felt it in his bones as he pushed himself upright. A dull ache came from his side. "I was stabbed."

Hafryn nodded. "Elania's furious. She'd have pulled Magus Brianna back across the veil to kill her again if she could. But a few more days and you'll regain your strength."

Danil gazed about the tent once again. "So we're still in the Fens."

Hafryn looked him over. "I'll let others more knowledgeable tell you how you got back. There's a whole gaggle of folk wanting to speak with you."

That only made the weariness grip Danil more fully. He took Hafryn's wrist and tugged him fully onto the pallet, throwing the furs over them both.

Hafryn chuckled in his ear. "I suppose they can wait, *fala*."

"We've not had peace and privacy for an eon," Danil said, resting his head on Hafryn's shoulder and burrowing so that the blanket covered his head. He didn't want to face the world just yet.

"It sure feels like it—certainly no peace, anyway." Hafryn gripped Danil's messy braid and gently tugged. "We may well have a wealth of it now, however, if we can stop Merlias from threatening the Roldaerian generals."

Danil felt a knot of anxiety loosen from his shoulders. "The army stopped its attack?"

Hafryn nodded. "The moment the magi lost their power. There may have been a few vengeful beheadings before Sonnen called a stop to it all. Even some Magi Guard were disappointed. But don't worry—Osriele's safe and well."

Danil thought of Hafryn's iridescent Trueform at the end of the pallet. It still retained its massive size from whatever Kaul had done to it. "What of you? When Kaul—" He stopped, feeling fresh rage and pain form a lump in his throat.

"I remember fighting him and the amulet. Kaul forced me to shift." Hafryn's voice dropped. "I didn't know such a thing was possible."

Danil pressed his face into Hafryn's neck. "Kaul's gone, and he won't ever return."

The leylines had seen to that. They'd stripped Kaul of his power and burned away any lingering, dark path that could lead him back into the living world.

Hafryn sighed. "I don't remember much of the battle. Flashes, maybe. It's all jumbled." He shook his head. "But I remember you, *fala*. And I heard Kailon."

Danil arched his neck to look at him in surprise.

"Sonnen's tried to explain it to me. When you used the House glyph to free me, I got entangled with your connection to Kailon. I remember riding the leylines. I felt Roldaer join with Amas once more." Wonder reverebrated in Hafryn's voice.

Danil sensed the leylines now, slowly filling up the empty channels across Roldaer like rainfall spilling into a stream. It was a cooling balm to his weariness. He yawned and pulled back the blankets to glance again at Hafryn's iridescent Trueform still drowsing at the end of the pallet. "Did you know your wolf glows, *fala*?"

"I'm aware." Hafryn sighed petulantly. "Merlias says I look ridiculous."

Danil snorted. "It's a gift from the leylines. She probably wishes her tail feathers shone so brightly."

"That's what I said, though perhaps with a bit of cussing."

A smile spread across Danil's face. "You're lucky Merlias didn't singe your fur."

"We may be past that." Bemusement tinged Hafryn's words.

Danil tilted his head again to look up at him. "Are you friends with an Eyrie now?"

"It's not the word I'd choose," Hafryn said, mouth tilting upwards. "But 'enemy' no longer rings true."

Danil supposed the same could be said of others in their party. He never thought a magus could be trusted, or that he'd come to admire the loyalty and forthrightness of Roldaerian guards.

But whatever other strangeness lay ahead for them, Danil knew it could wait. Healing sleep called to him and judging by the shadows under Hafryn's eyes, he wasn't alone. Tomorrow, they'd see what the changing world had in store for them.

He pulled the furs up under his chin and felt Hafryn curl contentedly around him, grateful they were both alive and together to do so.

~

BIRDSONG DRAGGED Danil from a restful slumber the following morning. Hafryn was already awake and dressed, watching Danil with intent from a stuffed chair as he stretched out the last remaining kinks in his body.

"Get dressed, *fala*," Hafryn said regretfully, pushing himself to his feet. "It's midmorning, and yon dragon grows impatient."

They left the tent a short time later, stepping out onto the wide granite outcropping. Danil slowed at the sight of the vast Roldaerian army encircling the hills. Pennants furled and snapped in the breeze, the smoke from cookfires rising for miles.

The immensity of what they'd been able to stop shook him. Even with dragons and the fiercest enchanters of Amas, they'd been destined to fall under the tide of the Roldaerian army. It made Danil appreciate even more the faith the Amasians had placed on him as custodian of the leylines.

Walking through the camp, Danil felt the weight of many gazes as folk stopped their work to call out greetings or touch the sleeve of his tunic. It surprised him only a little that Hafryn experienced much of the same now that his wolf Trueform was kiandrite-touched.

A flash of white hair caught Danil's attention as they walked among the tents.

Nera sat with a group of enchanters and soldiers, sharing tea and raisin dotted bread. She rose at his approach, a smile seaming her wrinkled face.

"What are you doing here?" Danil asked in happy astonishment.

Nera gripped both of his hands in greeting. "Did Hafryn not say? I suppose he was busy with other matters." Her eyes twinkled mischievously.

Hafryn had the grace to blush. "She made her way to the broken spire after we left and portalled into Aqila."

Danil looked at her in surprise.

Nera nodded. "If I'd known you were still in the Fens, I might have acted differently. Still, I had mighty plans to lay waste to the Magi Tower as retribution for the fall of Isfil. Found you amongst the rubble after my fun, Danil." She smiled. "I figured you'd want to be among friends. Imagine my surprise when I found all this."

Danil squeezed her hands. "Thank you."

Hafryn smiled at the silver dragon. "Come join us, Nera. Sonnen will want your thoughts on all that's happened."

Nera wrinkled her nose. "Representatives from the twelve Houses arrived before dawn with much fanfare. Sonnen went into the meeting tent with his game face on," she replied, then let out a scoffing laugh. "The Houses are still rather pompous, even after all this time."

"Kailon isn't," Danil promised. "You have a home there if you ever wish it."

It was the least he could do after all that had befallen them in Isfil. Nera had provided sanctuary and knowledge when they'd most needed it.

"I hear Kailon's filled with wild leylines and riotous living," Nera said, rubbing her hands together. "Perhaps it's time I re-joined such a world."

They waited as she finished her tea and respectfully thanked her hosts. One of the Roldaerian soldiers wrapped a piece of bread and pressed it into Nera's hand before they moved on.

The main meeting tent sat near the center of the camp, its blue canvas rising above all other tents. House glyphs had been sown in white along its trim, and Danil was surprised to see the royal pennants of Roldaer flying from its mast.

Inside, Sonnen and Osriele stood beside a large wooden table, with parchments and scrolls spread out between them. They were in deep conversation with what looked to be army commanders and members of the twelve Amasian Houses. Both Osriele and Sonnen bore serious expressions, but no animosity lingered in the air.

Seeing Danil, Sonnen's golden eyes grew warm with welcome. He turned to Osriele and bowed. "Noon draws near. Shall we pause for a meal before continuing with the finer details, Queen Osriele?"

Queen?

Danil mouthed the word at Hafryn. The wolf grinned.

A simple gold circled sat on Osriele's head, gleaming in the magelight. Her lips twitched. "Agreed, Prince Sonnen.

It's only fair that Custodian Danil is apprised of our treaty since he has his own part to play in it."

"Treaty?" Danil blurted, feeling overwhelmed.

Sonnen made a polite motion and waited for the representatives of the twelve Houses and the Roldaerian commanders to leave the tent. Those who stayed were members of the party into the Fens, along with Sonnen, Elania, Blutark, and Nera.

Osriele turned to an attendant. "A hot meal for the custodian, if you please. And refreshments for us all."

The Roldaerian manservant bowed and made his way outside.

The group retired to the chairs set around the warming brazier.

Danil was pleased to see both Commander Selen and Gethin looking bruised yet hale, although Selen's pale braid was missing, her hair clipped short to her skull. Her blue eyes held a vexed gleam as she took her usual position behind Osriele's chair.

Merlias noticed his gaze and leaned in. "Dragon mistook her for an army commander during battle," she whispered gleefully. "I'm surprised Selen kept her eyebrows."

"Or that the dragon kept its scales," Hafryn added in a whisper.

Commander Selen's jaw rippled as if knowing their conversation.

Sonnen cleared his throat meaningfully. "We have much to discuss, and already the day grows short. The Roldaerian army is expected to begin its march home tomorrow, with a new Queen due for her coronation back in Aqila."

Danil again glanced at Osriele, surprise trapping his words in his throat.

Osriele smiled, although it was tinged with regret. "My cousin has died on account of this war, Danil."

But Danil didn't recall seeing any royal pennants during the battle. He figured King Liam had wisely stayed far from the fighting. "I don't understand. Did he fall in battle?"

"In a manner of speaking," Osriele allowed. "By several accounts, King Liam was indeed with the army, cossetted by a squad of magi. But when my brethren were all stripped of their power, he disappeared—to be replaced by Lord Heron. Perhaps you recall him, Danil. He visited me at the manor in Aqila."

Danil thought of the balding, sweating magus and nodded. "He wanted to know your whereabouts before we left for Isfil."

"Heron wore a glamour powerful enough to fool even those closest to the king," Osriele said, face pale with anger. "As for my cousin's actual whereabouts, I can't say. In the rioting that followed Kaul's demise, Lord Heron was killed along with many of his closest allies."

Sonnen rumbled. "It does explain the Magi Council's increasing control over Roldaer these past years. Many have wondered why King Liam allowed such reign over his people. It would not be his wish for the blacksward to ruin his kingdom. "

Osriele looked saddened. "When Liam's demeanor changed, I should have thought to examine things more closely. Now that I am to be Queen, I must ensure such mistakes never happen again." She turned to Danil. "What remains of the Magi Tower will be torn down, along with the monuments magi have seen fit to erect across Roldaer."

Danil blinked in sudden realization. "You lost your power, too. The leylines spared no one."

There was no hostility in Osriele's eyes. "You tried to tell me, Danil. There are consequences when one does the wrong thing, even when they think their actions are justified."

"Have I put you in danger?" Danil asked carefully. "Roldaer's unprotected now."

Osriele smiled. "Our enmity with Amas is over. With time and teaching, I believe we will truly be allies." Her smile brightened. "You are evidence of what happens when the heart rules over greed and self-righteousness. Perhaps the leylines will find other Roldaerians who are worthy of them. Certainly, we will need such people to correct the damage wrought by the blacksward."

Danil startled with a rush of dismay. "It still spreads?"

Sonnen shook his head. "Fresh shoots already grow near Isfil, but the land needs time to recover. It is our hope, Danil, that you would aid your former kingdom in that quest. Until such time that Roldaer chooses its own custodian, we ask that you help to guide the leylines and assist them to flourish here once more."

Danil frowned, knowing that he couldn't be custodian to both lands. In his mind, the leylines laughed at his naivety, and he received a sudden image of a time in the future, where a crystal of green and purple burst through the surface to the waiting hands of a small child. It seemed that Roldaer would not be without a custodian for long. In the meantime, he would do all that he could to return the leylines to their former glory.

He smiled his agreement to the group. "I'll do all I can."

"What of the selasi?" Hafryn asked, hand sliding unconsciously toward his blade. "Do they still roam the blacksward?"

"With Kaul's power no longer here to twist them, the selasi are no more," Sonnen promised. "I daresay far worse creatures would have emerged to overtake Roldaer had it not been for Marama."

Eyes stinging, Danil thought of the brutal manner in which Marama died. After centuries of protecting Roldaer from the shadows, she deserved better. He cleared his throat with an effort. "The giant lizard-creature came because Marama could no longer protect us."

Sonnen nodded somberly. "She must have been a formidable presence before the magi stole her lodestone."

Hafryn turned to Nera and gently touched her shoulder.

Nera gave them a ghost of a smile. "Isfil was Marama's sanctuary. I'd likely have returned to Amas after the Great War had I not flown over the broken spire and seen her amidst the ruins. I couldn't leave her to suffer the pillaging of her leylines alone."

Looking pained, Osriele turned to Sonnen. "Now that our two kingdoms share a connection through the leylines, power will surely flood back to Isfil. With your aid, I'd like the spires to be the first place in Roldaer to be cleansed."

Flames of approval showed in Sonnen's eyes. "I would be honored to lend some of my finest enchanters, Queen Osriele." His gaze turned to Elania and Blutark. The enchanters nodded.

"Danil should go, also," Nera added. "Marama would like that."

Straightening, Danil said, "Isfil it is, then."

32

Discussions ended late in the afternoon, and Danil left the tent feeling hopeful of a treaty that would see both Amas and Roldaer flourish. Both Sonnen and Osriele were committed to the task and had capable attendants to see it through.

Turning to face the last warming rays of sunlight, Danil spied Merlias marching amongst the tents, the air about her shimmering as she prepared to take flight. "Merlias, wait!" He hurried to her.

The Eyrie enchanter turned to give him an irritated look. "What is it, custodian? It's been a long day, and all this politeness wearies me."

Sensing Hafryn move up behind him, Danil thought of the one thing that had bugged him since the battle against Kaul. The opportunity to discuss it in the tent hadn't presented itself, but Danil saw his chance now. "How did you know?" he asked as enchanters and soldiers walked around them. "When Kaul had Hafryn under his thrall—how did you know Kailon's glyph would break the amulet's hold over him?"

Looking between Danil and Hafryn, Merlias snorted. "Really, custodian? Why the leylines chose you is beyond me."

Danil glanced at Hafryn, who gave a mellow shrug.

Merlias rolled her eyes. "The Kailon glyph is an intrinsic part of you, custodian. I figured it would remind Hafryn of where his heart lay."

Hafryn raised a surprised eyebrow. "The power of love, Merlias?"

Danil blinked. It made sense now that he thought about it. The Kailon glyph had been newly inscribed on his palm when he'd first admitted his love for Hafryn all those months ago. That the wolf shifter also wore Kailon's glyph only further cemented their bond.

Merlias muttered something under her breath. "Give me a blade or enchantment any day. But if I must use foolish sentiment to save you idiots, then so be it."

Hafryn grinned in delight. "You wagered your life on love!"

"No, I wagered yours," she snapped, flaring. Her fingers twitched as if to form a glyph, but Danil saw her owl Trueform perched unruffled on her shoulder.

Hafryn's grin only widened.

"You're part of Kailon's House, now," Danil reminded her, seeing the glyph still inscribed on her palm. "You'll always be welcome."

Merlias glared at them both. "You're a pair of idiots. I am an assassin and enchanter of Eyrie."

"And a friend to Kailon," Hafryn added.

Seeing that they were both quite fixed on the idea, Merlias growled. The air shimmered, and she transformed within a furious whirl of sparks. The owl clacked her beak at them before taking flight, her derisive hoot echoing across the hills.

"I think she likes us," Hafryn observed, throwing his arm around Danil's shoulders and guiding him deeper into camp.

Danil was pleased to realize he didn't mind Merlias so much, either.

THEY RODE onto the beach opposite Isfil three days later.

Grey, powdery dust covered the pebbled beach like ash. An uneasy wind stirred over the waves crashing up against the two spires. Blackened rocks and rubble made it appear as if a fire had recently swept through. But on the dunes, fragile stems and greening shoots pushed through the sand and shivered in the ocean breeze.

Danil dismounted and made his way to the lapping shore, sensing both Roldaerians and Amasians trail behind him. Talis was gone, his body likely drawn out to sea, but markings on the rocks still showed where Brianna had made her curse. Danil crouched, uncaring when a wave hissed over his boots. The song of the leylines felt muted under his hand.

"We will find the missing Amasians, Danil," Osriele promised solemnly behind him. "I swear to you as Queen of Roldaer."

Danil nodded, scooping up a handful of wet pebbles and sand. "We should begin here."

Sonnen motioned to a handful of Roldaerians, who carried fragrant wreaths of healing aloes, thyme, and flowering brightstars. From each House of Amas, enchanters carried glimmering kiandrite crystals. Together, they set the wreaths and crystals upon the shore.

The dragon prince raised his hands. A large glyph came into behind, drifting up and expanding to include everyone in its iridescent shade.

"For the land torn apart, let us be those who heal it," Sonnen rumbled.

"*To the last breath,*" everyone intoned.

"May we always be guided by its radiant light," the dragon prince continued.

"*Until we return to the soil once more.*"

Danil took the merged crystal of Roldaer and Amas from his pouch and reverently lowered it to the sand. It tremored, its colors shifting from green to blue and pink, before the crystal winnowed its way below the surface.

Whispers flowed across the beach, loud enough that enchanters and Roldaerians alike turned in search of the source.

Flashing iridescent light drew Danil's eye to Isfil, where a specter in white stood in the shadow of the broken spire. His heart did a slow, heavy roll.

Marama.

The sand at his feet trembled before the crystal emerged once more. Danil bent to pick up the crystal, only to discover an unexpected weight. He pulled. The kiandrite lifted out of the sand, attached now to a shimmering staff made of wood and rock and seams of kiandrite.

Astonished murmurs spread across the beach.

Danil held the staff aloft. It vibrated like a living thing in his hand, the wakening song of Roldaer's leylines growing loud in his ears.

The white figure at Isfil brightened once more.

Understanding rushed through Danil. Turning, he

strode for Osriele. She stood amongst her advisors, simply dressed in gold-trimmed robes. A regal air hung about her, though she smiled warmly at his approach.

"Roldaer is yours now," Danil said. "Your duty to nurture. Your responsibility to protect. But let the staff be a reminder that we all stand together against darkness."

He held out the staff.

Eyes widening, Osriele gently took it. The crystal glowed earthy greens as if in welcome. Osriele tightened her grip. "We shall not fail, Danil of Kailon," she promised.

The leylines swelled to the surface, murmuring their agreement.

"Danil," Hafryn suddenly whispered reverently as he looked out across the waves.

Turning, Danil felt his gaze drawn once more to the broken spire. The glowing specter drifted to the furthest edge of the rubble, sparkling like a beacon.

Soft gasps and murmurs gathered across the beach. Sonnen stepped toward the water, mouth dropping in wonder.

"It's Marama," Nera said, her eyes watering.

"Great Lady of the Spire," Sonnen murmured before bowing deeply.

Marama's armor was no more, replaced instead by graceful white robes that left her glowing arms and legs bare. Pale hair floated about her as she took light steps beyond the broken spire and into the open elements. A wave crashed against the rocks, sending up a spray of iridescent, sunlit water.

When the wave fell away, Marama was gone.

"Free at last," Danil murmured.

33

The long journey to Kailon took months on horseback, slowed by the steady cleansing of Roldaer. It was draining work where even Hafryn was put to use, his kiandrite-blessed wolf sniffing out the bleakest boltholes where the poison held fast. But as autumn drew cool fingers across the land, the devastation left by the blacksward loosened its grip, nurtured by the rising song of Roldaer's leylines and the gentle urgings of enchanters like Elania and Blutark.

They drew close to Kailon, now. Danil could almost smell power on the wind, combined with raucous greetings that swelled to a cacophony in his mind. Grinning, he kicked his mount past the huts of Scara, waving at the villagers who'd returned to take up farming beyond the verdant hills.

Hafryn galloped beside him, letting out a happy whoop as they drew ahead of the rest of the party.

"This way!" Danil yelled, following the meandering gully between the hills.

Kailon's leylines urged him on, proudly singing of new

crystals emerging on the banks of the wildest rivers. They sang of a family of minks who'd made their den amidst the roots of a sprawling tree, and complained about the screeching bluewings who roosted in the gullies and made for sleepless nights.

Rounding the shoulder of a hill, Danil slowed to halt as he took in the vaguely familiar setting.

Hafryn overshot him and wheeled his horse about, his expression questioning.

"This is where we were portalled to Aqila," Danil said idly, bending to pat his mount's neck.

Hafryn gazed about. "So it is, *fala.*"

A new stream cut through the gully, framed by wide-fronded saplings and sweet-smelling rushes. Swinging from the saddle, Danil walked through the undergrowth. He felt the hum and swell of the leylines beneath him, urging him onwards.

Hafryn idly followed, plucking small orange flowers and twirling them between his fingers. His glowing Trueform gamboled through the rushes, tongue lolling.

Suddenly, the leylines called to Danil to stop. He paused amid a bed of wildflowers that danced and swayed in the breeze.

'*Kept it for you,*' the leylines sung. '*Safe and sound underneath.*'

Danil felt his gaze pulled to the rich brown soil at his boots. He bent, gently scuffing the surface.

A sliver of crystal glimmered. It was small and fragile, brittle along the edges as if it had been brutally cut from a larger piece. But it brightened as if waking from a deep slumber, pulsing a myriad of colors.

"Kailon's first crystal," Danil breathed, eyes tearing.

The leylines murmured smugly in the back of his mind.

Danil carefully dug around the crystal, scooping it out of the damp earth. It shone brilliantly and joyously as it tumbled across his House glyph, igniting them both.

Hafryn crouched beside him, basking in the changing light. His green eyes brightened. "Oh, you pretty thing."

The crystal shard blushed pink under the wolf shifter's warm regard.

"I didn't lose it, after all," Danil murmured, feeling his heart warm.

Grinning, Hafryn pressed a kiss to Danil's cheek. "Welcome home, *fala.*"

THE END

ABOUT THE AUTHOR

K K NESS is the pen name of identical twins living in Australia. They both share a love of characters whose antics make them happy, and enjoy competing against each other to see how much mayhem can happen in a book. They currently reside in sunny Queensland with various family and animal friends.

Visit their website for the latest releases and updates.

www.kkness.com